Wath Mill Allotr

Secrets, Lies and Two Leg Byes

David Beeley

Copyright © 2023 David Beeley

All rights reserved, including the right to reproduce this book, or portions thereof in any form. No part of this text may be reproduced, transmitted, downloaded, decompiled, reverse engineered, or stored, in any form or introduced into any information storage and retrieval system, in any form or by any means, whether electronic or mechanical without the express written permission of the author.

This is a work of fiction. Names and characters are the product of the author's imagination and any resemblance to actual persons, living or dead, is entirely coincidental.

The views expressed in this work are solely those of the author and do not necessarily reflect the views of the publisher, and the publisher hereby disclaims any responsibility for them.

ISBN: 9798375617015

This book is for Eveline May Beeley, my Rosangel.

Chapter One

Change never really changes

As Laura Watson walked towards the grave, she said to herself that this should be the last time. Absolutely the last time. Just as she had said to herself last harsh December.

The path from the lych gate up towards St Matthew's church in Newhill seemed steeper each year and at sixty-three her knees were beginning to rebel against this annual ritual. Arriving at the grave of William and Rosemary Mullins she put down her bag and felt slightly breathless. For eight years on the anniversary of William's death, she had trod this path and brought flowers for their grave or rather his grave.

The usual visitors to the church were a small Sunday congregation and occasional happy groups celebrating weddings or christenings or more sombre darkly dressed and grim-faced people arriving for a funeral. In the middle of this emotional spectrum were the irregular visits of notebook carrying amateur genealogists who would scan and peer at each gravestone hoping for clues to add volume to family trees. School parties complete with clipboards and pencils would learn the history of the ancient church as part of their local history curriculum. All would tread the same path as good Derbyshire folk had for centuries but today Laura walked alone with only the harsh cawing of rooks for company.

The early morning Derbyshire mist was lifting slightly yet still clung to the top of the solid square church tower unwilling to give up its hold on the small town. A watcher from the tower would have seen a woman on the edge of old age, dressed in warm black overcoat and red scarf. Her sensible brown shoes were chosen for comfort as was her long navy-blue skirt. Her role as teaching assistant at Newhill Primary School required casual smart but more importantly comfortable clothing. Her chestnut hair had more tinges of grey than last year, but Laura refused to bow to the vanity of colouring her hair. Not yet at least. A woman at ease with herself but today her usual black coat seemed especially proper. For eight years she had mourned yet only allowed herself the luxury of warm salty tears each December anniversary. Today in the morning mist. Alone.

As Laura laid the flowers down carefully, she did not look round in embarrassment as she once would have. Today she would speak aloud in her soft gentle voice not caring if any passer by heard her and wondered about her sanity, although modern earphones would probably not cause a second thought or glance. The curious may rather have wondered about the relationship between Laura and the occupants of the grave. At first glimpse the conclusion may have been a daughter visiting her parents' final resting place yet the dates on the headstone probably ruled this out. William had died, some said of a broken heart, eight years ago and his beloved wife Rosie just over a year earlier. No, Laura was not related to William or Rosie yet her love for the man twenty years her senior remained undiminished,

'Well William, here I am again, and it gets harder each year I have to say. That path is getting steeper or I'm getting older. I've brought flowers for you or rather for Rosie as usual as I know that she adored them as we both adored you.'

At this Laura could not resist looking round to make sure she was alone as she spoke aloud her long kept secret love, not that it mattered anymore of course. It was just an ingrained habit protecting her secret. She noticed a bright garland of flowers with a note saying RIP from the Polish Chlebek family. Laura smiled as it was obviously written in a neat and careful but childish hand. Probably eleven-year-old Rosangel Chlebek.

The flowers almost shone in the gloom and Laura smiled, happy that she was not alone in her memory of William Mullins, ex-headteacher, allotmenteer and changer of so many lives in Newhill. He had generously shared his lottery win, notably by buying the Wath Mill Allotments and thus saving it from the greedy grasp of housing developers. More importantly he had shared his calm wisdom and love. For William this had been primarily for his wife Rosie who had shared his life and now final resting place. Yet his heart had secretly yearned for the much younger Laura, a dual deep love never to be allowed to be spoken.

For her part she had admired and adored him since she joined his school as a new teaching assistant. Both were happily married, especially William and as his feelings grew for Laura, fondness grew into the pain of a secret love which could never be revealed, even to each other. He had even moved schools to avoid openly showing his feelings for Laura. He refused to risk his very long and happy marriage with his adored Rosemary, yet it was with a heavy heart that he left Newhill primary and the marriage threatening friendship with Laura.

Laura had quietly cried alone when William left Newhill Primary School and bravely greeted him cheerily when they occasionally met whilst shopping in the town. She always smiled and briefly chatted with the old man, usually hand in hand with wife, Rosemary. Yet Laura would sigh deeply with real regret that she had not been older or he younger when they first met and preferably both unmarried,

For years the old headteacher and the young vibrant teaching assistant were silently tormented by their love for each other and yet when they left at the end of the day she went home to her husband and he to Rosemary.

For his part Laura's husband Timothy had no inkling of his childhood sweetheart's unspoken love for another man, a much older man at that. He had always regarded himself as lucky to have married the girl he met at school. Love is blind but perhaps more so for men. Perhaps.   Rosemary on the other hand knew William as well as she knew herself. Fifty years of marriage did that. They had a joint memory bank and could predict each other's thoughts on matters large and small. Children came along and grandchildren and Rosemary would love to see William playing Champion in the Corner as the toddlers would strive to pull William on his knees out of the corner to replace him as champion. Knees were good back then. Their granddaughter Molly particularly enjoyed the game with her Grandad and the happy home was filled with squeals of delight. Looking back, these were the good days, the golden days although, of course, they didn't know it at the time. We never do appreciate the present for what it is. Just regret for a perceived past and hope for an uncertain future.

Rosemary watched with her usual calm patience as William put his professional endeavour into making his school the best he could even if at times his pupils sometimes took precedence over his own family. Later she bore her unwelcome cancer with steadfast bravery and fortitude and somehow it gave her a different perspective and insight into her life. The creeping fears came to meet her in the solitude of night. Of course, she knew of William's growing feelings for young Laura but did not confront him with her suspicions. Wives always somehow knew or at least guessed. Rosemary understood William and never feared that he would desert her for another woman. She liked Laura and could understand his deep fondness for her, yet her perceived role was to protect William from the worry about her fast-developing cancer and prepare him as best she could.

William Mullins was wise enough to know deep in his instinctive soul that Rosemary would know of his infatuation with the bright eyed, sparkling Laura. There was nothing that his wife did not know of him after fifty years together. They had met as teenagers and their bond had led to a mutual understanding of and respect for each other's thoughts. Yet he continued to allow himself the luxury of pretending to himself that Rosemary was unaware of his feelings for another woman. William was wise in so many ways, but wives of fifty years were invariably wiser.

Laura stood by his graveside, their graveside, united in death as in life, inseparable. She pondered, as she did in this cold lonely place on each anniversary, what might have been, the ludicrously impossible might have been. William and Rosemary were destined for each other, and Laura would never have contemplated any words or action which would jeopardize their marriage or her own for that matter.

Rosemary's death through cancer had come quickly. William had always imagined that he would pass away first and the shock of his wife's departure had diminished him as indeed had his own developing cancer. He was nevertheless pragmatic and resolute knowing that Rosemary would hate him to become self-pitying and introvert. In retirement he put his efforts into his plot at Wath Mill allotments on the edge of Newhill. A large lottery win had allowed him to buy the allotments site not for himself but to save a place of tranquillity and friendship from housing development. That creeping paralysis of unaffordable standardisation. He had been pleased to be able to help his family and others. However, cancer certainly could not be bought off with a cheque, money was of little use to him now. No foreign holidays or luxury yachts but he was happy and content to walk on a patch of good Derbyshire soil which he owned on behalf of his fellow allotmenteers.

The arrival of Laura Watson as allotment coordinator on Newhill Primary school's plot had sparked his fondness for her back into life. Nothing had changed, she was just as lovely with her laughing eyes and kindness, still happily married, still twenty years too young. Yet everything had changed. After deep contemplation at Rosemary's graveside, standing where Laura now stood in the December cold, he had decided that Laura could never be more than a friend, a special friend. This would, he knew, have been Rosemary's wise advice. It was not for him to break up marriages. Perhaps even now he was deceiving himself, he had never really seen himself as an object of female attraction.

Laura had called it their parallel unspoken love, platonic and pure and certainly unobtainable. Yet a chance meeting at the local garden centre after Rosemary's death had led to the revelation of their feelings for each other, both surprised and delighted. Both saddened by what might have been and yet somehow relieved that conflict had been avoided. Laura had enjoyed seeing William regularly at Wath Mill Allotments and sharing coffee and chat, yet it was an older cancer ridden man she saw though the qualities of kindness and wisdom still burned bright. For his part William felt joy at being able to see Laura regularly without guilt or complications. He knew Rosemary would have understood and approved. Laura kept him young, as did the lively children from the school as they learned gardening skills on their plot.

William had overcome his grief, had learned to accept it as old people do. They knew that all good things must end even great loving partnerships. He had over fifty years to prepare for the inevitability of life alone yet his granddaughter, Molly's, sudden, violent death in a car crash had proved too much for his heart to bear. The shock was of epic proportions The doctors had said that it was cancer combined with a heart attack, but it was generally accepted by those who knew him that it was a broken heart. To lose Rosemary his dearest and then Molly his delightful, darling granddaughter was too cruel, and many echoed the thought that he did not deserve such a fate.

Laura sighed deeply as she stood looking at Rosemary and William's grave. There was just the slightest tinge of jealousy that the older woman had enjoyed so much of William's life, yet she was so glad that he had finally revealed his deep fondness for herself. He had seemed genuinely surprised that she could have the same love for him. All too late but at least when the shocking news of William's death following his beloved Molly's death she had some slight consolation, knowing how he felt. He had loved two women and they him, yet he had chosen his wife as Laura knew that he always would.

'Well William, this is going to have to be the last time I struggle to get up here to give my report on what has been happening at the allotments. It sometimes seems silly, an old lady's nonsense, clinging onto a past which never really existed, never really mattered. Just might have been, what ifs.'

The December cold seemed worse each year and Laura sometimes wished that William's death had happened in a soft gentle spring, but the thought was a pointless one. It would have been far worse if William had been snatched away before that chance meeting in the garden centre had allowed them to reveal their strong feelings for each other. Her loss would have left an empty pitiless void but at least she had the warming consolation of knowing how William felt about her, had always felt about her. So many lost opportunities.

'As I told you last year Tolly Braithwaite passed away after spending years complaining that he had every disease known to man. The Newhill Horticultural society have named a cup in his honour in recognition of his many years as secretary and leading light in the town's Britain in Bloom entry. As you well know he was so pedantic and boring with his being a stickler for rules and constitutions and regulations. Still, he did an excellent job of keeping things going in his own way and his allotment was second to none. Tolly certainly knew how to grow prize vegetables. We now have the Tolly Trophy for the heaviest onion entry in the annual show. He would probably have won it himself each year, Using Tolly on the cup seemed a little odd but somehow proper as it was how he was known. Few remembered the Braithwaite name and even fewer were aware of his real first name.

Laura pulled her coat closer against the bone chilling cold and continued her news for William.

'You'll be pleased to hear that Tessa Tinton's son Alex is coming home for a year from Japan with his wife Kyoko and son Satoshi. His company is paying for this, and he's being seconded to a Japanese firm in Derby. Tessa is beside herself with excitement. Do you remember the days when we all called her Terrible Tessa, behind her back of course? None of us would have dared call her that to her face. She had a sharp tongue and very abrasive manner in those days, complaining and pointing out everyone's faults on the allotments. Your intervention pointing out to her that she had turned sour after her son left and that she needed to get her life and marriage back to what it used to be. She certainly turned a corner and husband Graham is truly delighted. They named their puppy Billy in your honour, a lovely cocker spaniel. Tessa is still membership secretary and popular with everyone, she has even stopped her addictive online gambling, you did a good job there William even though even you didn't dare do it to her face. As it turned out the letter which you sent her worked a treat.'

Laura could almost hear William modestly making light of Tessa's incredible transformation and would no doubt have put it down to merely putting forward a few home truths.

'Speaking of membership secretary's, you may be surprised to learn that Eileen Bisby is moving back to Newhill, her short prison term is over reduced by good behaviour apparently. She has been away since leaving prison, poor woman. Newhill seems to be divided by the case, some said it was a mercy killing of her husband to spare him from the agony he was going through with his disease-ridden body. More than a few said it was pure and simple murder. I'm sure that you would opt for the former and I would tend to agree but you know what Newhill gossip is like. It seems an age ago when she was membership secretary and a very efficient one too. Her calculated play to be chair failed, to most people's surprise at the AGM. Your intervention was crucial as usual. Your support of a young inexperienced girl Charlotte Webster as chair was a good move. She has been chair for eight years now and has been elected unopposed. The term of office is usually three years, but she has grown into the role and is very highly regarded. Your insight was key probably based on your gift of appointing the right people for jobs at school. Such care was taken to make sure that each person appointed would be part of a team with the needs of children as a first priority. This went from deputy heads to cleaners.'

'Of course, Charlotte or Charlie as she now prefers to be called, is working with us at Newhill Primary as a teaching assistant. She helps with Sam Chlebek on a one-to-one basis, helping him overcome his reluctance to speak openly. It certainly was a clever if bold move to contrive a meeting between her and Chris Poole. They were made for each other, and their twins are five now and are in Reception class. Only you could see that a young, bright but shy solicitor, one of your ex-pupils, would be attracted to a lonely bakery worker living with her parents. It was a brilliant move on your part and if they hadn't at once hit it off no one would have been any the wiser. A lovely family. Charlie was always your protégé on the allotments and she was like a daughter to you, I know she very much enjoyed your friendly relationship with her.'

Laura sighed deeply, remembering fondly the day that she had met William when he had shown her round the school with such obvious pride and later appointed her to the staff at Newhill primary school as a teaching assistant. That introductory pre interview visit had proved to be the seed of their deep fondness for each other. Only the large age difference and two happy marriages kept them from declaring the growing depth of their feelings for each other.

'I'm beginning to waffle and I'm due at school soon, so I'll just say that your old plot twelve on the allotments has changed hands once again. Several others have come and gone but I somehow think that the new ones will stick with it. Their names are Ben and Jenny Ellis, and they are awash with enthusiasm. They openly say they know little of growing vegetables or flowers, but they are soaking up advice and very keen to be part of our little community. He has mended the gate and is merrily cutting the central grass path and strimming round everyone's plot. He has already got your plot back to how you had it and I think he should be on the committee. They are both a great addition to Wath Mill with their work ethic and pleasant manner. You would certainly have approved of them both. He's an ambulance driver and Jenny works at Nora Wilson's bakery on the High Street.'

Standing still in the cold Derbyshire morning was beginning to take its toll on Laura and she wished that there was a bench to sit on whilst she held her one way conversation with William. She wondered if the church would allow one to be put in. A suitable plaque could be put on it to commemorate his life, their lives together. Without thinking too hard she was able to easily name people who would be only too happy to contribute, the Polish family, the Chlebek's, for instance. That reminded Laura.

'I almost forgot, Andy Chlebek has been elected to the County Council and his beautiful wife Sherrie has had a fourth child. I think his name is Jakob, but I understand that they may use the English spelling. He still has his allotment, but his workload has increased enormously, and we don't see as much of him as we used to. Rosangel is eleven now, I suspect that it was her who wrote the note with the flowers. A lovely girl takes after her mother in looks, she will break a few hearts along the way, and I know she is chuffed to bits to have three younger brothers to oversee. She loves responsibility. Sam, however, is increasingly a deep concern both for the Chlebek's and us at school. He has always followed Rosangel around but has almost developed into an elected mute. He looks to his sister to speak for him and will only whisper to her as his main means of communication. Even with his parents he always looks to Rosangel to answer for him. In class he never speaks, and Rosangel is, of course, in a different, older class. Next year she will move up to secondary school and then we don't know what he will do. We are trying to get as much outside help for him as possible, but this takes time and budgets are tight. Perhaps being in different schools to Rosangel will help make Sam more independent.... perhaps.'

Glancing at her watch Laura knew it was time to get to school, time to leave William. The end of her ritual of bringing flowers on the anniversary of his death and imparting news of his allotments and his old school.

'Well goodbye William... and Rosie of course. I'm getting a little too old to be standing around talking to gravestones and the cold seems to bite harder each year. I'm sure that the two of you won't miss me, you only ever really needed each other.'

Laura sighed and felt a deep sadness and reluctance to go for the last time but go she did, turning and walking slowly down the path to the church lych gate.

Leaving for the last time, until next December inevitably called her back of course. Deep everlasting love was like that. It certainly had no sell by date.

Chapter Two

Glitter Everywhere, Mince Pies and Warm Bed Socks

Thomas Tiler fumbled with the large bunch of keys trying to find the familiar main door key to Newhill Primary School. The January bone freezing chill did not help and it took longer than it should have to open the large church like green front door. Switching the alarm off with its small keypad was difficult at the best of times and he dreaded punching in the wrong numbers yet again. This would lead to a response visit from the police and phone calls to the security alarm company.

As a newly appointed headteacher, wrestling with the myriad of details necessary for the smooth running of the school, it would not be the first time he had taken too long to get to the alarm or hit the wrong buttons. It was usually the local community police who attended the alarm call and usually PC Eleanor Kent who attended. She would recognise the call to the school and would not rush. No need for the siren. It was usually a mistake by the new head trying to master the alarm system. Again. Not that she minded visiting her old school and talking to Thomas Tiler as he explained what had gone wrong this time.

It seemed strange to Eleanor or El as she preferred to be known, to be mildly rebuking the young bearded headteacher in what was Mr. Mullins' office in her day. Several times she had reminded Thomas of the importance of getting the unlocking and entry procedure right in her official voice. Her unofficial feelings were best kept to herself. He was of average height with tidy beard, large glasses and what was once known as a Beatle haircut, back in the day. Between the fringe, glasses and beard was a smile quick to appear. It was a smile which crinkled his eyes, making it sometimes difficult to ascertain their colour. They were either blue or grey depending on the light. His passport said blue.

No, PC Eleanor Kent enjoyed a non-urgent visit to the school to see the familiar surroundings. He was the most fanciable headteacher she had ever met. Not that she had met many below the age of fifty. Usually stern and mean faced, quick to rebuke and slow to praise. In her days at the school the headteacher William Mullins was different, he had been kind and pleasant and patient in his explanations but old not like the attractive Thomas Tiler. He was about her age thirty-three and she was certainly in the market for a new partner. She thought how strange it would be to make a play for a headteacher in her old school. Somehow wrong but outside school would be quite another matter. Definitely on the potential target list as she had discovered that he was married but separated from his wife. The next time she was called to the school when he made a pig's ear of the simple alarm system, she would try to discover if he could be interested in her in a non-official capacity. Well, worth a try. But not today. PC Kent was on duty but the alarm from the school didn't go off. Silence reigned at the small Newhill police station.

Despite freezing fingers Thomas managed to switch off the alarm and was grateful, as always, when the shrill entry alarm ceased. A sudden and very pleasing silence greeting the last digit being put in. He sighed with relief. He didn't mind the visit from the attractive police constable who wore her uniform very well but the phone call to the security company was another matter, always embarrassing,

It was not the first time that Thomas had gone into a school in early January before term started and children reluctantly left their Christmas toys to meet friends and compare presents. The cry, 'What did you get for Christmas?' would echo round the playground and classrooms. For the better off it was a good question to ask and answer but for the less fortunate, trickier to answer and certainly not one to ask.

As he entered the building, he was met by the usual school smell so evocative and full of memories. Years of polish and plasticine, wet coats and boiled cabbage seemingly embedded into the very walls. For parents coming into school for Parents'

Evenings or summer plays it was an aroma of the past, their past a comfortable familiar never changing smell in a rapidly changing world.

A stranger travelling through any town in England could instantly recognise three vital cogs in the town's life; the church whether Norman square tower or elegant gothic spire, the allotments site which were distinguished by their conglomeration of sheds, water butts and intense cultivation and of course the Victorian school. These latter buildings were recognisable by a concrete playground surrounded by a wall and solid stone-built walls with gable roofs. Occasionally there would be two church style doors with stone carved signs saying Girls and Boys. Clear distinction for the Victorian minds. Newhill Primary School, St Matthews church and Wath Mill allotments would certainly not disappoint visitors to the town. Not that there were many tourists. The finding of a hoard of Roman coins at the allotments site had led to small items on local news and television but not enough to encourage a flood of tourists. Old Derbyshire mining towns could not rival York or Bath for attractions. Newhill was a small, friendly working town with a population rooted in agriculture or the mines. Down to earth with a deep patient, work ethic and dry sense of humour. The quiet enduring backbone of English society. Thomas Tiler was born in Ashbourne of solid agricultural stock, and he instinctively understood the children at his school and their parents. Understood and liked and the feeling was certainly mutual.

For Thomas it was the first time he had opened up a school and come in during the Christmas holidays as a headteacher, the one in charge, the one responsible for...well, everything really. On paper the governors were in charge, but he would be the one to lose his job if an Ofsted inspection revealed weakness' in provision, teaching or leadership.

Thomas poured fresh water into the urn and switched it on, others may come in later to prepare classrooms and lessons. For now, he had the luxury of peace and quiet if not warmth. He risked taking off his winter coat and decided to have a look round whilst waiting for the water to boil. He spooned coffee into his large England cricket mug, one sweetener but no milk in the fridge, at least none which he would risk. Black coffee it would have to be, but at least it would be hot. A search of the variety of tins revealed mince pies and several with biscuits in, the ones none of the staff wanted. Several parents had donated tins of chocolates or biscuits to the staffroom at the end of term and teachers and assorted staff had descended on them like hungry gannets.

Picking up two mince pies Thomas began his look round the school whilst eating the very welcome festive treats. Living by himself in a small flat or rather bedsit near the White Horse pub just off the town's High Street he appreciated any food which was not ready made or microwavable. The pies were heading towards stale, but the sealed tin had given them a few days grace, possibly enough to avoid food poisoning.

The central hall with classrooms going off were festooned with Christmas decoration, trees and sparkling glitter on almost every flat surface. The magic of Christmas festivities and joyful anticipation with its unique feel of cheerful goodwill had quickly faded, and the carols were silent. Thomas enjoyed the end of term with parties and entertainments, everyone in the right spirit or nearly everyone. There were notable exceptions amongst the staff which he had inherited in September.

Thomas had decided that a SWOT assessment of the school would best be left until he had time to be in place for a term, Strengths Weaknesses, Opportunities and Threats. A good methodical way of looking at a school, especially a school where the dreaded Ofsted inspection was due. An inspection which could reveal elements and hidden secrets about Thomas which would see him forced to resign. If he was lucky. Ignominiously sacked if he were not. The governors would no doubt prefer the image of a happily married family man, but Ofsted inspectors couldn't care less about his marital status but the other issues, the ones he had fought to overcome for years may well concern them. This problem was shelved for the moment as he finished the second mince pie and arrived back at his office to pour the black coffee. An extra sweetener may help, he thought.

Taking a large blank sheet of paper, he divided it into four quarters with a black felt tip pen. At the top of each quarter, he put Strengths, Weaknesses, Opportunities and Threats.

Thomas always enjoyed this exercise; it gave a clear overview of the school's current standing and enabled him to understand the direction in which the school was evolving and the dynamics of change. A coherent plan could then be developed over three years to overcome threats. enhance opportunities build on strengths and improve or eliminate weaknesses.

In the strengths quarter he wrote new head committed and enthusiastic. Keen to succeed. Under threats he wrote Ofsted inspection and falling numbers. he paused before adding potential forced resignation of new head. A cold-water moment but Thomas was pragmatic and understood the need to be realistic. A poor Ofsted could lead to him being without a job, but his long-hidden secrets had that same potential to make his first headship both short term and his last. He sighed and moved on. The shadow was long, dark and seemingly endless or more realistically two overlapping shadows. One he might survive but not two.

At that moment he heard the door open and got up to investigate. Laura Watson jumped slightly when Thomas appeared in his casual cord trousers and checked shirt covered by a thick blue jumper. Not his usual suit, Laura thought quickly, makes him seem friendlier somehow, more casual.

'Good morning, Laura and I suppose that I should say Happy New Year, I wasn't expecting anyone in yet'

'And the same to you Thomas, did you have a good Christmas?' Laura replied and instantly regretted her mistake. She knew well that he was separated from his wife and living in a tiny bedsit. Possibly went home to parents in nearby Ashbourne for the holidays but knowing the young headteacher he probably stayed working alone. He deserved better, she thought.

'Not too bad thanks, what have you got planned for today? Not finishing off the biscuits and mince pies, are you?'

Laura laughed and suspected that he had already investigated the staffroom tins of edible treasure. 'Not with my figure, I need to lose weight not gain it. I thought that I would bring in some milk for anyone daft enough to come in on this cold morning and begin to tidy away the Christmas decorations. Nothing worse than coming into school in a flat January to be greeted by the faded and false trimmings. Get the new term underway. When the dreaded alarm didn't go off, I knew that someone had beaten me to it.'

Thomas smiled, 'The milk, and of course you are very welcome. Will you join me in a first coffee of the year?' He liked and admired the older woman; his leading teaching assistant and it was typical of her that she was both first in and organised enough to bring milk for the staffroom. Why didn't he think of that? I must do better next time, if there was to be a next time.

Taking off her coat Laura replied, 'No I'll have one later thanks Thomas, I'm quite keen to get the reception classroom cleared first that's usually the worst. I'll see you later you are probably busy, drawing breath after your first term. Did you enjoy the experience of being in charge?'

'I did actually, it was hard work and strange in the first few days not to get a classroom ready and I felt lost when everyone disappeared to their rooms to greet the children on the first morning. I began to wonder what a headteacher actually did. The lull before the storm. I was really tired, but it was a good tired and the children here are very friendly and welcoming.'

'Well, I know that you have the full support of the governors and parents and virtually all the staff, including myself and I have worked with some great heads I can tell you, I'll talk to you about that later if I may, over that coffee.'

Thomas was both intrigued and somehow not surprised at this mysterious statement. When Laura left, he wrote under Strengths the name Laura Watson. Under weaknesses he wrote Laura Watson retiring. Such a pity, she was a great role model and support for him. She would be missed in the inevitable battles to come.

Under strengths Thomas added, Greater ethnic mix and Diversity. The West Indian family, the Shakespeare's and the Poles the Chlebek's had been joined by several Italian, Indian, Pakistani and of course long-term Irish families. It was good to see and class photographs would reflect this evolving mix of races and religions. A testament to tolerance and the willingness of the English to welcome and incorporate those wishing to live and work peacefully in England. There was even talk of a Japanese boy joining the school for a year. World Culture Day would certainly be interesting. Thomas found this increasingly ethnic blend invigorating and wondered about the background of the Shakespeare's from Trinidad. There was surely a story there. He must remember to ask Keith Shakespeare, Billy's dad, when he next saw him. Nice family as most were.

With a sigh Thomas began to fill in the quarter of the sheet of paper headed Weaknesses. He wrote, 'some teachers resistant to change'. Under Opportunities he decided to be positive and added 'Ofsted Inspection' to counter its position as a threat. Thomas continued until the sheet was full, if uneven. There were more threats and weaknesses than strengths and opportunities. Sitting at his desk in the cold office had made his back ache so he stood and carefully stretched out his muscles. Time for another cup of hot coffee and maybe a couple of biscuits although the chocolate ones were probably long gone, devoured by staff needing a sugar boost in the frantic last week of the Christmas term.

Walking through the high-ceilinged hall towards the reception classroom where he rightly guessed that Laura would be busy, he stopped by the display cabinet. Most of the cups were battered and tarnished with age, some with coloured ribbons representing the winning houses at various sports and competitions. All houses were named after Derbyshire rivers, large and small. Echoes of the four houses of Hogwarts he thought. The Sports Day Trophy carried the yellow colours of the Derwent as did the football trophy whilst the green ribbons on the netball trophy and rounders cup stood for the mighty Midlands River Trent. The lovely River Dove with its beautiful dale of the same name was appropriately represented by blue colours and their forte seemed to be academic as they were current holders of the House Points Trophy. Thomas smiled to himself as he remembered walking by the Dove with his then new girlfriend Beth when he slipped and got wet feet. Elizabeth Jane Galley had later become his wife, Beth Tiler. The couple had drifted apart without real cause, rhyme or reason and she now called herself EJ, more modern she said. A break with the painful past although she still used her married surname, Tiler. But on that sunny day in Dovedale they had laughed happily together and kissed, their future together seemingly secure. Thomas always light heartedly swore that she had pushed him into the river although she always laughingly denied it. Good days. The early magical days of love and Thomas looked back fondly at those times. At night he wore bed socks to keep warm in his cold, lonely bed sit but he would easily swap their comfort to go back to that glorious wet footed kiss by the Dove. He missed Beth enormously especially her warm body at night and yet she lived alone in their house whilst he slept alone in a one roomed flat. At least he hoped that she slept alone. There had been rumours and suspicions about Declan the sports teacher at Oak Tree Lane where Beth was the Special Needs coordinator. Thomas had never liked the way he laughed with Beth as he himself once had.

'You've noticed have you Thomas?' Laura Watson said, making Thomas jump having not heard her come into the hall. He was confused as he was deep in thoughts of his wife and past times.

'Sorry Laura, I didn't hear you there, Noticed what? I was just wondering why Newhill's river Warne had no red ribbons on trophies last year'

'Who knows, it changes each year as the Year Six move on. Derwent were strong last year, good athletes. Nothing stays the same, next year the Warne team should do better. They have young Shakespeare and the Chlebek's, I wouldn't be surprised to see lots of red ribbons this time next year,'

Thomas silently hoped that he would survive long enough to see that. 'I was just coming to see if you were ready for that coffee yet.'

Laura laughed easily.' And I was about to come and say the same. I would appreciate a hot coffee and a chat, don't worry I won't keep you long', she assured him.

'What about this large trophy? Thomas asked, peering closely at the crisp new inscription. The William Mullins Cup.

Won last year by Newhill. 'Pretty impressive. Not a house trophy I assume.'

Laura smiled, no it is the local cricket cup for primary schools in the area, usually very competitive and hard fought. Last year we had a very enthusiastic PE teacher, who left in the summer for a deputy headship at Mapleton Road. The year six were particularly talented and very keen, didn't like to lose. They easily won the cup and thoroughly deserved it. Unfortunately, most of the kit was their own and we don't have much left of our own, but we still have the cup at least until the summer.' No chance of keeping it this season though.'

As Thomas and Laura walked towards the staffroom cleaners had begun to appear grumbling about the state of the Christmas wreckage from the last week. Thomas greeted them warmly and wished them season's greetings. That seemed to appease their moans. Being acknowledged by the new head gave them a feeling of being part of the team and Thomas knew how important support staff were in the team structure.

Arriving in the small, cluttered staffroom Laura began to prepare coffee whilst Thomas rattled tins to find the remaining biscuits.

'Tell me Laura, the William Mullins cup, was this the same Mullins who was once head here at Newhill. I presume that you would have known him, was he a cricket man?'

Laura handed Thomas his coffee in a Chatsworth House mug but declined a biscuit. They sat nursing the welcome warmth of the coffee mugs and Laura noticed the open biscuit tin on the chair next to Thomas, mainly soft pink wafers, the rice crispies of the biscuit world, unwanted, the ones left until choices were gone.

'Yes, William was certainly a lover of cricket, developed it at both his schools. He was the one who appointed me as a lowly teaching assistant in this very room as a matter of fact. And now I'm retiring at the end of the year. I'll certainly miss Newhill.'

'And Newhill will certainly miss your leadership. What happened to William Mullins, is he still around? Was he the one who donated the trophy and put his own name on it?'

A painful shadow seemed to cross her face as she replied, looking down at her lap.   'No, all the schools in the cricket league donated to a fund to set up the trophy. He was never one to blow his own trumpet. William died of cancer eight years ago, he's buried in St Matthew's churchyard with his wife Rosemary.'

Thomas sensed that he had touched some sort of nerve and quickly changed the subject. 'If I can't persuade you to stay on for another year, if your mind is made up who do you think should replace you as leading TA?'

'Yes, it's time for me to go, my innings is over as they say in cricket and my husband Tim, and I want to do some travelling before we are too old.'

'I think that you deserve that after all you have given to the school. I only hope that the Ofsted inspectors arrive before you go in July. You are a great asset to the school, appreciated by everyone, none more so than me.'

'That's kind of you to say so Thomas but that is what I wanted to talk to you about. I was wondering if you would allow me to continue to act as coordinator on the school's plot at Wath Mill allotments. It's going really well and would keep me in touch with everyone. When I'm away on my travels or rather our travels, Charlie Poole has agreed to keep an eye on things. She is chair of the allotments committee, at least until October when her term of office ends. Which brings me neatly onto your question of who should replace me. I know Charlie has not been long in her role as T.A, but I have seen her in operation as an efficient chair of the committee and I think that she is an outstanding teaching assistant. The twins are at school in reception now so it would be convenient for her and good for the school. You would have to interview formally of course, and it may ruffle feathers amongst the more established older TAs but believe me she would be worth it. She is quiet and unassuming but an enthusiast, always keen for the children to make progress, they all adore her. She's calm in a crisis and would be a real leader of the non-teaching staff as well as....'

Thomas laughed as he interrupted Laura's flow of admiration for Charlie Poole. 'I had already pencilled her in and was planning to sound her out when I next see her. Perhaps you could do that for me as you seem to be her publicity agent.'

'Sorry Thomas, I should have known that you would have figured it out for yourself without my interference.'

'No, it makes me feel that your endorsement makes my first assessment the correct one. Charlie is the right choice, if she wants the promotion and if the formal interviews go well. Have a word if you would.'

Thomas took a sip of the rapidly cooling coffee. 'Now you hinted earlier that not all staff are fully supportive of me as head in particular and the school in general. Off the record what did you mean or rather who did you mean?'

'I am leaving at the end of the year but that is irrelevant, you should be aware of Mary Anderson Year Five teacher. She is poison behind her smiles. She is sly and a focal point for any discontent, always trying to stir things up. Her words and actions don't always match. The parents see her as a traditional old-fashioned disciplinarian and yes, she is strict and gets good results from her class, but they are afraid of her. I believe she manipulates the end of term test results to enhance her status. I think she applied for your job even though she didn't get the deputy headship two years ago. Watch out for her, she is the bad apple.'

'Thank you for your frankness and honesty Laura. Unfortunately, I believe that you may be right. I'll certainly bear your warning in mind but for the moment keep this between us, if you don't mind. On a lighter note, I'm thinking of organising a new cricket team at Newhill to win the William Mullins Trophy again. It seems that no one has won it twice in a row and I like a challenge. I know that Kevin Bolton at Snelston is determined to win the cup this year.'

Laura grimaced, 'Kevin has an allotment at Wath Mill, not a nice man. The male equivalent of Mary Anderson if you ask me. Not popular with others on the allotments. I think that to start a new cricket team from scratch and win the cup would be a mountain to climb but I would certainly like to see Kevin Bolton's face if you manage it. He has a grudge against the Chlebek's, and William Mullins before William passed away.

Laura said she would get back to clearing the infants' classrooms before she got too negative. Thomas was left with much to ponder. Back in the office he wrote 'winning the Mullins trophy' in the opportunities section and placed the initials M.A. in the threats quarter.

Thomas would need to overcome the twin personal demons if he was going to face the threats to his headship and the future of his school. And he certainly now felt that sense of ownership. Newhill Primary was indeed his school, and he was certainly well on the way to falling in love with it. He was grimly determined to save his school and make it the best he could for each and every child in his care.

Chapter Three

Little Billy Shakespeare: Wicket Keeper/ Detective

Little Billy Shakespeare lay in his bedroom, the smallest of four, in the detached house, which was a coincidence as he was himself the youngest and smallest of four. His three sisters towered above him as did absolutely everyone in Year Six at Newhill primary and indeed many of Year Five. Everyone from the age of...well forever had called him Little Billy. He lay back with hands behind his head. A Saturday meant no school and he could plan his day without disturbance, a wet blustery Saturday however severely restricted his planning. Helping his dad on plot seventeen at Wath Mill allotments was out of the question. February was always a quiet time with little to do there. Too cold and wet with sliding mud underfoot. A pity as he always enjoyed working there with his dad, the two men of the house. Both happy to be away from the hustle and bustle of three teenage girls.

Billy was eleven but looked eight. He had been born at Queen Elizabeth Hospital in Birmingham to Keith and Faith Shakespeare from Trinidad. He thought as he had done a thousand times that he could not blame his parents for his lack of stature. Both were of average height, stocky with full, ample figures as his mother, Faith would say. A testimony to good wholesome West Indian food. Billy had inherited his parents deep brown eyes which matched his easy smile. Like his father he had tight knit curly hair, cut short and a rich light brown coloured skin. The first impression of Billy was usually one of a happy smiling boy, small but nevertheless happy.

Since arriving in England, his parents had flourished, he as a talented landscape gardener and she as a cook in one of Moseley's many ethnic independent restaurants. Keith had no idea where the name Shakespeare had come from in Trinidad but understood that he was unlikely to be descended from the famous writer. Any connection was tenuous at best, but Keith was fascinated by the tales and indeed rich language of the Bard of Avon. At home in Trinidad, he had soaked up information about the great playwright and would love to read out the words of Hamlet, Othello or Henry the Fifth. The great speeches. It is not always easy to understand the Elizabethan language, but Keith enjoyed using his deep rich voice. A real pity that he was in no way an actor and certainly had no pretentions in that way. However, his reading aloud attracted the attention of Faith Baptiste, and she loved the resonance of Keith's voice. The attraction was certainly mutual, and they were soon engaged and married. When their first child, a girl, came along. Keith hunted through his Shakespeare books and found the name Cressida from The Merchant of Venice. Faith said the name several time to the gorgeous tiny baby and she seemed to smile and respond to the name. So, Cressida Shakespeare it was, and she was the joy of Keith's life. The decision to move to England was a brave one, looking back Keith always said it was the bravest thing he ever did, apart from asking Faith's father for his daughter's hand in marriage. The small family moved to Moseley in South Birmingham and a second daughter was born. This time The Merchant of Venice supplied the name Jessica and again Faith approved. A year later an unplanned but successful pregnancy gave them a third daughter and they felt truly blessed. This time Faith insisted on having some more say in the naming of her daughter, Keith agreed and prepared a list for his wife to choose from. All taken of course from Shakespeare plays. She rolled the names over and over aloud. Maybe Desdemona but definitely not Lady Macbeth. The third delightful baby had been born in a gale which shook the windows of the hospital, so Miranda from The Tempest seemed just right.

   Billy loved his tall willowy sisters, Cressida was now nineteen and applying for university, Jessica was seventeen and the musician of the family. Jess sang in a girl band, all seventeen, they had formed at school. At school sixteen-year-old Miranda was an athlete specialising in the long jump and high jump. Her coaches were confident that she could go on to the highest level. Yes, Billy was proud of his tall good-looking sisters yet somehow dad always quoted the three witches' scene from Macbeth when the girls left the house together. 'When shall we three meet again?'

Dads could be very strange, Billy decided.

Five years after Miranda's birth Faith Shakespeare found herself in the delivery room at Queen Elizabeth's in very familiar surroundings and, as usual, the nurses seemed amused by her surname. Some tried to be witty with jokes about the name, but Faith knew that they were only trying to put her at ease. She had heard most of the puns and quotes before but laughed as if they were fresh and new to her. After five years she did not recognise any of the staff, unlike the first three births and the new staff seemed so young even the doctors, especially the doctors. Faith felt that it should be she putting them at their ease by telling jokes. Still, she knew they meant well.

Not for the first time Faith Shakespeare wondered if she should have married a man with a different name, Dickens, Wordsworth or Tolkien. Perhaps not. Different jokes, that's all and she would never swop Keith for any man in the world even if he had had the surname of a notorious murderer. He was always laughing and kind, the best of fathers and she loved his deep voice often quoting his beloved namesake. He had hated having to stay at home looking after the three girls whilst she went to hospital. Faith knew well that he would be unable to settle, pacing and waiting for a phone call. Pacing and worrying. He would try to take his mind away from the worry by making a meal for the girls. Cressida, then eight years old had reminded him, no, warned him severely that it should not be chicken nuggets. He had vaguely known that chicken should be well cooked to avoid salmonella, so he had once put the nuggets into the microwave for twenty-five minutes to ensure that they were done. The iron hard nuggets entered family legend and they would afterwards laugh about dad's cooking prowess or rather lack of it. Keith had felt slightly put out; he was only thinking about everyone's safety. after all. Chicken nuggets never appeared again on the menu.

The nurses began the usual call to push and said that they could see the top of the head and Faith, knowing full well the procedure pushed, and a baby boy was born quickly and easily. The baby had been wrapped up and after the briefest of meetings with mum had been whisked away to be examined. He had been declared perfectly healthy just tiny. Wrapped up snug in a white shawl he was passed to Faith, and she cried to see his perfect brown face and wisps of black hair.

She kissed the forehead of her first boy knowing that he would be the youngest and last in their particular line of Shakespeare's. Keith would be ecstatic. He had tried to introduce his daughters to being Aton Villa supporters like himself and Warwickshire fans and had taken them to Villa Park and in the Hollies Stand at Edgbaston. They had loved being with dad on these occasions but showed little inclination to learn the intricacies of 3-5-2 and the offside rule or the difference between leg spin and off spin. Faith had loved to see Keith taking his girls to football or cricket armed with sweets and refreshments to keep them quiet, a little ironic since the Holt End at Aston Villa and the Hollies Stand at Edgbaston were well known for their full vocal and raucous support for the home team. Thousands of Brummie voices urging on their teams in a good humoured but loud and passionate way. Vociferous but always fair.

Not for nothing was Edgbaston known as the Bear Pit, it was where the England cricket team had most success driven on by the noisy spectators. Keith's girls let it go over their heads and just enjoyed sitting by their dad and watching him shout, cheer or groan. He had even once almost caught a six hit into the stands. Almost.

Back in the small ward Faith knew that her own personal noisy crowd would soon respond to the phone call and dash to her bedside. But for the moment she enjoyed the quiet and serenity of her time alone with her precious baby boy. Her experienced head said it was probably wind but her heart sang and said that he was smiling. And he had continued to smile at life ever since.

Faith had asked the nurse not to tell Keith that he had a son just that it was a safe delivery and mother, and baby were well.

She wanted to see her beloved's face when he met his son for the first time. It was not long before he came in anxiously with three young girls in tow. They were all desperate to see mum and the new baby. Faith noted the lack of application of hairbrush or comb. Keith would not have thought of that. Cressida had warned her two younger sisters not to jump up on their mother just sit on the bed. All eager to see the new arrival and ask when he would be coming home. Faith kissed her husband and looked into his deep brown eyes with the question in them, perhaps the ultimate question.

Faith handed the tiny baby to her husband,
'Keith, meet your son, definitely the last of our Shakespeare's. Four is enough even for you.' He had openly wept with the utter joy of the moment and the girls wondered if he was sad but of course knowing dad he was never sad, so they laughed and tried to touch the baby's head with loving strokes. Keith handed the baby carefully back to the security of mum's embrace.

'Well done my love,' he said sitting on the bedside chair, 'we've all missed you.'

'Not chicken nuggets again,' she chuckled.

'I've been thinking about names,' Keith began tentatively, 'obviously I didn't know until a moment ago that we had a son, but it was always a choice of two, so I have had some suggestions ready.'

'If you are going to suggest Othello or Hamlet I'm going to have to say no definitely not.' Faith braced herself for the suggestions or probably only one suggestion knowing Keith. After three daughters they were well accustomed to choosing girls names from Shakespeare plays and she was veering towards Portia or Juliet, but those discussions were now academic. Keith and Faith had quietly hoped for a boy but didn't dare voice their hopes and jinx it by discussing boy's names. But this tiny baby in his mother's arms was living proof that dreams could really come true.

Faith looked at her husband who had proved a gentle loving partner and superb father to their three lovely daughters. She knew well that this child was destined to be an Aston Villa supporter and would end up at Edgbaston cheering on England.

At that moment she saw that he was shyly working out how to voice his suggestion and felt that she could never be happier than she was at that moment. She instantly understood what he was trying to say and decided that she would relieve him of the difficulty. She reached out and took his hand.

'Yes Keith, I agree that we should call him William, it's a good English name as we are English now and I'm sure that there will be few William Shakespeare's in the country. A good name though, one to be proud of.'

Keith was always amazed that Faith could read his mind so easily and he felt that his heart would actually burst with love and pride. He could not find the words he wanted but his tears flowed freely and that was enough. He took baby William carefully in his arms again and kissed his tiny head.

'Girls this is your new little brother, his name is William. William Shakespeare just like the famous writer.'

Eight-year-old Cressida looked thoughtful and added, 'Perhaps we can call him Billy and keep William as his Sunday best name.' she suggested.

Jessica beamed, 'Yes, I like that, little Billy Shakespeare.'

Whilst everyone laughed five-year-old Miranda snuggled up to her mother's side aware that she was no longer the youngest and felt quite grown up but still it was good to have a cuddle from mum.

A staff nurse on the ward passed this happy scene and smiled to herself. She thought that the baby would probably curse his parents for the burden of jokes which he would have to endure but then she realised that he would grow up cushioned in the love of a delightful happy family. Many would give a fortune to be in his position, a stable family with three older sisters to spoil him and certainly he would be well loved and cared for.

Eleven years later Billy lay in bed on a cold wet February morning and weighed up his options. He had been sad when his dad had got the job as head gardener at Fitzwilliam Hall in Newhill with its courtyard restaurant and walled garden. Not sad about the job or leaving their old house in Moseley but like his father moving away from Birmingham and Villa Park threatened their precious football afternoons or long warm afternoons watching cricket at Edgbaston. Father and son had anxiously checked the road map.

'It's OK son its only about forty miles and a good road. Just over an hour I reckon. It used to take us that by bus and train sometimes to see the Villa. We could always start watching Derby County instead, it is a lot closer,' Keith said mischievously.

Father and son looked at each other for a brief moment and together said,' No, no way.' They had laughed and high fived each other, their claret and sky-blue allegiance secure, their love for each other reinforced. Derby County indeed, the very idea!

The move to Newhill had proved successful and they had bought a four bedroomed house, which was superbly convenient for the park, the garden centre, Wath Mill allotments and Newhill Primary School. The town offered less than Birmingham, but Newhill was a friendly town and Keith applied for an allotment soon after registering the children at school. Tessa Tinton, the membership secretary had shown him the available plot seventeen, next to her own at the top end of the site. He was surprised that an allotment plot was available at once. Not like the heavily oversubscribed sites around Birmingham.

Billy listened to his teenage sisters mildly arguing about the order of bathroom time. Billy was not a teenager and reckoned that a look at the hot water tap would do. He had been given the smallest bedroom whilst nineteen-year-old Cressida had her own room, at least until she left to go to university in Sheffield. Jessica and Miranda, closest in age at seventeen and sixteen, shared in a good natured and companiable way. It was a room of mysterious whispered secrets and giggling comparisons of the merits of boys and pop music, make up and fashion magazines. Billy shuddered and was truly grateful to have his own tiny room.

From downstairs came the warm comforting smells of a family breakfast and the less welcome sound of some screeching group of so-called musicians. Billy dressed in his usual jeans, tee shirt and trainers topped with his old sweatshirt with Aston Villa badge. Strange how Father Christmas always knew what he wanted. This year it had been a beautiful Gunn and Moore cricket bat. Each morning he went through the ritual of stroking the bat and tapping the large colour poster of Aston Villa for luck. Today they were playing away at Crystal Palace so he and dad were football free but would carefully check the scores throughout the afternoon.

Billy had tried hard to be a success at football, but his size worked against him despite his knowledge and experience of watching the Villa. He was quick and played on the wing but was often knocked off the ball by larger players. Determination could only get you so far. He had once tried to be a goalkeeper, but the ball kept flying mysteriously over his head out of reach and he was soon sent back out to the right wing.

Cricket proved almost as difficult. Billy had hoped to be a tall loose limbed fast bowler terrorising batters like the legendary West Indies giants or patrolling the boundary chasing the ball with long strides, but the setback was always the word tall. He had long accepted that he would always be the smallest in whatever group he was in and tried to make up for his lack of stature with effort and good humour. He played with a smile on his face,

Keith Shakespeare never spoke it out loud, but he really felt for his son, always trying never conceding defeat always enjoying his sport. As an umpire for his local club in Moseley he had faced many wicket keepers at the other end, and it had dawned on him that they were usually small and quick. That was Billy all over and in cricket there were usually no physical encounters with larger players. The suggestion was made, and Billy took to it quickly, he had found his sport and his position or rather his dad had. Billy Shakespeare; wicket keeper, legend in waiting was created.

Chapter Four

A Little Deodorant and Some Serious Chats

As Billy Shakespeare went downstairs his mum, Fath asked if he had washed, especially behind the ears. What was it about the behind the ear's thing? Mothers seemed obsessed with washing behind the ears. Billy tried a bold approach.

'I tried to get into the bathroom, but it was crowded with sisters, and I didn't have time to wait so I put on some deodorant instead.'

One mum and three daughters stopped eating breakfast and looked up startled. Keith continued with his cornflakes oblivious to the earth-shattering statement.

Jessica broke the silence, 'You've never used deodorant in your life. Have you even got any?

The four females looked at each other bemused. This was news of epic proportions. Little Billy taking care of his personal hygiene and on a Saturday too!

'It's OK I tried yours Cressie, but it was horrible, so I experimented with the others I found in your bedrooms.' Billy smiled expecting the howls of outrage and protests to their mother.

Keith looked at his son and reckoned that he would have to talk to him about the perilous dangers of upsetting the female of the species. The odds were stacked against him especially in this female orientated house. Father and son exchanged a conspiratorial smile of male allegiance amidst the cries for him to be sent away to an orphanage.

'At least then we could then have a bedroom each,' Miranda piped up.

'Don't worry yourself ladies, I only used dad's deodorant. Yours smelt terrible anyway.' Keith spluttered his tea out and decided that Little Billy must have a death wish. He would go far if he survived his sisters' wrath ...and his.

Billy grinned and knew that he was safe. He stood to go back to the bathroom for that wash avoiding the playful punches as he went, skipping quickly past his dad's attempt at a headlock.

'Keep my bran flakes warm for me.'

He reckoned that a wash on a Saturday was a waste of water, but meeting Rosangel Chlebek today was well worth an extra squirt or two of dad's deodorant.

Faith called after him, 'And don't forget to wash behind your ears!'

Billy ran the cold water tap and splashed around before tiptoeing into his parent's room to add an extra layer of spray.

Being eleven was wonderful as he had no commitments, and he could go out alone with few restrictions. Newhill didn't have the potential perils of Moseley and Birmingham. He had arranged to meet the three Chlebek children and possibly Grace Bisby up at the park. They felt too old and sophisticated to play on the swings and slides but there was an old wooden shelter where they could hang out.

Billy didn't actually need to brush his tight knit black curls but nevertheless put a brush across his head. A touch of aftershave was added, and he went down to continue his breakfast. The consensus whilst he was upstairs was that a girl was definitely involved. On his arrival the combination of after shave and deodorant confirmed their suspicions.

'Most certainly a girl or aliens have taken our Little Billy and replaced him with a robot,' Jessica declared.

'When did you start shaving son?' Keith asked, knowing full well that he had certainly not.

Billy grinned and resumed eating his bran flakes.

Faith added more toast to the basket and looked closely at her son. She knew Cressida's boyfriend well and had both met and approved of him and suspected that Miranda and Jess were opening discussions with local boys, but she had hoped that her youngest could remain her baby for a while longer. Time passes so quickly she thought, pouring orange juice for Little Billy, and it would not be long before Keith and her would have the house to themselves. The happy noisy bustle would be replaced by silence if any house could be considered silent with the frequent deep laughter of her lovely husband. It would be companionable, precious moments together. She supposed that the children would return for visits, especially at Christmas. The volume of noise would return, and they could go to the Christmas Eve service at St Matthews together once again, a family ritual. Of course, they would be older and taller, well perhaps even young Billy too if he had a growth spurt.

Faith had the sudden inevitable realisation that one day they would be returning to the nest with babies of their own and a tiny tear of joy escaped to roll slowly down her face. Cressida noticed and frowned.

'Mum, what's wrong, are you alright?'

Everyone looked up towards Faith, suddenly worried.

'Nothing is wrong, in fact everything is just perfect' she assured them, and this was true as far as the Granny in waiting was concerned.

'It's not because Little Billy didn't wash behind his ears, is it?' Miranda asked.

This broke the moment and Jessica said, 'He probably ran the tap and splashed water about so we would think that he had washed, such an old trick.'

Billy reached for his toast, suddenly aghast that his secret was out. How did women always know these things?'

Keith Shakespeare ate his third piece of Marmite covered toast and smiled to himself, yes, he would certainly have to have a talk to Billy about females. In his capacity of husband with three teenage daughters he had become something of an expert and in a quiet moment together on his allotment he would try to pass on some of his knowledge. Little Billy had much to learn.

Rosangel Chlebek, the cause of Billy Shakespeare's double dose of deodorant and hopeful splash of unnecessary after shave was particularly quiet that Saturday morning at breakfast. Usually, she revelled in the role of second in command to her mother at mealtimes. Dads didn't count in these affairs of the kitchen. She would keep order with Sam and Mikolaj, her younger brothers. Mikolaj, at eight, was usually lively and needed his big sister to remind him of the correct way to conduct himself properly at mealtimes. Jacob the toddler was a law unto himself. Today they sensed that Rosangel or Rosie as she was often called was preoccupied and rather than take advantage, they ate their honey hoops quietly to avoid attention. You never know with sisters; it may be a trap.

Sam was nine and rarely spoke, allowing Rosie to act as his mouthpiece. When asked a question he would at once look to his adored big sister to speak on his behalf. This had been the way since he was a toddler when he would follow her everywhere she went.

Andy Chlebek was checking some papers for the County Council meeting at the breakfast table, a habit Rosie usually disapproved of but today she said nothing. Andy had worked hard from being a postal worker in Newhill to the Town Council to representing Newhill Central ward on the larger county council. He still worked for the post office but in an indoor managerial role now. Better paid but he missed the outdoor life and meeting his customers directly. He and Sherrie his beloved and beautiful wife, were proud of their Polish heritage and its high work ethic. He had kept up his allotment at Wath Mill, plot thirteen, despite the many calls on his time. They had continued to live in their old, terraced house behind the Market square although he and Sherrie acknowledged that it was fast becoming too small for their needs and indeed status. A move to a larger house was being seriously contemplated.

Sherrie began the washing up even though the boys had not yet finished their toast. She glanced at Andy and gave a tiny movement of her head towards Rosangel and indicated a question with a slight frown. He at once knew what she was asking, and he gave a slight shrug to show his lack of knowledge. Andy was always busy but for him and indeed Sherrie their children were a priority.

Folding his papers away into his nearby briefcase he told his sons to help their mother clear the table and wash up. With mouths full of marmalade covered toast they pushed back their chairs and began to obey.

'When you have finished what is in your mouth first boys,' he said quietly but firmly.

Rosangel began to stand and help almost automatically.

'Not you Rosie I need your advice in my study. Come on, it will only take a moment.'

Sam looked slightly anxious at the sight of Rosangel going upstairs with their father. The study was a tiny box bedroom. To call it a study may well be an overstatement but would suffice till they could afford a bigger house. Andy sat on his swivel chair and Rosie took her place on the small stool. On another day she would have loved to help and advise her dad but today she was serious and quiet.

'Rosangel, you are my first born and very special to me and your mum. You are fast growing into a lovely, caring and intelligent young lady and we love you beyond words but today you seem sad and preoccupied. What is filling your mind with worries? I can see that you are not yourself. Are you feeling ill?

'No, I'm perfectly well dad I would tell you or mum straight away if anything was physically wrong.'

Andy knew that she was the epitome of a sensible girl but noted the word, physically.

'Is it Sam you are worried about, we too would like him to speak out more and he does rely on you to talk for him. The school is doing their best for him. Mrs. Poole is very kind and understanding. I'm sure that he will cope in September when you move to secondary school. He tried to sound reassuring, but both knew that Sam would struggle without his big sister, both were worried and dreaded September.

'No, it's not that, I do worry about Sam of course but it's not particularly that today, at least not more than any other day. To be quite honest I feel a bit down about one of my friends.

Andy sighed, 'Is it a boy? I know that Billy Shakespeare really likes you but he's a good lad from a good family. Of course, he's an Aston Villa supporter but no one is perfect. Andy began to wonder if he should have left this chat with his beloved daughter to Sherrie and began to flounder. This was unknown territory for him, and he began to regret being so quick to offer help. Girls and their developing bodies and relationships were something of a mystery to him and he usually fell back on the traditional last retreat of fathers everywhere. Ask your mum. The tiny study seemed suddenly extremely small and unusually warm. He well remembered the panic when Rosie had been seven and had suddenly asked him where she came from. He had turned a shade somewhere between pink and white and looked round for Sherrie's practical, wise support but she was shopping in Newhill. He blundered his way through mixed up tales of birds and bees and people who loved each other and differences in boys and girls but was sinking fast, praying for the seventh cavalry to arrive in the guise of Sherrie. She would know how to answer a daughter's hard questions and as if in response to his desperate prayer the front door opened, and his wife came in laden with shopping bags and Mikolaj and Sam in tow.

Rosie had felt relief but nowhere near that felt by Andy. At last, she would get a straight answer to a simple question. Sherrie put down her bags and ushered her sons into the living room.

'Mum, thank goodness you are here, I asked dad where I came from, Poland or England and he seemed very confused.'

Today in the study Rosie smiled at her father's discomfort knowing full well what he was fearing. Her mum had already had a long discussion on affairs of the heart long before it had occurred to her father. This had been admirably confirmed by simple, honest lessons in sex education at school taught in a sensitive manner.

She spoke quickly to allay his unease. 'It isn't Little Billy; he's a good friend and I know that he likes me a lot and I like him. He is fun. No, it's Grace Bisby I am worried about. Her granny is coming back to Newhill to live, and it has been years since Grace has seen her. Grace is very worried about seeing her after all that happened, but she won't open up and talk to me about it. I'm her best friend in the whole world and its sort of my job to help. Guard her back sort of thing.

Andy gazed at this almost perfect copy of the wife he worshipped. Same shape of face, large brown eyes which usually sparkled with a mix of curiosity and calm and a deep blond mop of hair. The small nose was identical. This morning

Rosangel had shown that same compassionate and caring side of her nature. This was truly a child to treasure and love.

'What can I do to help dad, if she won' t tell me what the problem is. I'm worried about her.'

'Well Rosie when faced with a dilemma I usually say, go and ask your mum but in this particular case I believe that I can offer some help. You and Grace have been friends since you first went to Newhill Primary school together. She is, like you, an intelligent girl and I feel that all she wants is a friend to be there for her. When she is ready, she will talk to you, and you will know what to say. But the first move must be from her. If she is as worried as you fear, then she will appreciate having you there to confide in. That's what friends do, and you are good friends, and they are the best kind.'

Rosie stood and hugged her dad; he was truly an understanding father and she loved him even more for it.

'Thanks dad, that helps a lot. I'll follow your advice. I'm meeting her today with the others in the park, but I won't push her. I don't want to lose her even if we don't end up in the same secondary school, we'll always be best friends.'

Rosie went downstairs feeling somehow lighter and smiled at her mum who had finished the washing up without the somewhat limited help of her sons.

'Come on boys brush your teeth and get your coats, we are going to the park to meet Grace and Little Billy.'

Sam and Mikolaj rushed upstairs with a heavy clatter almost pushing past Andy. Rosangel followed more calmly towards the bathroom to brush her own teeth. Sherrie went over to her husband and planted a brief kiss on his lips.

'Well?' she asked looking up at him whilst thanking God that she had a husband who was understanding of the needs of their children and was willing to respond with compassion and wisdom.

Andy looked down with serious face. 'It turns out she wants to marry Little Billy Shakespeare, but I said you wouldn't approve of an Aston Villa supporter in the family.'

'What! No. What was it really about? You aren't serious, are you? She's only eleven, much too young...' then she saw Andy's grin and punched him on the arm.

'What is she really worried about, is it Sam?'

'Our daughter is quite a remarkable young lady she is actually worried about Grace and has shown care for her friend. I think that she is a credit to you and me. She is intelligent and thoughtful and anyway she has agreed not to marry Billy until she is at least twelve.' The next punch was followed by a heartfelt hug.

There was a swirling noisy rush as the three Chlebek's headed for the front door putting on warm winter coats and scarves. Baby Jacob had already been changed and put down for a nap.

'Be back by twelve for lunch and take care crossing the road. Stick together, Rosie, watch out for the boys. Unnecessary advice but it was Sherrie's duty to issue the standard warnings. The front door slammed, and silence fell on the tiny house.

'Well, Mr. Chlebek you have, as usual, dealt beautifully with the needs of your children. Perhaps you would like to join me upstairs to help with my needs, we are free until lunch time.' Andy grinned and thought that he didn't really have that amount of time he had lots of paperwork to do but looking at the gorgeous figure of his wife moving towards the stairs he stirred and began to follow. She looked over her shoulder at him with a seductive sexy smile. No man on the planet could resist such a request for help There was always time to help in whatever small way he could.

Life was certainly good on this wet February morning in the Chlebek household.

Chapter Five
Bad Apples Old and New

The blustery late February day had calmed, and the evening was cool and fresh with the setting sun producing vivid cloud scenes, changing and evolving. An evening to stand with a cup of hot coffee and warm coat to admire the Derbyshire sky.

For three people all on their way to the bi-monthly meeting of the Wath Mill allotments committee there was little time for more than a glimpse at the beauty of the sky. All three of them individually decided to walk to Tessa Tinton's house. No one could remember how it had come to always be held at the membership secretary's house. Perhaps because it was the most central of the current committee's homes or more likely that Tessa was a great host. A fresh baked cake was cut and ready and the smell of coffee filled the home, mingling with the aroma of carrot cake or lemon drizzle. Why change if Tessa was willing to act as host to the small committee?

Steve Shaw was well prepared for the meeting with his papers ready for his treasurer's report, copies of which were ready to hand out as he knew that some people liked to see the figures. Not that they didn't trust Steve, it was just easier to follow his latest financial update with the figures in front of them and perhaps look at them at leisure later. Not that they were complicated, and the financial position was sound, well more than sound. Most allotment sites would be envious of Wath Mill.

Steve's thoughts turned to the recent rumour which he had heard. Eileen Bisby, the old membership secretary at the allotments was apparently returning to Newhill. It was a famous case in the small town a few years ago which had sharply divided opinion. Eileen had smothered her husband John to death to save him the misery of years of accumulated agonies which even strong painkillers could not relieve. Her loving compassion was treated as manslaughter, but her motives were considered by the court. She had, however, spent several years away from Newhill and her precious daughter Amanda and granddaughter Grace.

Steve walked through Market Square just as most of the shops were closing for the night. The Duke's Head was far from closing and Steve thought of the days when he had had to battle an addiction for alcohol. Once upon a time he would have called in for a pint and a rum and coke as a matter of course and then later return home to an empty house. Two failed marriages to beautiful shallow girls had drained him economically and he took comfort in greeting the bottom of bottles when he returned from the nightly binges in various pubs. He had liked to frequent different pubs so as not to get a reputation as a drunk. The dustbin men had sometimes complained about the number of bottles in the recycling bin. Steve had put it down to jealousy.

Those days of failing marriages, no children and the stress of intensive ever-changing work in IT had taken its toll on the forty-four-year-old Steve, He knew full well how he had disappointed his parents when their high hopes for him had been cruelly dashed by spectacular failure at Limerick University. His father had died still bemused by his adored son's lack of a degree of any classification after three years whilst his mother never forgave Steve for his underachievement.

It was hard to look back at those bad times but Steve thought that it was good to reflect and see how far he had come. He had lost the election as chair of the committee in a closely fought election to Charlie Webster or Poole as she was now. Surprisingly this had reduced his stress level and perhaps even more surprisingly he had taken over from old Tolly Braithwaite in running the Newhill Horticultural show and was the leading light in the Newhill in Bloom competition entry.

Steve's mother had been pleased to see her beloved if somewhat wayward son at last achieving some status on his own merits. She conceded that her late husband, Donald, would have been almost happy with the way things had turned out.

Steve wondered how his mother would react when he told her his special news. She would probably be pleased for him, but this news had an added twist, and he was not quite certain of the reaction.

Turning the corner Steve saw Charlie Poole coming, like him, towards Tessa's house. They greeted each other warmly, once rivals but Steve had appreciated the way that Charlie, or Charlotte, as she had been known then had ensured that he would continue to have a role on the committee and to save face as the Chinese would say.

'Hi Steve, what do you reckon, chocolate cake or lemon drizzle?' Charlie Poole asked smiling. Tessa's cakes were legendary, and they made boring committee meetings an event to look forward to.

'I quite like the chocolate one, hard to resist and even harder to eat whilst giving a financial report.' he replied.

'Will it be good news or bad? 'She asked, knowing or at least guessing the answer.

'As you know Willam Mullins bought the site from his lottery win and left us enough in his will to ensure we were never in the red. That together with the annual membership fee means that we have the ability to take on projects and improve the site each year. I feel something of a fraud as treasurer, it's too easy.'

Avoiding a large puddle Charlie looked at the still handsome man and noted the grey at the side which somehow gave him a distinguished look. More gravitas.

'I have to say that we appreciate you being treasurer, I know how busy you are with the Horticultural society and Britain in Bloom. I don't know how you find the time.'

'Less time drinking in pubs and more time enjoying sunsets like these and Tessa's chocolate cake, of course. I quite like keeping in touch with the committee even though it's a minor role. My allotment keeps me grounded even though I'm helping to look after another plot these days.'

'Another plot? If I had known that you had enough time to work on two plots, I would have asked you to do mine. The autumn digging seems worse each year or I am getting old. But seriously have you enough time to look after two plots?'

Charlie stopped and looked at the man who was once her rival for chair. He automatically stopped as well.

Realisation dawned on Charlie, her female intuition finally kicking in.

'Leona? I had noticed that you often seemed to be chatting together.'

'Yes, we are getting married, we are keeping it quiet, it will just be a small wedding. We've both been married before, twice in my case. I thought that I would announce it after the committee meeting tonight.'

Leona Maria Pontes was a care worker in the Woodlands residential home. It had a good reputation, mainly due to the diligence and effort put in by workers such as Leona and her friend Anna. Both had come from Portugal at the same time. They had plots two and three next to the school plot at Wath Mill. Leona could not be said to be beautiful but rather attractive in a wholesome sort of way. Her dark eyed striking looks, fuller figure and Portuguese accent had first attracted Steve's attention, but her common sense and easy laughter had become attributes which had led him to ask her out for a meal. Despite both being married before they felt like nervous teenagers on a first date. The Italian meal had gone well, and she had insisted on making him an authentic Portuguese meal if he wished. Steve had agreed with a grin and their goodnight kiss at the end of the evening had been brief but without any sense of awkwardness. Instinctively he knew that Leona would be good for him. Unlike his two earlier marriages. His mother would surely like her as he did.

Charlie Poole hugged Steve and offered her warmest congratulations.

'I am really pleased for you, I was going to ask you to consider taking on the chair at Wath Mill but I can see that you will be too busy, two allotments, wow. This is great news. Laura will be chuffed; she is next to Leona and really likes her. As obviously you do. That has made my day.'

As they arrived at the Tinton house Steve opened the gate for the still beaming Charlie. 'There's more news I'm afraid but I'll save that for later otherwise it will be less of a committee meeting and more of a gossip shop'

Charlie laughed, 'And why not, good news is always most welcome especially in dreary February days like these. I do hate

February's' She paused slightly remembering telling her late friend William Mullins the same thing many years ago. She still missed him.

Steve noticed her hesitating and the sudden lack of a smile. He changed tack.

'Well, what do you reckon, will it be lemon drizzle or carrot cake, fancy a ten pence bet?'

Charlie's smile reappeared, 'I'll go for the lemon cake you can have the carrot.'

Steve rang the doorbell just as Graham Tinton was leaving with Billy their cocker spaniel, on a red lead.

'Hi Charlie, Steve I'm just taking Billy here for his evening walk. I can enjoy this sunset and we'll be out of your way, but I'll certainly be back before you all demolish the chocolate gateaux which Tessa has made.'

Gaham steered the Billy the cocker spaniel past the two guests and did not notice their shared grin. Both wrong. All bets off. Billy was reluctant to leave the house with its delicious aroma of chocolate, The way to a spaniel's heart was definitely through his stomach and Billy was never one to show reluctance to forage for food to supplement his meals.

Once settled in the lounge with mugs of tea and plates for their generous helpings of cake they began. Papers were placed wherever it was convenient. It was a small meeting and very informal. They could have sat around the table but that would have seemed too impersonal. There was an agenda and reports to be made but it was more a loose framework for the meeting, which everyone had agreed should be no more than an hour long.

Laura Watson was late, and everyone looked up when the doorbell rang. Steve went to answer the bell as Tessa was busy cutting more cake.

Taking off her coat, to be hung up by Steve, revealed her large comfortable green Wath Mill allotments sweatshirt. Laura sat on the large comfortable sofa, next to Charlie. Soon her hands were full of a cake laden plate and a mug of tea.

'Not like you to be late Laura, been sky watching, have you?' Tessa observed, noticing that Laura had obviously been hurrying to the meeting. 'Everything alright?'

Laura resisted biting into the gorgeous cake as she knew that it would seriously reduce her ability to communicate her news. Instead, she took a sip of tea from the mug with its 'I love Tokyo' motif.

'Sorry, everyone but I ran into an old friend Julie, we worked together at Newhill Primary school for a short time. She is a Teaching Assistant at Snelston school now. We chatted and Julie could certainly chat but anyway it turned out that we had a common acquaintance. I say acquaintance rather than friend. Kevin Bolton on plot fourteen.'

There was a collective groan at the mention of his name.

'Actually, I was going to bring up Kevin's name as an issue under any other business.' said Charlie who of course chaired the informal meeting.

Steve's plot was next to Kevin Bolton's and his heart sank, 'What has he been up to now, nothing good I assume.'

Kevin Edward Bolton was a teacher at nearby Snelston and took his son, Jason, to that school despite living in the Newhill catchment area. He had had an allotment for almost two years and in that time his opinions had managed to upset most of his fellow allotmenteers. He was forty-four, stocky with short clipped grey hair. Never slow to offer his viewpoint, he was not afraid to enter into verbal conflict and seemed to enjoy the battles. Few were left unsure about his strongly voiced opinions. Politically he lay somewhere to the right of Genghis Khan and Attila the Hun. He considered himself well balanced, but others said that this was because he had chips on both shoulders.

Kevin made sure that everyone knew that he had once had a trial at Derbyshire cricket club, and he still maintained that the South African coach had it in for him. Despite not achieving at that level, although he wrongly believed that he would have, given proper opportunity he played as a solid bullying batter for Newhill. At his only school he had been overlooked twice for the deputy headship and once for the headship. For his latter attempt at management, he had not even been granted an interview which his experience would normally call for. The governors were well aware of his bombastic manner and knew that his style was not one of cooperation and cohesion.

Years before his father, Eddie, had been soundly defeated by Andy Chlebek, the Polish postal worker in the Town Council election. Eddie, like his son, was opinionated and despised anything remotely foreign. As a somewhat shoddy builder Eddie refused to employ non-English workers even though this led at times to having a less skilful workforce. Unfortunately, Andy's plot and Kevin's sat next to each other at Wath Mill. Andy would try to avoid times when he knew that Kevin would be there.

Kevin refused to communicate with Leona and Annie, the Portuguese care workers and Spiros the rarely seen Greek chef on plot five but he reserved his most contemptuous abrasive and domineering remarks for Keith Shakespeare, the jovial Trinidadian. As a weekend umpire Keith had sometimes come across Kevin batting for Newhill and did not like his manner. He had come across too many like him. Words were often sly and behind the back but obvious.

After one match whilst enjoying a beer Keith was approached by Kevin.

'If we had television cameras I would never have been given out, I clearly snicked the ball before it hit my pads. That makes it not out in my book.' Kevin had challenged.

'Well in my experience and after careful consideration the scorebook and I both called it out, there were no two sounds, clear sign that you had not hit it.'

Keith disliked conflict, he reckoned that life was too short to let bitterness spoil his cricket.

'Let me buy you a drink Kevin, a pint of bitter I presume?'

'No thanks we can buy our own and I still reckon you were biased out there today.'

This was both harsh and incorrect. Keith noted the word we. Kevin seemed to have set himself up as spokesperson for the nation.

Kevin went on relentless in his attack, 'Tell me who do you support when England play the West Indies?'

Keith noticed his son drinking orange juice nearby and considered his answer to this abrasive, rude and unnecessary question.

'I love my cricket and I love watching England whether on television or at Edgbaston. A fine century or a spectacular catch or good spin bowling deserves applause whether the player is black, brown white or a deeper shade of purple. I will be the first to applaud the skill, I reckon that I am blessed to be able to watch my old country and my adopted one play each other, I can't lose, can I? Something you seem to be good at.'

Kevin grunted and walked away as Billy Shakespeare came over to his dad immensely proud of his calm rebuff of what could only be considered a rude interruption.

'Nice one dad. I was there as back up for you if he'd turned ugly.'

Keith looked down at his diminutive son and solemnly thanked him.

'Thanks son but just remember, always keep calm in such circumstances, no matter what the provocation. Violence never solved any argument. If you back down to such attitudes they will win, use intelligence and wit, not your fists'

The idea of his small son fighting physically against aggressive racist challenges made Keith smile but inside he felt a profound sadness that his son should have to endure such pathetic medieval attitudes.

'He's a teacher at Snelston,' Billy said, 'but I'm really glad that I'm not in his class or even school.'

'So am I son, so am I. let's go home and see what we're having for tea.'

Laura Watson sat with the plate of chocolate cake on her lap and having had a sip of tea to calm down her breathlessness decided to be brief. Worrying about her increasing lack of breath could wait until later, but it was beginning to be a nagging concern.

'Well, my friend Julie was telling me about Kevin Bolton. It seems that his wife came into Snelston school demanding to see the head, Ian Newsom. She was steamed up and wanted action. It seems that her obnoxious son, Jason, in Year six had seen a pair of girls turning a long rope for another girl to skip. Normal playground stuff.'

Tessa wondered where this was going.

'To cut a long story short, as I said my friend could chat for England, Jason took another skipping rope and hit one of the girls with the rope, called her names and made her cry. All to impress his group of friends. Of course, the dinner ladies on duty outside sent Jason to the head. Ian, being a reasonable man calmed the situation and explained to Jason why hitting girls was wrong or hitting boys for that matter. He ensured that Jason would never repeat his action, or anything like it.'

'So why was Jason's mum angry? Charlie asked

'It seems that she wanted the little girl to be rebuked and spoken to in the same way her precious son had been.'

Steve, Tessa and Charlie all said 'What!' at the same time.

The head apparently couldn't believe that she was not only serious but wanted to have this little girl punished for having the temerity to cry and report the incident leading to Jason being in trouble.

'Steve said, 'It's been a long time since I was in a playground and it's a bit alien to me, but I can't see what the girl had done wrong to bring forth such anger in the boy's mother.'

Charlie added, 'Why didn't his dad, Kevin, intervene to calm things down. It seems that the head, Ian, had acted perfectly reasonably. Kevin is on the staff at Snelston after all.'

Laura had taken a small bit of cake whilst Charlie was speaking, and she couldn't resist any longer.

'That's the amazing bit, he had left his class to go with his wife to complain about his wonderful son's punishment as they insisted on calling it.'

Charlie decided that she was glad to be at Newhill primary and not working alongside Kevin Bolton or worse with his obnoxious son but thought that the meeting should get back on track.

'I was actually going to bring up Kevin Boltons attitude at Wath Mill under any other business, but your story Laura seems to have brought it forward. We have had several complaints about people feeling uncomfortable when Kevin is there. Your story seems to have more than confirmed our concerns.'

Laura had taken the opportunity to finish her cake and wash it down with a sip of her rapidly cooling cup of tea.

Tessa had already stood up, 'More tea anyone, do help yourself to more cake'. If you don't eat it Graham and that greedy dog of ours will finish it off. I'll put a slice away for him, not the dog, he's fat enough already.'

Charlie saw that the agenda was turned upside down but persevered whilst declining a second slice of cake, 'We have had a formal complaint from Kevin Bolton. He has looked at the constitution and regulations and it states clearly that dogs are not allowed on the allotments site. He says in his letter that he has often seen Meg, your lovely beagle, Laura and Billy your cocker spaniel, Tessa, on the site. They have been going there since they were puppies and sit calmly near your plots not doing any harm. Everyone loves them, apart from Kevin apparently, they have become sort of mascots.'

Laura and Tessa were shocked, their dog was no trouble at all, and they could not imagine going to the allotments without them. It was part of the dog's routine exercise.

Steve could see their upset. 'It seems irrelevant and petty minded, but Kevin is a heavy smoker even around his son, but he doesn't waste an opportunity to point out everyone else's faults. The Chlebek's and the Shakespeare family seem to bear the brunt of his venom. I have seen his son Jason hanging about Kevin's plot next to mine and he is a good-looking lad with his long blond hair, a star cricketer for Snelston apparently. Kevin never fails to sing his praises. But it seems to be a very dysfunctional and certainly unpleasant family.'

Charlie, like Steve, didn't have a dog but loved to see Meg and Billy calmly waiting on the plots for their walks. Certainly, the children working on the school plot, number one, enjoyed petting the two dogs and walking them up and down.

'Before we decide what to do about this very unpleasant man and indeed his son I would like to go back to a nicer item, not on the agenda but important, nevertheless. On behalf of the committee can I offer our sincere congratulations to two of our site members, Leona and Steve here, who will be getting married. Two plots merging into one as it were.'

This news lightened the mood and congratulations were added.

Steve almost blushed.' There is a little bit of extra news. As you know Leona and I have been married before and Leona has a little girl. from her first marriage My fiancé is younger than me and she is going to have a baby in the summer. I am going to be a father for the first time.'

Tessa said, 'This does call for more cake.'

Chapter Six

A Little Paraffin Goes a Long Way

The park was unusually quiet considering that it was Saturday. The early morning March rain and stiff breeze had blown itself out leaving a penetrating cold, wet grass and puddles across all areas of badly pitted tarmac. Benches, swings and roundabout were wet and unlikely to dry out anytime soon. A feeble sun offered neither warmth nor drying out capacity

Apart from a well wrapped up dog walker throwing a tennis ball for his West Highland terrier only the Chlebek/Shakespeare/Bisby gang braved the park that morning.

A small wooden shelter with benches offered little but had the virtue of a fairly dry place to sit.

'We really must get a proper name for our gang,' Billy Shakespeare suggested, swinging his legs which, he could do comfortably as his legs didn't reach the ground.

Rosangel considered this for a moment, 'Are we a gang? I mean we don't rob banks or kidnap people, and why do we need a group name anyway?'

'It was just an idea, what do you think Grace?'

Grace Bisby thought deeply as she often did. She was modest and did not consider herself pretty or beautiful, especially when compared with her best friend Rosangel. Grace had long brown hair with not a curl in sight and she perceived her ears to be too large but her habit of pushing her hair behind her ears exacerbated this. In fact, Grace considered herself plain and ordinary with a mouth a trifle too wide. But she was wrong. When she smiled her face lit up and her eyes sparkled but of course few people actually smiled naturally into a mirror. Others saw the quiet depth of her character bordering on sadness. Grace would have liked to have been a little taller but recognised that this would come with time.

'I think that it is enough to just be friends, friends who help and support each other. We all go to the same school at least until September. Until then when we are split up, we can just enjoy each other's company. It won't last forever,' Grace replied thoughtfully.

Sam looked troubled by the very idea of school life without Rosangel, not feeling able to communicate. September would bring real fears for him.

Rosangel noted the words, 'help and support each other'. Was this a sign that Grace was asking for help or at least a sympathetic ear as her father had suggested might be the case if she showed patience?

Meanwhile Billy and the younger Mikolaj were debating what to do with their free morning. Sam, as usual listened but did not contribute. The weather was certainly restricting their options.

'We could always try to solve the mystery of the missing tools and watering cans at the allotments.' Billy suggested brightly.

Mikolaj asked if Billy wanted to be the new Sherlock Holmes.

'No but between us we should be able to put our heads together and work out who is responsible. At least it's better than sitting around being bored.' Billy replied but he was far from bored, time spent near to Rosangel Chlebek was never boring.

Mikolaj declared himself to be hungry and his sister made a bold and decisive decision.

'I agree, we can use our powers of deduction, but we need sustenance to think clearly. Has anyone got any money? I've got two pounds.'

A collection of coins produced, enough for chocolate biscuits, crisps and perhaps cans of orange,

'Well, Little Billy Shakespeare, wicket keeper, detective, would you do me a favour and take the boys across to the supermarket to buy what we need? Grace and I will stay and work out a strategy, I would be really grateful for your help.'

Both Sam and Billy were reluctant to leave Rosangel but for very different reasons. Billy was delighted to be given such a responsible role by his favourite girl. Grace was nice but Rosie was somehow special.

'Go with Billy and listen to what he says and be careful crossing the roads.' Rosangel said to her brothers conscious that she sounded just like her mum.

Grace looked at her friend after the boys had walked away to the High Street. A short walk but they would take time deciding on what to buy and work out if they had enough money.

'What was that all about Rosie? We don't usually buy snacks so soon after breakfast and as for working out a strategy......'

Rosangel knew that this was her moment, the moment to be a good friend. She moved closer to Grace and took her hand.

'Grace, we have been friends since we met at school on our first day playing in the sand and water. Our friendship has been very special to me. I have three brothers and I love all of them deeply although they can be annoying at times. You are like a sister to me, and I know when you are sad, what is troubling you? Let me help, please. Are you worried about secondary school, it's not for months and we'll probably be at the same school and hopefully the same class.'

To Rosangel's surprise tears began to roll down Grace's face and she began to sob, frightening sobs which came from deep inside her. Her anxiety had been released and Rosangel wished her dad was there to offer his advice, but instinct took over and she held Grace tight and allowed her almost sister to cry herself out.

Grace finally reached for a handkerchief from her coat pocket and began to apologise for her anguish. 'I'm sorry Rosie but I'm glad to have you here for me, I need to have someone to share my feelings with me. A special friend like you, I'm so lucky'

Rosangel sensed that a second bout of tears was about to start, whatever was troubling her was truly serious and she wondered if she was up to this. It seemed to need a parent or teacher, was she capable of helping.' She gently took her own handkerchief, silently thanking her mum for insisting on not going out without a clean hankie and wiped away her best friends' tears. Grace took the clean dry hankie and loudly blew her nose. The sobbing episode was ebbing if not finished. Time to help.

'Keep the hankie, you may need it later.'

Grace smiled a weak smile and promised to wash it before returning it. Rosie was truly a very good friend, one who understood.

'Take your time Grace but the boys won't be too long.'

Grace drew a deep breath and held Rosie's hand between her own.

'Do you know what DNA is Rosie?

Rosie looked puzzled and tried hard to recall what little she knew.

'I know it is short for a long word and that dad sometimes uses it when researching our family history, especially the Polish part. I don't really understand it, but I think that it is what makes us all unique but links us to our family. Why is DNA troubling you? I don't understand.'

'As you know my granny killed my grandad, not a shooting or stabbing but she put a pillow over his face to stop his agony. A mercy killing, they call it, he was seriously ill and dying.'

Grace paused and collected her thoughts although these same thoughts had increasingly haunted her dreams and wakening hours.

Rosangel instinctively knew the words to say without rehearsal.

'She must have loved your grandad very much to do that, but it was years ago. Why are you so upset by it now?

'I can barely remember my granny and never met my grandad apart from in old photos. She was put in prison for a short time, the courts took into consideration her compassionate reason to do such a terrible thing. Later she went somewhere for what they call rehabilitation and counselling. I've not seen her for years and now she is coming back to Newhill to live with us, she's like a stranger to me, I'm scared to meet her, what will I say to her, how will I feel?'

'I reckon that you will know when the time comes, she must be anxious to meet you again you were just a toddler when you last met. How does DNA come into all this?

Grace's face darkened and she looked down at her shoes and small tears began to roll. Rosangel wondered if she had another dry handkerchief. This was obviously serious.

'Promise that you will never tell anyone about this Rosie, I couldn't bear it if anyone knew what I fear.'

'Whatever it is we will face it together and being together makes us stronger. You know that I don't have to make any promises because we are sisters, not blood relations but nevertheless sisters who look out for each other. You can tell me anything and it will remain secret between us.'

'I'm scared, very, very scared that my Granny's DNA is nearly the same as mine and that her ability to carry out a mercy killing may be in my blood, my instincts. Will I ever do such a thing?

'I'll try to find out more about DNA, but I know that you are the kindest girl I know and that you haven't a vindictive bone in your body. I am 100% sure that there is nothing in your make up that would lead you to harm anyone. Your granny was in exceptional circumstances and had to go through a dreadful ordeal to save the husband she loved from pain. She must have been very brave.'

'In the daylight my mind understands that it's just that I have bad dreams and I know that some people in Newhill regard her as a murderer. I'm very worried about meeting her again, what will I say?'

'Grace Bisby, you can't rehearse or know what you will say, it will just happen and I've no doubt that you will know exactly the right thing to say, she is your granny and I believe that she loves you deeply and can't wait to meet you again.'

'Thanks, Rosangel, you are the best friend any girl could ask for, my special almost sister, no wonder Billy Shakespeare loves you so much.'

Rosangel blushed and laughed.

'Don't be daft, now dry your face, if we've got a dry hankie between us, the boys will be back soon. Do you think they'll bring custard creams or ginger nuts? I would bet on chocolate digestives myself.'

At that moment a chewed tennis ball rolled into their shelter and stopped at their feet. Outside an enthusiastic West Highland terrier wagged its tail and excitedly waited for the ball to arrive. Rosangel, who had a good throwing arm, picked up the soggy ball and threw it as far as she could. The dog owner shouted his thanks and Rosangel was left with a wet hand, but the dog did not respond as expected. He tensed and pricked up his ears. Turning his head towards the allotments he lifted his head and sniffed. He barked a yapping warning bark, the ball entirely forgotten.

Grace and Rosie looked at each other and stepped outside the shelter. Across the park and small river there were two fires at Wath Mill allotments. Not the heavy bonfire smoke type but angry flames rising high.

The dog walker was on his mobile phone contacting the fire brigade.

'Oh God, where are the boys?' Rosie exclaimed, looking frantically around.

'They would have had to pass us to get across the bridge to the allotments and we haven't seen them,' Grace tried to reassure her friend, but Rosie was anxious and felt responsible for them, or at least two of them.

'We weren't exactly looking out for them, were we?

At that moment the boys arrived laden with crisps, drinks and packets of biscuits, their approach hidden by the shelter.

'What's going on?' Billy asked as he noticed the twin flames and the anxiety of the girls.

'It looks like big trouble Billy, fires as bad as that don't start in two places at once, not accidentally at least,' Grace added.

Rosangel knew that her father was at work and her mother was safe at home with baby Jacob. Her brothers were here safe with her and even in her anxiety noted that Mikolaj had opened the chocolate digestives. Typical.

Little Billy scanned the allotments trying to see if his dad was there. It was Saturday but he hadn't said that he would be going to tend his plot today.

Grace had no personal link to Wath Mill apart from the times she helped Laura Watson on the school plot. It was a Saturday and unlikely to have anyone on that particular plot. Grace as an only child had the unwanted luxury of not having to worry about siblings, her mother was at home and her best friends were here.

Sam and Nikolaj began to make inroads into the packets of biscuits.

Rosie calmed down a little as she had her brothers here in her care, like a mother hen.

Grace looked at her friend, her nearly sister, and decided that she would make a great mother. Strangely Billy Shakespeare was thinking the same thought.

'It must be two sheds,' Rosie said, 'who has a shed?

'We do.' Billy said quietly 'and I think one of the fires is at the top end near the hedge where our plot is.'

They all looked at him and could see his obvious worry.

''Is your dad working up there today?' Grace asked, fearing the answer.

'I don't think so but I'm not sure. He didn't say at breakfast, he may be, I've got to go over and check.'

'Or we could just phone your house to see if he is there,' Grace said calmly.

After an uneasy wait for the call to be answered Billy sighed with relief and grinned.

'Dads at home mending the flat tyre on my bike.'

The relief was greeted with friendly hugs and pats on the back.

'What about the second fire? It seems to be near the bridge and our school plot,' Mikolaj added, opening a packet of cheese and onion crisps.

Grace tried to look closer but said, 'The school don't have a shed but the two Portuguese ladies, Leona and Anna, share a shed and they are near our plot.'

'We should investigate,' Billy Shakespeare, wicket keeper detective announced somewhat grandly 'But my mum warned me not to go near.'

The sound of fire engine sirens filled the air.

Rosie agreed with Faith Shakespeare, safety first but added that they could go over to the old mill near the bridge and watch the firefighters at work from a safe distance. There was only the wooden bridge access to the allotments, but the firefighters were professionals, and the river was close, plenty of water.

Grace looked at her friend and agreed, 'Perhaps we can actually share the drinks and biscuits before Mikolaj eats everything himself.'

Thick smoke was beginning to drift low over the river Warne, spreading across the park. Others arrived curious to see what was happening,

Rosangel smiled, 'Well Billy it looks as if you have a case to solve after all. Two separate fires, stolen tools and watering cans, it must be a case for our detective sleuthing skills.

Billy grinned, 'Hang on though, I thought that you girls were supposed to be working on a crime solving strategy whilst we were doing all the work at the supermarket.'

Rosangel and Grace smiled at each other and shared the moment of real companionship and love.

'So, we were Billy, but we got somewhat side tracked by DNA and a terrier.' Rosie said enigmatically.

Billy frowned and decided that despite having three older sisters, or perhaps because of it, he would never understand the mysterious workings of girls' minds. Still, it was kind of fun to try.

They walked across the park towards ruins of the old Saxon mill to find a good place to watch the firefighters at work. Shouted urgent calls made them stop and turn.

Andy Chlebek and Keith Shakespeare were hurrying towards them across the park. Both men had heard about the fires and left what they were doing at once to make sure their children were safe. A flat tyre and council meeting took a poor second place to their role as fathers.

After ensuring that everyone was indeed safe and not involved, Keith stole two biscuits from Billy and walked over to his plot and strictly ordered his precious son to stay with the others.

Arriving at his plot, his shed was merely a large pile of hot ashes with metal tools left and the firefighters were carefully raking through to make sure it would not flare up again. The police had by this time arrived and PC Eleanor Kent was taking notes from Kevin Bolton and his son Jason, he of the long blond hair. Keith had little to add except to say that plot seventeen was indeed his and that it was his shed or had been. He had not been present or witnessed anything. Yes, it was locked, the padlock being visible charred and still hot in the white ash.

Keith walked slowly and grim faced back to where the others were waiting. He passed Leona and Anna's shed, now a smouldering heap of ashes with occasional flare ups of garden chemicals which burned like tiny fireworks.

On Andy's instruction Grace was phoning her mum to assure her that all was well Amanda Bisby had vaguely heard the sirens, both police and fire engines but was unaware that Grace was at all in the vicinity.

Andy noted Keith's grim face, most unusual for him but he had just lost his shed and it was unlikely to have been insured. A loss of hundreds of pounds, probably.

'It's not the shed although it will need to be replaced to say nothing of the tools, it's what the Boltons were telling the police.' Keith's face was tight and angry.

' They say that Jason Bolton found the two shed fires and phoned the fire brigade, trying to be a hero obviously. No, they have had the barefaced impudence to say that Grace here might have been somehow involved in starting the fires. A load of nonsense!' Even had the nerve to suggest that Grace might have stolen tools and watering cans as well.'

All turned to look at Grace whose face crumpled into tears, Rosangel held her tight and whispered in her ear.

Keith was fuming and increasingly angry at the thought of Grace Bisby being accused of being an arsonist. The very idea was ridiculous.

'I've a good mind to go back there and punch him into next week, there was no call for that obnoxious slur. They suggested that Grace might, and I emphasize might have done it as she had her granny's bad blood.'

Andy held onto his friend as it was clear that he was about to go and commit assault in front of a police officer.

'Hold on Keith, I would also like to set him straight but there are better ways, trust me.'

Little Billy raised his voice to make himself heard above the commotion, 'It is impossible for Grace to have set fire to two sheds, she has witnesses plus we know Grace. She is the last person who would do such a dreadful thing apart from Rosangel of course and why just those two sheds?'

'An excellent point Billy, were you with her all the time this morning? Andy asked.

Billy's heart sank as he realised that he and the boys had gone to the supermarket. Plenty of time to go to the allotments and start two fires. Should he lie for his friend?

Grace was inconsolable but at this point Rosangel spoke up clearly and took away Billy's moral dilemma. 'The boys weren't with her all morning, but I was, and I will swear on the Bible that neither of us went anywhere near Wath Mill allotments. If anyone is going to punch that horrible excuse for a man and his creep of a son, then as Grace's best friend I demand the right to be the one to do it!'

Andy felt a surge of pride in his brave caring daughter. 'But I'm afraid that your testimony would be dismissed as you are her friend and would be biased.... I'm sorry Rosie.'

'I agree dad but that man over there with the West Highland terrier knows that Grace and I never left the shelter until we threw the ball for his dog and its then we all noticed the fire.'

Keith went straight over to talk to the dog walker, and he confirmed what Rosie had said. As PC Kent left the allotments to collect addresses from witnesses Andy gave a concise account of the morning's events, together with the name of the dog walker. He went on to say that legal proceedings would be taken against such an unfounded evil slur if an instant apology was not forthcoming, in writing.

It was Rosangel's turn to feel proud of her dad whilst Andy remembered that the allotment chair Charlie Poole's husband, Chris, was a local solicitor.

El Kent remained calm and aloof but felt that she had a good understanding of the situation for her report.

'Well! Little Billy declared, 'this detective work is dead easy we've solved our first case.'

Rosangel looked at him, boys didn't think things through, 'We all know that Grace didn't and wouldn't set fire to anything, but someone did.'

'I've had enough excitement for one morning.' Andy said.' Let's all go to the Garden Centre café and have hot chocolate.'

'...and cake dad? Mikolaj pleaded.

'I think that you have had enough biscuits and crisps for today son but perhaps we all need cake. My treat.'

Grace smiled and tried to look happy at the idea of hot chocolate and cake, but the shadow of the Bolton's insinuation had bitten deep into her soul. If they could think her capable of crime because of what her granny had done years ago, how many others would be silently thinking the same?

Andy could see her pain and walked alongside her putting his arm around her shoulder.

'You know Grace, I am blessed with four children, three fine boys and a girl who is not too bad,' Andy said winking at his beloved daughter, 'but as far as I'm concerned, I really have two daughters, you and Rosie here and I promise you that I will defend you with every ounce of my strength. No one will accuse you of anything without answering to me. Do you understand what I am saying?'

Grace moved to hug Andy closer, 'Thanks Mr. Chlebek.'

'You are after all beautiful enough to be Polish.'

Keith smiled at his friend's kind, loving and caring words He added 'And clever enough to be from Trinidad Grace. We are all with you, don't waste worry on those Boltons.'

Chapter Seven

Preferably Nearer White than Black

Thomas Tiler loved making daily lists and getting up early, fresh and ready for whatever the day would bring. Early April meant that the shy morning light came into his small one roomed flat to make an alarm clock superfluous. Even after the changing of the clocks at the end of March Thomas rarely overslept. 'Spring forward, fall back' was the old saying although Thomas felt that he would have preferred Autum to the American, 'fall'.

Since leaving his family house to live alone in such small accommodation he had developed a settled routine. Not that he needed a change of address to have routines. Thomas was organised and this quality had always served him well as a young teacher, deputy head and now headteacher at Newhill Primary school. As a husband however, his love of the comfort of familiar convention, forward planning and lists could be seen as tiresome and unexciting. His wife Beth or EJ as she preferred nowadays felt that she could write a book on the subject. Thomas never forgot birthdays; they were carefully plotted in the diary, but unexpected surprises were beyond his scope.

Today Thomas sat, as he usually did, at the necessarily small Formica table which had cutlery plate and glass for cranberry juice laid the night before. His weekly routine was always porridge, bran flakes, fried egg, corn flakes and chocolate hoops. Today being Tuesday, it was bran flakes for fibre. Predictable, some said bordering on the obsessive. At the weekend, however, Thomas tried to train himself to be more independent of the breakfast routine, but it was hard. Saturday was usually porridge with maple syrup which he enjoyed and on Sunday he would scan his cereal choice pretending that he didn't know what he would choose. It was however usually corn flakes with a sprinkling of chocolate hoops. His wife could have written down his menu and even safely predicted his free choice weekend fare. Thomas held few surprises, just two secrets, secrets which were rarely far from his conscious mind, their shadows darkening his otherwise happy days. If being alone could be said to be happy.

At the side of the breakfast plate sat his open diary and the cheap notebook with the heading Tuesday. The first entry was always, 'breakfast' which he would circle when complete. A hundred per cent success so far. His diary was unusually almost empty for the day, but he had learned that this could rapidly change as events unfolded. Thomas felt that this lack of structure was so alien to him that he hoped to become less rigid in routine and timetables. As a teacher this was comparatively easy, as a head almost impossible. He understood his shortcomings and tried to overcome them, perhaps too late to save his marriage though.

The diary was little help in formulating the daily list, He had to call his chair of governors to request an informal meeting about falling numbers and upcoming Ofsted, there was an appraisal meeting with the Year one teacher Daisy Morgan at one o'clock, that should be the easy meeting with the enthusiastic young probationer and a meeting with Mr. and Mrs. Tinton and son Satoshi at ten o'clock. That should be interesting, and he looked forward to welcoming them and showing them round the small school.

That left the first session between nine and ten. If there were no unexpected disturbances, he decided that he would use this time to select the cricket team.

Having washed up the dishes he packed his brief case and glanced at the time. It promised to be a fine morning, so he thought that a walk to his school, it was still wonderful to say that, seemed right. His school. It may not be perfect, but he was working hard to make sure that it was the best he could make it.

The air was April warm with a slight breeze and it felt like a potentially good day. Locking the door behind him he strolled past the White Horse pub and turned up the High Street where he passed the bakery owned by his landlady Nora Wilson. She was putting more crusty loaves, bloomers and sourdough onto the window display. Glancing up she saw Thomas and waved cheerily. He was a good tenant, and she liked the young headteacher. He returned her wave, and she beckoned him in. Entering the small bakery was a delight for the senses.

'Morning Thomas, getting your exercise early are you, would you like me to save you a tiger loaf, I know that it's your favourite?'

'That would be great Nora, could I take it now though, you may be closed by the time I go home.'

It was almost impossible to resist the bread, cakes and baguettes once inside the shop. Nora's assistant Jenny placed a tiger loaf in a paper bag and handed it over the counter with a smile. As Thomas paid, he thought that his office would smell wonderful for the rest of the day, good to welcome visitors with.

'How's school going Thomas? You must be well settled in by now.' Nora asked.

'I think that I'm still in my honeymoon period, but having my own school is special so long may it continue. Well, I must be going, wouldn't do to be late.'

He left the bakery clutching his loaf and briefcase. Nora watched him walking up the High Street toward Market Square.

'That lad deserves better than living alone in my tiny bed sit. He should be at home with his wife. I wonder what went wrong for them?' A new customer entered, and the question was not answered or even pondered upon.

Thomas walked past the war memorial where several names from two world wars had been inherited by pupils at his school. Passing the Town Hall, he cut through onto the Leek Road and was soon entering the school.

Ritual took over and he hung up his coat and went to the staffroom to make himself a mug of coffee, having placed his tiger bread safe on a shelf near his desk. The office was now beginning to look like his own, familiar education books adorned the shelves and motivational posters filled the walls. His desk was neat and tidy with stationery, pens and pencils carefully at hand. A framed photograph on his desk showed Thomas with Beth in earlier carefree days standing on a hill overlooking Ashbourne. Happy days, and not so long ago. His Derby County mug, a present from Beth, was steaming with hot coffee. He felt comfortable and ready to begin the day's work.

Several staff passed his open door and greeted Thomas with cheery good mornings. A good sign he thought, his own early work habit was beginning to be replicated, at least by some staff, Mary Anderson was a notable late comer, as usual.

Thomas took his A4 ruled pad and turning to a fresh page he wrote Cricket at the top and began a list.

1, Check existing equipment
2. Set date for trials
3. Announce setting up of new team in assembly (Wednesday)
4. Trials Day
5. Arrange friendly match (Possibly Snelston or Oak Tree Lane)
6. Pick team

Methodical as usual he checked his diary for a free evening straight after school and pencilled it in. He looked again at the letter from the chair of the local schools' cricket league informing him of the cup draw for the year. In addition to the typed letter was a handwritten piece giving details of the arrangements to hand back the Mullins trophy, proudly held by Newhill. No doubt a wonderful day for the school, but all that was in the past. The team had moved on to secondary school with their extensive personal range of equipment and their coach had been promoted to a nearby school. He had seen a team photograph of them looking smart in their all whites with the trophy proudly set in front, in a place of honour.

The departed coach, Brian Perry, was now Deputy Head at Mapleton Road Juniors, and he would no doubt be bringing his cricketing expertise to his new school and new team. Thomas noted that the cup draw had coupled Newhill with Mapleton at their school grounds. Certainly, a tough start.

Looking down at the rest of the draw, Thomas noted that his wife's school, Oak Tree Lane, was away to Wootton Central. A shadow passed over his mind as he remembered taking Beth to see Derbyshire play Yorkshire one sunny August Sunday, He had spent all the game explaining the simple but time embodied complex rules to her. She didn't seem to mind but Derbyshire lost and somewhere along the way since he had lost the affections of Beth. Thomas moved on to clear his mind of such thoughts but could not help glancing at the photo on the desk. He sighed deeply.

Who to arrange a friendly with? Most schools at this time of year were looking towards end of year tests, the results of which were so important. His eyes fell on Snelston Fitzwilliam Primary school, drawn at home to Warneside CE juniors. Kevin Bolton, their PE teacher was known to be a keen competitor and would no doubt be happy to play an early season friendly against cup holders, Newhill. It would be a tough one but would give an indicator of Newhill's strength or more likely weakness.

He added a note in his daily list to phone Kevin Bolton to arrange a friendly, although any match between keen local rivals, Snelston and Newhill was never actually too friendly, especially with the overbearing Kevin in charge of the opposition.

Thomas finished the now cool coffee and walked down to the PE storeroom. A look at the dusty assortment of pads, stumps and ancient bats convinced him that he was being foolish to even try to retain the Mullins trophy. He tried to sort out the kit which was in much need of tender loving care but only succeeded in disturbing the dust and indignant spiders. The bats needed linseed oil and the pads some whitening. Even a minimal outlay on basic equipment would cost money, a luxury which the school could not really afford, and he wasn't even sure that the small numbers available for selection would justify it. But Thomas had a stubborn streak and part of him yearned for an obvious success in his first year as headteacher. Ofsted would not be impressed; they were concerned with test results and number crunching not trophies.

'You can't hide in there all day Thomas, you've got to come out sometime.'

Thomas jumped slightly and turned to find a smiling Charlie Poole. She was the epitome of freshness, not unlike his tiger loaf he thought.

'I was just checking the cricket equipment, its filthy in here, I'm thinking of restarting the Newhill cricket team.' Years as a teacher had taught him that any child starting a sentence with 'I was just...' was usually guilty. It worked for many adults too, as a rule of thumb.

Charlie smiled at his somewhat naïve sporting ambition 'Good idea, won't be as good as last year's superstars but worth a go, won't do any harm and will certainly be welcomed by the children. Billy Shakespeare for instance will hero worship you forever, he is desperate to be school wicket keeper, he plays for a local club under 12's where his dad umpires. He at least will have his own pads and gloves.'

Thomas left the storeroom and made a mental note of this valuable information.

'I was actually thinking about you when you appeared like magic Charlie.'

Charlie laughed easily, 'Thinking of me in a dark room, I'm a happily married woman Thomas,' she scolded in a mock serious tone,

As soon as she uttered the words, she could have bitten her tongue off as too late she remembered that Thomas' marital status was far from happy.

Charlie could not retrieve the well-intentioned but poor choice of words.

'I'm sorry Thomas, I didn't mean, I was just...., a poor joke I'm afraid.' Charlie flustered.

Thomas understood at once and helped the floundering young woman, 'No offence taken Charlie, no I meant to say that I was wondering about the school PTA. I know that you are on the committee as a parent now the twins are here. How are they doing by the way?

'They absolutely love it and can't wait to get in each day. They are real individuals but manage to come home covered in paint most days. Jamie loves stories whilst Annie prefers to be more active.'

'That's good and twins are certainly good for our dwindling numbers, no I was wondering if the PTA...'

Thomas didn't finish as Charlie intervened; she had much experience as chair of the committee at Wath Mill allotments.

'How much do you need for, let me guess, new cricket equipment?' Charlie asked relieved that he had skilfully understood her error and was glad to be back on safe ground.

Thomas laughed, 'You must be able to read my mind, am I so obvious?'

'Not hard finding you in the PE storeroom and wanting to keep the Mullins Cup, Laura is the school representative on the PTA committee so together we could make a good case for you. We had a good Christmas Fair and so our bank balance is healthy, but had you thought of getting sponsorship? My husband's solicitors firm often supports local charities and as you know Chris is on the governors. Between him and the PTA we should be able to rustle up about £500, would that be enough?'

'That would be wonderful, I would be most grateful, and we wouldn't look too shabby playing other teams. I think that it is important to look the part when representing the school.'

'Leave it with me Thomas, now I must get on. I'm with Sam Chlebek before assembly.' Charlie said glancing at her watch.

Instinctively Thomas looked at his own watch. 'Thanks Charlie, you have just reminded me I have a meeting with potential parents in a few minutes.'

Back in his office Thomas felt slightly grubby after rummaging through the fusty sports equipment. His mind went to his hand shower and its curtain which he hated. At home Beth and he had installed a new shower unit which felt luxurious by comparison. The water pressure was good, and the cubicle was comfortably large enough for two.

'Your visitors are here Mr. Tiler' his secretary, the very competent Jill Taylor said popping her head into his office. At fifty-three she looked after Thomas like a mother hen.

For the second time that morning a woman had startled him out of his thoughts although he had to admit that the warm delicious thoughts of Beth and he in the shower was a very pleasant one. Better than cricket equipment.

'Thanks Jill, show them in.'

Jill paused and looked at the young head as a sergeant would inspect his new recruits. 'Give me your jacket I'll give it a quick brush, its covered with dust, where have you been? I assume your shirt is clean and ironed.'

Thomas grimaced as he handed over the suit jacket. The blue shirt had been clean yesterday but as for ironing, he had reckoned that his jacket would hide most creases. Perhaps in future a jumper would be better, less formal. Feeling crease exposed Thomas went to greet his visitors, the Tinton family.

Jill sighed, 'We really must get him better organised with his clothes, I wonder if he can iron shirts, an ancient and noble art. Did he even own an iron? I'll bet his wife kept theirs.' Her office of course had a clothes brush, and she vigorously brushed the jacket whilst making a mental note to check her job description. Still, he was well worth the effort she had served several heads and reckoned that Thomas had the potential to be one of the best, at least since William Mullins.

Meanwhile Thomas shook hands warmly with Alex Tinton and he introduced himself and his Japanese wife, Kyoko and eight-year-old son, Satoshi.

Thomas was at once entranced by the slim very beautiful mother who bowed in the traditional way. Satoshi shook hands and he too bowed deeply from the waist. Kyoko's outfit was simple with muted shades of brown, yet it gave an air of nonchalant grace and elegance. Satoshi wore the usual trainers, jeans and a yellow polo shirt.

The office was small but had two chairs for visitors, Jill brought in a wooden chair for the young boy, anticipating, like all good secretaries the need, He bowed and thanked her. She found herself wanting to bow in response but instead asked if everyone would like tea or coffee. Somehow the idea of making tea for someone familiar with the legendary Japanese tea ceremony was daunting. There was relief when the exquisite and dainty Mrs. Tinton asked politely for coffee, like her husband.

An orange juice for the boy seemed right with a plate of biscuits. Like his mother Satoshi had the usual Japanese straight black hair and his eyes were a good mix of Derbyshire stock and the Asian he too had clear porcelain like skin. Although only eight he seemed older, taller and he had obviously inherited this from his father.

Thomas thanked Jill and welcomed the family to the school. Firstly, he checked the boys date of birth to make sure there was room in his year group. This was a formality, and he knew that there were plenty of places available.

As usual he asked why they wanted to enrol in his school.

Alex Tinton sat back and briefly outlined their story. He had been brought up in Newhill and his mother Tessa had an allotment at Wath Mill. Whilst teaching English in Japan, Tokyo to be precise, he had been offered a job, a very well-paid job, by a large international car manufacturer. They wanted someone to teach their managers and technical engineers English so that they could communicate better in factories abroad. At this moment he glanced at his wife and his eyes said everything. They shone with adoration at the telling of such happy memories.

'I was lucky enough to meet Kyoko on a training course I was running and was amazed that she seemed to like clumsy ugly Englishmen who spoke mediocre Japanese. We shared a passion for history and films. To cut a long story short I went to meet her family and eventually plucked up courage to ask permission to marry their second daughter. My time in Japan became extended although I know that my parents, and in particular my mother found the idea difficult. Young Satoshi here was born eight years ago, and he speaks both Japanese of course and reasonable English.

Kyoko Tinton recognised that her husband was beginning to ramble, lowering her eyes, she added. 'Alex has been given eighteen months here in England to work in a car plant near Derby. Education is important to us both and we would like Satoshi to continue his studies in an English school during this time.'

Thomas felt that he could watch and listen to this Japanese lady, for she was indeed deserving of that title, for a long time. Her accent was delightful, and he could see exactly why Alex had married her. A lucky man indeed.

Kyoko discreetly moved the fast-reducing plate of biscuits away from her son.

Alex asked if there would be room for Satoshi at Newhill. His parents had visited them in Tokyo, and his mother had mentioned that Newhill Primary had a good reputation.

Thomas confirmed that the class where Satoshi would be did indeed have a place available. He thought it best not to mention that there were several places and not just the one.

Thomas went on, 'But I always like to leave such a major decision to the children. Perhaps I could show you all around and then Satoshi can ask any questions before deciding.'

Satoshi stood and bowed, 'Thank you Mr. Tiler, I would like to look round, but I really only have one question, if I may?'

'Before you ask, I have a question of my own, does the name Satoshi mean anything, in English I mean.?'

Kyoko smiled, 'That is a good question Mr. Tiler, Satoshi would be loosely translated as 'clear thinking' something he sometimes lives up to.'

'And your name, if I might be so bold?'

'Kyoko simply translates as 'mirror' Mrs. Tinton added.

'Now Satoshi what was your question?' Thomas asked taking an instant liking to the boy, his instincts on these matters were usually sound.

'At home we play baseball, it is our national passion, my team is the Tokyo Swallows, and I love playing for my junior team, but I know that it is not played much in England. I would love to try your English cricket and I have seen matches on television. It is similar to baseball, slow to build up then with very exciting endings.'

'Not always exiting Satoshi, there are many dull draws,' Alex intervened, 'I'll take you to Derby to see a county game in the summer, but we had better get on with our tour, Mr. Tiler is probably a busy man.'

Mr. Tiler stood wondering if the gods of cricket were looking after him. A possible £500 for new equipment and a potential new team member, all in one morning.

One week later Satoshi had his wish and he stood with other potential team members at the cricket trials. He had quickly struck up a friendship with Mikolaj Chlebek and they chatted together while waiting for instruction.

Thomas was slightly disappointed with the low numbers but thanked them for coming. He had brought a bag with bats, balls and a motley collection of batting gloves.

As you know we are holders of the Mullins cup and I think we have a good chance of winning it again this year. This produced an enthusiastic response which Thomas didn't fully share as he looked round at the potential players. Not an obvious team of winners.

Not wanting to waste the decreasing light he organised bat and ball exercises to assess basic skills. Satoshi clearly had good hand-eye coordination and he seemed to have made friends easily, especially with the Chlebek children. Quite an ethnic mix he thought and a fair splattering of girls. A sign of modern times, a good healthy sign and the rules were clearly open to mixed teams at this age.

At the end of the session Thomas sat in his office, glad to be in the warmth as the cold of early April had begun to creep into his body. Turning to a fresh sheet of paper in his pad he wrote out his first team for the arranged friendly against nearby Snelston. The new equipment would hopefully arrive by then, but the team would need to supply their own clothing. He had ended the training session by saying that he didn't expect brand new cricket boots, trousers and shirts with white sweaters.

'Just do your best to get as near white as possible. Trainers are fine and think of it as a colour range, preferably anything nearer white than black is ideal. Do your best.'

Billy Shakespeare grinned, 'Isn't that racist Sir, what's wrong with black?'

'Firstly, Billy if you look at professional cricketers, they wear white in order to see the ball better against their kit as you well know, secondly we are Newhill and want to look smart and thirdly you are not black but more an adorable toffee colour and I don't pick comedians just cricketers.'

Everyone laughed and Billy enjoyed the joke, The new headteacher was proving popular. Thomas noted this camaraderie and decided that Billy would be his captain. He certainly had the experience, if not the height and the others would respond to his leadership

The friendly match came and went remarkably quickly. Thomas had cut the grass as short as possible with the school petrol mower, but the rest of the outfield was long, the equipment had turned up much to everyone's excitement. As requested, the kits ranged from cream to whiteish. Mothers had scoured the charity shops for white trousers, shirts were a lesser problem. Only Billy really looked the part with his blue wicketkeepers' gloves (small) Thomas looked at his team and felt a surge of pride as they had all made a real effort to make Newhill look smart.

Kevin Bolton had arrived with his team, and they looked fearsome even in warmup. Jason Bolton was of course captain and opening batter. He and his father were the picture of sporting confidence. Thomas began to doubt his ability to score and umpire at the same time... it looked so easy on television.

Newhill started well by winning the toss. Billy chose to bat first, but the team peaked before a ball was bowled. The Snelston bowlers were devastating in their speed and accuracy. Satoshi and Billy had a partnership of four runs, but wickets tumbled easily. Grace Bisby, batting at number eleven, was clean bowled first ball by Jason Bolton who collected seven Newhill wickets. Thomas had found it difficult to keep score in the book as well as umpiring. He was struggling and at the end of the innings he announced all out for eleven. The Snelston team were triumphant

Jason Bolton led the jibes and crowing whilst his father muttered darkly about girls ruining the game and its traditions.

Thomas realised that playing such a strong team as Snelston as a first friendly was probably a monumental mistake, but he put a brave face on it as he gathered his team around him.

'The match isn't over till it's over. If they can get us all out for a low score, we can do the same. Just do your best.'

Billy added, 'We are Newhill, we are the cup holders it's time to fight, come on guys keep your heads up.'

It was decided to let Rosangel open the bowling as she had shown some ability as a spinner. When questioned about this unexpected skill by Thomas she had replied, 'I looked it up on the internet. I just need more practice.'

Despite the motivational efforts of Thomas and captain Billy Shakespeare the match ended after three balls. Three balls and three boundaries. The necessary eleven runs had been easily passed. The Snelston team ran on to congratulate Jason whilst Rosangel stood dejectedly watching their cheering. Some had muttered about girls not being suited to cricket, but Rosangel glared at the captain and opening batter, the one who had hit three straight fours, the hero of the hour.

Rosangel was not particularly consoled when Billy walked down the pitch to see her.

'Never mind Rosie, you tried your best.'

Rosangel felt her Polish fighting spirit rising and her eyes flared, 'We will smash them next time Billy, mark my words. I won't let this happen again'

Billy decided that he had never loved anyone at that moment as much as Rosie Chlebek when she was aroused by indignity.'

Snelston had humiliated Newhill so much so that Kevin had suggested that they should have another game at once to make their journey worthwhile.

Keith Shakespeare had watched the match and its brutally short ending. He felt pride in his son as captain and his attempt to defy the odds with the new boy from Japan, but he hated the fact that it was the arrogant Kevin Bolton who had won. He did not win with magnanimous grace but chose to grind in the degree of his team's victory by suggesting that they start again. Keith was pleased when Thomas declined.

Thomas felt that he had let his team down and they were certainly deflated. At one point he had been concentrating on the scorebook when he suddenly realised that play had stopped, and everyone was waiting. Flustered he called, 'Play' and the Snelston bowler, the long blond haired one sneered, 'Shouldn't we wait for the next batter to come to the crease?

Afterwards Keith Shakespeare took Thomas to one side

'Mr. Tiler, ... Thomas, I'd like to thank you for setting up a cricket team again at Newhill, but you can't do it all by yourself. If you wish, I could umpire, and you could then concentrate on scoring and helping the team from the side lines. Let me know when the matches are, and I'll get Ben Ellis to help me cut the grass. Ben doesn't have children at Newhill or any children at all for that matter, but he is a real enthusiast and would love to help, he has an allotment near mine.'

In the background Thomas could hear the Snelston team chanting that they would win the cup. He feared that they could be right. Thomas thanked Keith and was grateful for the offer of support. He thought, or rather knew, that his first year as a cricket manager could well be his last. He was fairly certain that his secret or maybe both secrets were about to be revealed.

Before the much-anticipated match Thomas had opened a curious envelope addressed simply to the head. No stamp, so hand delivered.

The anonymous letter had confirmed all his darkest fears, it was short and simple and just said, 'We know about you.' The four words had been cut from a newspaper and cellotaped on a sheet of paper and put in an envelope in the school letter box.

Chapter Eight

Plant Swap Day

It had been the perfect Saturday in May, at least as far as the weather was concerned. The warmth of the sun and clear refreshing air had been appreciated by everyone in Newhill and a few commented that May was the best month of the year with its promise of a long summer. Some even said that there was no country on the planet equal to England in May and probably no county as fine as Derbyshire at this time. The people of Yorkshire and Cornwall would probably argue this point fiercely and with some justification. It was like Christmas without the bitter cold, August without the heat and drought. The trees looked magnificent and there was growth everywhere you looked, images of a Merry Olde England with may pole dancing on the village green, the gentle melody of 'Greensleeves' being played and the promise of plentiful harvests. It was a good day to be alive, an idyllic day, one to treasure.

But as night fell not everyone went to bed with a sense of contentment.

Ben and Jenny Ellis had retired to bed after a busy day, he had done a shift as an ambulance driver, and she had worked at Nora Wilson's bakery. As days went it had to be considered a good one. Ben had no major call outs and all had been mild and successful, a boy had fallen from a slide in the playground and a fractured collar bone was suspected, he had attended a small fire on the industrial estate, but no one was injured, and a ninety-seven-year-old man had called with breathing difficulties. The fine day meant few car accidents due to fog or skidding and it was too early for sunburn cases. For a Saturday night there were only a small number of drunkenness incidents and its inevitable aggression and aftereffects. It had been a time for beer gardens and families. Even Derby County had won after a long journey to Plymouth Argyle and Derbyshire had

had a strong batting day against Sussex at the County Ground in Derby.

Jenny had enjoyed her shift at the bakery, she and the owner, Nora, had chatted and gossiped with each other and the many customers. As usual she had brought home a large crusty loaf as she knew well that Ben enjoyed his Sunday morning tea and toast in bed with the television on with repeats of gardening programmes.

A good day yet even as they cuddled in bed, as they always did, Jenny felt an emptiness. She loved Ben to the end of the earth, but the usual sadness crept over her, and her unwanted tears came quietly.

Ben held her close and stroked her hair, He asked the usual question but already knew the answer. The problem ate away at him but for Jenny it was far more intense, they were both in their mid-thirties and they had tried, my God they had tried so many times to have a baby of their own, a warm delicious cuddly baby of their own. They had a room ready, and Jenny often bought items ready for the big homecoming, when it came. But it never came. The nursery remained empty and so did she.

Ben's heart went out to her, he knew she would be a wonderful loving mother and he hated the fact that she felt this way so often. They had talked repeatedly of alternatives, fostering or adoption. The doctors had declared them both healthy and capable of pregnancy, but nothing happened. It was so unfair, there were so many children in the world uncared for and unwanted, but it felt as if they were being punished. Ben had often had to attend cases of emergencies involving pregnancies and he would sigh with a deep jealousy. If only it could be Jenny.

'What started it off this time, my love? 'Ben asked gently.

'Charlie Poole came into the bakery with her twins, Jamie and Annie, and they are adorable, just started school, so bright and lovely, then Leona from the allotments came in later for her Pasteis de Nata, you know, those Portuguese custard tarts. They sell really well but we always set some aside for her and Steve. She is well on in her pregnancy, and I asked how she was. I asked and I smiled but I really wanted it to be me. Why can't it be me Ben, why not me?'

Ben was a kind and gentle soul who loved to help, sometimes over enthusiastically but he couldn't answer the question asked so many times. Sometimes a loving cuddle was never enough but they eventually drifted off to sleep wrapped in each other's arms.

Meanwhile Keith Shakespeare went round the house preparing for bed, he liked to lay the table for breakfast and make sure that lights were switched off. Mugs were prepared for the early morning tea in bed He would usually help himself to a biscuit from the tin emblazoned with a picture of a magnificent stag on the Scottish Highlands. He needed this to survive the long ascent of the stairs to base camp. He tried to finish it before cleaning his teeth to ensure that his wife Faith did not know of his raid on the tin. But of course, wives always knew. How? nobody knew. In the past he would lock the front door and loved the feeling of security that his family were all in the house and safe inside, but things were changing, His eldest, Cressida was out at a music event, he wasn't sure what a gig was, but she was with her boyfriend and safe in his care. He was a good sound boy who was liked and trusted. The door remained unlocked, and the arrangement was that Cressida would lock the door on her return, so they knew she was inside and safe. Sadly, he realised that one day it would be just him and Faith. Even little Billy would leave but not yet. The thought was daunting, four marriages, four weddings but hopefully no funerals. For Keith it was a bitter sweet moment but it dawned on him that he and Faith would be grey haired grandparents. He had heard the old joke that grandchildren were your reward for not actually killing your exasperating rebellious teenagers. These thoughts filled Keith's mind and he felt blessed that he and Faith had so many special moments to share in the future. This monumentally happy thought called for a second ginger biscuit, and he returned to the stag on the tin, his friend.

Earlier he had gone into Billy's room to switch off the light and tuck him up, usually the boy was reading a cricket book or one of his old Aston Villa programmes, but Keith had found him with hands behind his head staring at the ceiling. Keith was about to give his usual talk about putting his reading away and snuggle down for sleep when he realised that his son was deep in thought. He sat on the edge of the bed, which just about took his considerable weight.

'No reading tonight son? That's not like you.' he said, leaving a space for an answer.

'I was thinking about our last cricket match against Warneside school. It was a league match, and we were so close. Satoshi was brilliant again and Sam and Mikolaj scored runs. Rosangel got two wickets, her spinners are getting much better.
'

Keith interrupted, 'I know son I was the umpire if you remember, you were a little unlucky and the team are getting much better but what else is worrying you?'

Billy wondered how his dad could read his mind, 'Jason Bolton never misses the chance to lord it over us at the allotment, he keeps saying how they are going to win the Mullins cup and they probably will, Snelston are much better than us. He seems to enjoy upsetting us, there is really no need.'

'Some people are like that Billy, you will meet them occasionally, you must not rise to them. Dignity is the answer, they are hoping for a response from you, rise above it son, rise above it, you are the better person.'

Keith was saddened by his son's unhappiness but instinctively knew that there was something else beyond a close cricket defeat or the taunting of a boy from another school.

'And what else is keeping you and me from sleep?'

'Sorry dad, it's just that, well. It's just that, I don't know how to... 'His voice trailed off as he struggled for the right words.

'Just speak your mind Billy as I've always taught you to do.'

Billy sighed deeply, 'How do I make girls like me, I'm so small, it doesn't seem fair.'

The age old question asked so many times in so many different languages throughout the ages. Keith's heart went out to his son, and he saw a witty, cheeky kind boy with enthusiasm and many skills, but he had self-doubt. He realized that his answer was an important one and he thought carefully.

'Do you mean girls in general or Rosangel in particular?

'Just Rosangel, we have always been friends, but she is beautiful and tall, and I am just Little Billy, good enough to make people laugh but...'

'I too felt the same at your age and I had many disappointments and tears along the way but then I met your mother and life changed for the better for me. We were almost destined for each other; you will meet someone who will love you and you will want to spend your life with her. It may be Rosangel or someone else, I don't know but I do know that whoever it is she will be the luckiest girl in the universe.'

'Thanks dad, that means a lot to me.'

Keith tucked his precious son up and went to switch off the light.

Entering his own bedroom, he sighed.

He realised that he could not solve his children's problems for them he just had to try to prepare them for whatever disappointment and triumphs they would inevitably face.

Faith was reading her kindle, her usual Val McDermid mystery, she didn't look up.

'You've been visiting the biscuit tin again, haven't you?' she said with a smile. Wives knew these things.

Gaffer McGrath, one-time lower league professional footballer and now landlord of The White Horse public house in Newhill was finally glad to bolt the door of his establishment. There were still jobs to do and glasses to clear. At least there were no ashtrays to empty these days. The last customer, Kevin Bolton, had seemed reluctant to leave. Probably wife troubles he thought. But he was wrong.

Kevin was a well-built sturdy man, a sports teacher at Snelston school and he could hold his drink well but even he swayed slightly as he walked home. He always felt overlooked on the ladder of success. Several disappointing interviews at his own school and even more rejection letters from other schools had ensured that he was still just a sports teacher when at his age he would have expected more, much more. He had stopped applying for other more prestigious jobs as he could not bear the usual, 'Thank you for your application but unfortunately on this occasion.......' letters.

The whole process left an accumulated bitter taste in the mouth which several pints of beer had not washed away. He tried to obscure the memory of his morning visit to see his mother at the Birch Trees residential care home. Not that he didn't love his mother, he certainly did but he hated seeing her in the home. Dementia had come early to Eithna Bolton and the passing of her husband, Eddie, had accelerated the slide to her room at The Birch Trees. As Kevin walked slowly and carefully home, he breathed deeply, but the smell of the care home stayed in his nostrils. It always hit him when entering the faded building with its threadbare carpets and shabby interior. It was a combination of strong disinfectant and cheap air fresheners and urine and stale boiled cabbage and dirty toilets in desperate need of replacement. It was less than half full, residents who could afford it went to the more sought-after Woodland's care home in Newhill. It was popular and well run, clean and bright with its friendly atmosphere and pristine facilities. But that cost money and Kevin did not have the salary to pay for a place there and he deeply resented the fact that he couldn't support his mother in the way she deserved.

He knew that the Portuguese girls. Leona and Anna with their allotments worked at the Woodland home and they always seemed enthusiastic and happy caring for their clients. The comparison with the Birch Trees was stark, there the home did not attract a team of workers with the best of attitudes. Only the ones who could not get other jobs went to the lesser run-down home. The moaners and the clock watchers, the lazy and the incompetent. It was a downward cycle which Kevin could not break.

He had entered the building after taking a deep breath of fresh air, as if that would last him for the next hour. He wondered if he preferred to be with his mother in her room with its flaking paint and broken television or in the depressing lounge. There the residents sat in large, battered chairs in a semi-circle facing the television, some rocking gently backwards and forwards, many asleep to escape the drudgery, some mumbling to themselves and some watching mindless television. A visitor had once added subtitles to the picture with the remote to allow the hard of hearing to enjoy the banal programmes, but some had said it spoilt the effect. The well-meaning visitor left, and normal service was resumed. No subtitles.

An assistant in a stained blue uniform informed Kevin that his mother was in her room,

Kevin walked down the familiar corridor carrying a small bunch of brightly coloured flowers, the only brightness in the building. He knocked gently and entered to find his mother still in bed and sitting up but dozing. She looked painfully thin, and her hair was untidy and uncared for. Kevin replaced last week's flowers in the vase and put them in water. The faded blooms were consigned, like the residents, to the waste bin of life. He made a clumsy attempt to arrange the flowers artistically but only succeeded in spreading them out.

The sound of the water being poured into the vase woke his mother.

'Kevin is that you? Is Jason with you?' Eithna Bolton had long ceased to expect Kevin's wife to go with him, she didn't care but occasionally Jason came, although he, like his dad, hated the atmosphere of stale decay and approaching inevitable death.

Kevin forced himself to smile as he went over to kiss his mother, she seemed paper thin and taking her hand he sat in the torn leather chair at her side. It was an old hand with dark liver spots and purple patches. It was a hand that had once tended him with care and love as a baby and toddler. It was a hand which had wiped away his tears and put plasters on scraped knees. It was a loving hand which now shook slightly without control.

'I've brought you some flowers mum', Kevin said, unaware that he said the same thing on each painful visit, a simple way to break the ice. Eithna was old, not passport dated old but prematurely dementia induced old.

'They are lovely son, did you bring Jason with you?' she asked again, with decreasing hope of seeing his long blond hair and good looks again.

'Sorry mum he has cricket practice this morning, perhaps next time.' The lies tripped easily from his lips, lies intended to let her down gently, the truth was too painful. Jason had consigned his grandmother to the list of hopelessness. He could barely remember her as anything other than the shadow of her former self, robust and lively. Only her love remained.

Kevin wiped her mouth of porridge with one of several tissues he had brought. Experience had taught him that boxes of tissues would be empty or unavailable. This was not the Woodlands after all.

'You are a good boy, Kevin. Always have been, how is school doing?'

'Very well mum our cricket team is unbeaten, and Jason is an outstanding player.'

'And what about you?'

The inevitable question was deep and bit hard with its shadow of failure, a career stalled and unlikely to improve any time soon. There was only his invincible cricket team and Jason as compensation.

Later, walking home, Kevin went through every painful detail of his usual morning visit to see his mum in that dismal place. If only he could afford better for her.

The house was in darkness as he entered, perhaps another drink, perhaps not. As usual he chose to sleep in the spare bedroom nominally to avoid disturbing his wife but these days there was little point of doing otherwise. Her bed would be warm but only in temperature. As he undressed and got into the cold sheets he thought of his mother, she would no doubt be asleep, he hoped so. At least sleep offered some escape from reality for her. Pulling the sheets close around him Kevin allowed the tears to fall, and they didn't stop for some time. He needed a mother's loving hug, but those days were gone.

Sunday afternoon and the sun came out from the high clouds to warm the Wath Mill allotments. It was Plant Swap Day and two pasting tables had been set up and covered with cloths for the traditional cakes and buns. Everyone tried to include ingredients grown on their plots, The cakes were as varied as the plots themselves, carrot and courgettte cakes, rhubarb pies, rich moist delicious fruit cakes, gooseberry buns and jars of damson jam. Spare plants which people had in excess were placed nearby for anyone to freely swap. A Kelly kettle was set up and plastic mugs prepared. Each year everyone brought a variety of chairs and people sat happily trying different cakes and exchanging recipes. Charlie Poole sat by Laura Watson discussing the latest committee meeting.

Charlie had a paper plate on her lap with a slice of rhubarb pie.

'If I step down as chair as I really should who will take over? I've done it eight years now, its traditionally three for heaven's sake.' She bit into her pie and watched out for her twins who were trying each cake in turn. Jamie in a methodical way, Annie less so.

Laura put down her thick slice of fruit cake made by Anna with a Portuguese recipe, and thought about the question of careful successional planning, 'I thought about Ben Ellis, but he is more practical and certainly enthusiastic. Committees wouldn't be his kind of thing, I would say. He might appreciate being made site manager. That would allow him free rein to organize work parties and he could strim the site to his heart's content. He does keep us tidy.'

Tessa Tinton arrived with son Alex and his wife Kyoko and her grandson Satoshi. Everyone one was introduced, and all were enthralled by the slim and elegant Japanese lady and the son who bowed deeply to each person he was introduced to. A respectful boy.

Sam, Mikolaj and Billy took him under their wing and Satoshi was intrigued to see the variety of English cakes. Tessa had baked a chocolate gateau covered with her own raspberries. Very tempting but not one for weight watchers or diabetics, especially diabetics. Tessa loved seeing how her friends at Wath Mill responded so positively to her daughter in law. Kyoko had brought a tray of beautifully presented rice cakes each individually flavoured. She was inundated with questions and offers of coffee mornings.

It was a mellow afternoon and a few regretted having Sunday lunch beforehand. Kevin worked on his plot, conscious that he had not brought any contribution to the feast, An outsider again. Jason had no such reservations, and he could barely manage his fully laden plate. However, he still found time to taunt the Newhill children about cricket, boasting as usual. Snelston would definitely win the cup this year

Faith Shakespeare was explaining her family name to a slightly confused Kyoko when she noticed Kevin working alone. She decided to go over and invite him to join them. It was a time for comradeship and sharing. If he had not brought a contribution then so what, he could help reduce the large excess of refreshments.

Kevin saw the large West Indian woman coning towards him and was at once curious.

'Won't you come and join us Kevin, we really have too much, and the cakes are very good.' Faith said. 'Jason is already helping us get rid of the chocolate cake. Please do come and join us.'

Kevin felt a swirl of emotions and was genuinely touched that Faith would go out of her way to invite him into the circle of friends. She drove home the invitation. 'My husband is getting the tea ready, he may need help with the Kelly kettle, he's never used it before.'

Kevin hesitated unsure on how to respond to Faith's kindness. 'But I don't have a cup,' he mildly protested, and I forgot to bring anything.'

'Nonsense Kevin, we have cups and all you need. Your joining us is all we would ask.', Faith would not take no for an answer and Kevin found himself walking towards the large group of plot holders chatting, laughing and eating with full appreciation. Perhaps this would be a good day to become more friendly. Less conflict and bitterness. Perhaps. The thought was broken sharply by a piercing scream. The pressure on the boiling hot kettle had caused it to fall, spilling much of its contents onto Keith Shakespeare's right arm.

Faith cried out and ran but not as fast as Kevin who sprinted down and grabbing a plastic tub of cold water took Keith's arm and gently poured the water slowly over the agonizing burn. Ben Ellis saw that the action was swift and right. He took the allotment first aid kit and did what he could before offering to take Keith to A and E. He lightened the moment by joking that he did know the way there.

The earlier speculation about the mysterious shed fires and thefts of tools was forgotten in the drama of Keith's accidental scalding. Ben said that an ambulance was not necessary, and transport was organised for the Shakespeare family. Billy was shocked and frightened as he went with Ben and his parents. The conclusion was that it was an unfortunate accident and that Kevin had proved exceptional in his prompt first aid.

At the far end of the allotment Rosangel and Grace were deep in sisterly conversation and were not aware of the accident and commotion. They had had some cake but decided not to have too much unlike the boys and the awful Jason.

Grace looked at her friend and asked, 'If I tell you a secret will you promise not to laugh or make fun of me? It's important to me at least I think it is.'

'Is it about your granny? You know we are best friends and special best friends don't mock each other do they, now what is it?'

Grace hesitated slightly but fully trusted her friend. 'There is a boy who I really like, he doesn't know but I would like him to know, and I don't know what to say to him or how to approach him.'

Grace was serious and Rosangel intrigued. Grace had never shown particular interest in boys before, 'Who is it, is it someone at our school?'

Grace replied, 'No he goes to another school, but he's our age'

'And does he have a name?

Grace cast her eyes down, 'Please don't laugh when I tell you.'

Rosangel was intrigued and promised not to laugh.

Grace drew breath and said quietly. 'It is Jason Bolton and I really do like him'

Rosangel was open mouthed with astonishment.

Chapter Nine

I Can Resist Everything Except Temptation

Thomas Tiler sat at his office desk and doodled on a pad of clean paper, he found that it helped him concentrate and formulate ideas. He was alone in so many ways. The others had all gone, the noisy excitement of children rushing to leave at the end of the day and later the staff, weary and looking forward reluctantly to an evening of planning and marking, weighed down with bags Finally, the cleaners had left after emptying his office bin and trying to hoover around the young head. He had said goodbye to most of his staff as they passed by his open door. A few children had come to retrieve confiscated items with promises not to bring them to school again.

Thomas had drilled home the fact that there was one and only one rule at the school, his school. All knew it off by heart, you could do anything you wanted, say anything you wanted but your words and actions must not upset or hurt anyone else. Today a boy had come to get his Spiderman figure back from the head's office.

A barrack room lawyer in the making he was confident that he was on firm ground with his rehearsed argument.

'But my spiderman in school didn't hurt anyone else and that's the one rule, isn't it?'

Thomas had smiled, he admired the young boys daring and logic.

'You are quite right, that is the one and only rule, but it did upset someone, your teacher, Mrs. Danby, was not happy with you playing with your Spiderman when it was quiet reading time. The other children were disturbed by the sound effects you added, and I am upset that you were not reading quietly like the rest of your class. Do you agree young Master Mapplebeck?'

Eight-year-old George Mapplebeck sighed and admitted defeat, it was sometimes hard to argue with teachers and this headteacher was both logical and popular with the children.

'Yes sir, but can we ever have a vote on changing the rule?' he asked, taking the precious Spiderman figure and perhaps pushing his luck.

'No George you can't change the rules just to suit one person,' Thomas replied with a smile.

George knew that he had lost but at least he had his Spiderman back. Turning he said, 'Have a good evening, Mr. Tiler and thanks.'

'And you, George, take care now.'

Thomas admired the courage of the young boy; he had made his point politely and when defeated had shown no resentment or anger. These were qualities which Thomas was keen to develop in the pupils in his care, George Mapplebeck was a likeable rebel, and he would probably go far.

The school fell silent and the warmth of the May day began, like the old radiators, to cool. For Thomas it was a fairly short walk to home, but home was merely one sparse room with a small cooker, table and single bed. The bathroom was shared with others along the corridor in similar bedsits. It was not home, his real home, so Thomas decided to stay at work until his seven o'clock meeting with the Friends of Newhill committee. When he was appointed as head it had always been called the Parent Teacher Association, but the PTA by definition excluded anyone else who wished to support the school. Keith Shakespeare, with newly bandaged forearm and Ben Ellis had spent time cutting the grass and trying to make as good a cricket pitch as they could. Keith was a parent; however, Ben was not a teacher or parent, but his enthusiastic support was valued, and he would be welcomed under the new banner of Friends of Newhill.

Thomas had been unsettled by today's events and found it difficult to work well in the ever-cooling office. He went into the staffroom and microwaved his evening meal. It was one course and simple to prepare, a cheap meat pie. Boiling water was added to a pot noodle he had bought to keep him going. Perhaps fish and chips on the way home.

Thomas had the good sense to use a tea towel as a napkin as the chicken noodles had a habit of trying to spread down his shirt front. The pot was not large, but it was hot and warmed his body if not his soul. Quality of taste did not enter into it. The pie was piping hot but bland. On the desk next to his doodling pad were two anonymous letters, if their brevity could be described in that way. The first had been crumpled and straightened out several times whilst the second was merely a photocopy, clean and fresh.

Earlier in the day PC Eleanor Kent had asked to see him and his secretary Jill Taylor had shown her into his office and Jill had closed the door, raising her eyebrows in a silent questioning manner at Thomas. The Kent family were well known in Newhill, and Jill remembered Eleanor as a former pupil at the school. She knew that El was recently divorced or at least separated from her lout of a husband. The mix of an attractive police officer and the lonely headteacher did not bode well. Jill still had hopes of a reconciliation between Thomas and his wife Beth. The long-term secretary was down to earth, competent and straight speaking but discreet, when necessary, yet she read many romantic novels and she yearned for a happy ending.

Once the door closed Eleanor had said that she was here about an anonymous letter. Thomas had felt a dark shudder of shock hitting his stomach. He tried to make his face neutral and impassive, but this was the stuff of nightmares for him. The words of his earlier anonymous letter, 'We know about you' were emblazoned on his mind with increasing horror. Someone knew his secret or rather secrets, his days as headteacher were numbered. He had analysed each word to try and glean some clue about its origin, but he was no forensic expert. Fingerprints may have helped but he had handled the crumpled paper often enough to ruin any chance of that and who would be checked? If the fingerprints were not on police file they would remain, as intended, anonymous. Not that he had any intention of showing the brief four-word statement to the police. They would see it as trivial but may well enquire as to what information the sender knew. What could cause such concern? They might dismiss it as a child's prank, but Thomas certainly didn't want to take any risk. The police had to be kept out of this mess but here they were or rather here she was.

Eleanor had taken a sheet of paper from her pocket. It was a folded photocopy of another very different anonymous letter.

It was written in large stark capital letters.

It read, 'GRACE BISBY SET FIRE TO THE SHEDS AT WATH MILL ALLOTMENTS.'

Thomas felt a huge sense of relief, the letter was not about him or his secrets, yet it raised many uncomfortable questions, and he asked somewhat stupidly if he could handle the paper, fingerprints and all.

Eleanor replied patiently 'It's a photocopy and the original didn't have any on it., we checked.'

Thomas felt some confusion, still happy that he was not the prime target but worried that Grace an eleven-year-old at his school was. 'How did you know that Grace goes to this school?'

'I attended the original incident at the allotments, two shed fires well apart so definitely deliberate. The ones who reported the fire and called the fire brigade indicated that Grace might be involved as her grandmother, Eileen Bisby, had been convicted of the manslaughter of her husband. Guilt by blood, I suppose it was a mercy killing, one of those sad cases. At the time I dismissed the information as nonsense but then this was posted to the station. I wondered if you could give any background.'

Thomas recovered himself. With a deep breath he composed his answer, grateful that he was not the one accused but increasingly angry that Grace should be implicated in such a thing.

'Grace Bisby is in Year Six, she is a lovely girl, calm, kind and intelligent. She is a member of the gardening club who have a plot at Wath Mill but they are always supervised there, Laura Watson is the teaching assistant who leads the club. I would stake my life that she is not involved in this arson. She has my full and unreserved support; I know her well as she is in my cricket team and a more delightful girl you could not wish to meet. I will speak up loud and clear in any court of law. I'm sure that Laura will say the same.'

Eleanor admired the strident loyalty of the young head for one of his pupils, 'Don't worry Mr. Tiler, or may I call you Thomas? We have put the fires down to vandalism, probably an errant bottle of cheap cider and a bit of bravado. We have an eye on several possibilities, but your Miss Bisby is certainly not on our radar. This note smacks of malice of the worst kind. We won't be taking it any further in view of what you have said.'

Thomas was a swirl of conflicting emotions; his passionate defence of Grace was heartfelt but his relief at not being the victim of at least one of the anonymous letters was a tremendous relief. The first letter remained in his drawer. No need to complicate matters, the two letters were obviously unrelated, just a coincidence. Nevertheless, a strange coincidence.

In his euphoria at having a reprieve Thomas noted the friendly request to use his first name and saw, not for the first time, that Eleanor Kent was very attractive and pleasing on the eye. Since his separation from Beth, he had noticed that there were so many young ladies who stirred his imagination, everywhere he seemed to come across desirable girls, but he was nevertheless married although without its benefits.

The ugly thought that Beth might not be showing the same restraint with Declan, the very fit and handsome teacher at Oak Tree Lane, caused him anxiety. He paused, wondering whether to ask Eleanor to join him for a drink after his meeting and when she came off duty. A possible fish and chip supper and maybe more. Was it possible to proposition a police officer on duty? Was there a law against bribery? Was his spartan bedsit a suitable place for romance, there was only one chair and of course a bed. These thoughts ran through his mind in a second or two.

By coincidence the police officer in question was asking herself the same question about professional codes of conduct.

At that moment Eleanor's radio crackled into life and pressing a button she responded, 'I'm at Newhill school, I can be there in three minutes.'

'Sorry Thomas I must go, a domestic getting out of hand, thank you very much for your help. If you can think of anyone who would send the anonymous letter don't hesitate to give me a call. Here's my card with my number.'

As she left Thomas wondered why life was so difficult at times, he had been on the verge of inviting the attractive police officer out for a drink, a starting point but one with a corresponding deep moral dilemma.

Thomas glanced at his watch and putting the two anonymous letters into his brief case he went to the toilet mirror to check that no delinquent chicken noodle had managed to stain his shirt, or worse trousers

It was usual to hold the Friends of Newhill School committee meeting in the small staffroom and the experienced members knew to wear warm clothing even on this spring evening. The committee often referred fondly to themselves as the FONS and they were the hard-core supporters of the school, ever eager to work hard to raise funds and help with projects. The new head had shown himself willing to work in partnership with themselves for the benefit of the children.

As people arrived Laura Watson, the school representative, offered a choice of coffee or tea, coats were removed, and the chat was friendly. Thomas regarded this as the parents' opportunity to support and give feedback so attended the meetings but did not chair them. Faith Shakespeare held that role. She had considerable experience of such committees at the Birmingham school attended by her three daughters when they were primary school age and now her youngest Billy would know that his parents supported him and his school here in Newhill. It was much smaller than the one the girls attended but principles were the same. Faith was a good chair who allowed all to voice opinion but made sure that the meetings did not ramble on.

Faith opened the meeting when everyone was seated, most with a hot drink which was appreciated.

A short agenda had been circulated and Faith hoped to move quickly to the main item, the organisation of the Summer Fair. This was usually a main source of income alongside the Christmas one.

'As you know Laura will be retiring at the end of the year and she will certainly be sorely missed. We will no doubt be thanking her later and properly for her many years of work here at FONS'

There was a general warm sound of agreement and thanks directed to Laura who hadn't expected this. It was not on the agenda and even at her age she found herself blushing and hoping for the next item to appear.

Faith went on, 'However Charlie has kindly agreed to step in to represent the school. Welcome Charlie. I know that we are lucky to have Thomas at our meetings, but he is here in more of an advisory capacity. I know that in many schools the head doesn't go to the PTA, and some can't even be bothered to have one. Our children are very lucky. This will be a last summer fair for Laura and a first for Thomas. Let's make it a good one. I hope that you all have come armed with some ideas.' Faith smiled.

Thomas nodded his acknowledgement of the complement and support but cringed inside at the dark distressing thought that this could be his first and possibly last Summer Fair as a headteacher.

Faith went on, 'After the treasurer's report Thomas has asked if he could have a short added item of his own. Sherrie, perhaps you would do the honours.'

Sherrie Chlebek had three children at the school and one, Jacob; to follow later. She had a decidedly vested interest in the school doing well. She had been particularly pleased to hear that Charlie Poole would be joining the committee. Her second child, Sam, was almost an elected mute and Charlie was his mentor on a one-to-one basis. They had a very good relationship and mutual respect. A simple sheet outlining income and expenditure for the last two terms was passed round. The balance was healthy, and donations had been made to the school for cricket equipment and seeds and child sized tools for the garden club to use at the school allotment plot. The school library had benefitted from a stock of new books and new playground equipment added. Sherrie spoke clearly and succinctly, secure in her knowledge of her subject. Thomas made notes on a pad, balanced on his knee. It was a novelty not to play the lead role in these meetings, but parents needed to know that he was fully involved and supportive.

As Sherrie talked through the accounts Thomas felt pleased that everyone was on first name terms, there was no formality or hierarchy, and this led to a friendly atmosphere.

Thomas could not help but notice Sherrie's ever so slight Polish accent and he found it both charming and pleasing. It was difficult to imagine that she had four children. Her figure was just the right side of voluptuous, almost perfect he thought, and she was certainly stunningly beautiful. His mind drifted away from the accounts and began to imagine the speaker as a Miss Poland contestant and the image of Sherie in a swimsuit came unbidden to his mind. He forced himself to concentrate, did they even have the ridiculous Miss World contests anymore and would Mrs. Chlebek be disqualified as a married woman?

Thomas was almost startled from his almost inappropriate thoughts of the beautiful treasurer when Faith moved to his added item.

He pulled himself together and thanked Faith for this opportunity to speak.

'I will try to be brief, I know that the summer Fair takes a lot of time and organisation and that your efforts are appreciated by the staff and children. On behalf of the school cricket team, I'd like to thank you for the new cricket equipment. We haven't managed a win yet, but we are getting better and I'm sure that we will be making every effort to keep the Mullins cup.'

'On a serious note, I want to make you aware that the school is due an Ofsted inspection and this is in the context of falling rolls. We need more children otherwise it is a downward spiral. It might even lead to staff redundancies. School closure is not on the immediate horizon, but it is important to present a positive image at all times to attract new parents. Faith was not alone in thinking that the newly appointed head was already giving a very positive impression.

Sherrie smiled warmly at Thomas, 'The Chlebek's have donated three children with one to follow, we are doing our bit and we wouldn't have them at any other school, mainly thanks to you Thomas and your staff of course. I can safely say however that a fifth contribution is unlikely.'

Charlie Poole grinned, 'Our twins have recently joined the school and Chis and I will stand up for the school and give our full support, our contribution may not however finish with Jamie and Annie, at least I hope not.'

Sherrie laughed with everyone else but was thinking how difficult life was at home at the moment. Her husband Andy had a job with the Royal Mail as a manager and was on the County Council representing Newhill. He was often tired and too busy and increasingly irritable. The opportunity to enjoy each other fully and perhaps even welcome a fifth Chlebek child seemed unlikely.

Looking at the handsome bearded head with his easy smile led Sherrie to make unfair comparisons with Andy. But this was a comparison with the Andy of recent times and not the good looking Polish young man she loved and married. Was her marriage in danger? she thought. Of course not, it was just a bad patch they were going through, and Andy would not be on the council for ever, but he had mentioned that he would love to be an MP one day, then she could foresee real problems. She would try hard if only for the sake of her beloved children. Sherrie found herself gazing at Thomas, following every word and thinking how carefree he seemed. But she was wrong.

Laura Watson and Charlie Poole noticed the obvious chemistry between parent and headteacher and glanced at each other. This was not good and in that silent glance they decided that action to prevent this blossoming any further may have to be taken.

After much discussion of new ideas for the Summer Fair and the practical logistical organisation the meeting ended, and Thomas prepared to set the alarm and lock up. He was aware that Sherrie had taken her time to put on her coat and was the last to leave but first she took the opportunity to speak to Thomas, privately.

'I would just like to thank you and Charlie for all your efforts to help Sam with his speech issue. I know that the two of you are doing your very best for him.'

There was a slightly difficult pause and Thomas was not sure how to respond to this beautiful woman. He mumbled his thanks and said it was a pleasure working with Sam.

Sherrie wished him good night and the alarm was set and door locked.

The setting of the alarm reminded Thomas of his earlier meeting with PC Eleanor Kent. She was indeed a temptation, and he might well have asked her out for a drink but for a domestic incident on the Leek Road which led to her rushing off. Eleanor was attractive and had seemed interested in him, but Sherrie could only be described as stunning, and she had also seemed interested in him on a personal level.

Thomas walked to his cold and lonely bed sit and decided to call in for cod and chips with mushy peas. They would not help his dilemma or his problems but would take his mind off his thoughts. Sherrie was married but El was not. He too was married but unhappily separated and he was increasingly finding it difficult to actually picture his wife, Beth's face apart from photographs.

Why was life so difficult and yet so exciting and threatening at the same time? A fish supper would not help solve anything but then what would?

Chapter Ten

A Tropical Derbyshire Paradise

At Newhill Primary the school bell rang at 3.30pm, the signal for release, it was a sunny afternoon in May and the weekend loomed long, full of wonderful promise. It was the perfect time and for many, children mainly, there was a happy movement to the school gate where parents waited chatting in groups whilst scanning for their own offspring.

Coats were being dragged or worn off the shoulder, hair was dishevelled, paint and pen marked hands unnoticed. The move towards the gate was a mixture of tiredness and shouting, shoes seemed somehow heavier than on the way to school yet some managed to skip or playfight. Homework was crunched in hands or pockets; semi wet paintings were carried like trophies to delight parents and be pinned proudly with magnets on grandparents' fridges. Some like Rosangel Chlebek had gathered their siblings together like mother hens.

This unregimented file of children moved like a camel caravan on the Silk Road. It was a buzz of shared news, plans and preparation for the inevitable end of day question.

'How was school today?

This was always met with the traditional answer, 'Fine'. No more no less.

The follow up bonus point question came.

'And what did you do today?'

'Nothing much', came the reply as bags, paintings, lunch boxes and homework were passed without due reverence to exasperated mothers whose duty it was to at once admire unidentifiable images in wet paint.

Not all shared the tired moving wall of childish excitement. Thomas Tiler made a point of being outside as the children left with various degrees of alacrity.

'Nothing much!' he groaned inwardly. So much for curriculum development, individual learning plans, focused child centred learning and finely tuned planning. All the efforts of his staff boiled down to the children reporting that nothing much had happened at school today. Some children elaborated and said who had fallen over in the playground or about the new playground equipment.

Thomas smiled and chatted with a few parents and wished children an enjoyable weekend. Gradually the stream of humanity finally petered out and Thomas walked back into school, wondering if he would have anything like an enjoyable weekend. A spur of the moment decision led him to go to the school office where Jill Taylor was completing her filing and order forms. She looked up when Thomas appeared, trying to look casual.

'Jill, you've been a secretary here for some time, do you know anything about anonymous letters?'

'Put them in the bin or burn them,' she said firmly. 'I can respect complaints or constructive criticism when the writer has the courage to sign their names but anonymous letters reek of cowardice and malice. They are not worth worrying about. You haven't had such a letter, have you?

'No, well yes but it's not directed at me or any staff member for that matter but it's about one of our pupils and that makes it far worse. It was sent direct to the police.'

Jill was discreet and professional in outlook. She reckoned that he would tell her the name of the child if necessary. At least that explained why a police officer was in the school earlier.

'The same principle applies, if there is no truth in an accusation then it's not worth wasting your time even thinking about it,' Jill added.

Thomas knew that she was absolutely right. Unfortunately, one of the letters, the one to him directly, was right, possibly on two counts and could not be denied. Someone knew his secret and no amount of paper burning could alter that. On the other hand, the malicious note about Grace Bisby could not possibly be true and he decided to confide in his experienced and trusted secretary. Perhaps confrontation was better than hiding away. Burnt paper could easily be replaced by another note of malice.

'Jill, have you got a minute?' She nodded, realising that this seemed to be seriously troubling him. 'Of course.'

'Come into my office, its more private.'

Once his office door was closed the two sat, the young tousled headed, bearded young headteacher and the older secretary who glanced at the clock, her hairdresser appointment was due in half an hour. Duty to school and her sense of intrigue kept her from mentioning this.

Thomas sighed deeply and composed his thoughts, clarity was important.

'Did you hear about the shed fires at Wath Mill allotments?' Thomas asked, knowing that Jill was usually well informed about local events, especially those of an unusual kind.

'Of course, Laura runs the school plot there and Charlie Poole has an allotment, she's actually the chair. The Shakespeare's and the Chlebek's also have allotment plots and I believe the Tinton's have one too. Satoshi's granny not the younger Tinton's.'

Thomas smiled, he had been right about the range of Jill's knowledge. Her office was a central hub of information, it was the GCHQ at Cheltenham's equivalent in Newhill.

'You should go on Mastermind, do you know everything?'

'One hears things,' Jill smiled, wondering where all this mystery was leading.

'Do you know who started the fires, I say fires as there were apparently two separate sheds burnt down well apart, so no chance of it being accidental.'

'The police reckoned that it was probably vandals, a random act of mischief,' she replied, her informant was her friend Eve Kent, mother of the attending police officer.' Laura and Charlie had confirmed this suspicion during coffee break one morning.

'One of the sheds belonged to Keith Shakespeare and the other to two Portuguese ladies, care workers at Woodlands care home.' Jill completed her comprehensive report.

Thomas was both amazed and amused. 'I was only joking about the Mastermind thing, but you really do know everything.'

'Oh yes, and the police considered racism as a motive but concluded that it was more likely cheap beer or wine and showing off.'

'Mastermind nothing, you are wasted as a secretary you should have been a barrister.'

Jill was aware that she might well have to be late for her appointment for her hair to be coloured at the Lavish Locks hairdressers in the High Street.

'How does all this affect our school? The gardening club are always supervised, they can't be involved.'

'Someone believes that one of them can, at least that's what the anonymous letter states, very clearly. Grace Bisby is the one accused.'

Thomas had expected Jill to laugh at this ridiculous suggestion, but she was grim faced.

'Oh, dear God, have that family not suffered enough? Grace's mother will be mortified. We must fight this with everything we have Thomas, Grace is a delightful girl, and she is no more capable of setting fire to two sheds than I am of becoming a Japanese Sumo wrestler. She often comes into the school office with her friend, Rosangel, to ask if there is anything they can help with at breaktimes.'

This statement was most definitely a positive affirmation of his feeling that the anonymous letter was one of mere mischief, one for the waste bin.

'That's what I said to the police, without the sumo reference obviously.' Thomas replied.

'I know that some malicious gossips in Newhill have got it in for the Bisby's, Eileen Bisby, Graces grandmother, helped put her husband out of his utter misery. He was in pain and suffering every minute with end of life cancer and the doctors weren't able to help. If he'd been a dog a vet would have done the right thing and put him to sleep and no one would argue, but a human is made to linger on and suffer agony. I think that Eileen did what most would do in her position. I certainly like to think that I would have the courage to help the one I loved achieve peace.'

'Does Grace know about all this?' Thomas asked, wondering if the note had come from one of the malicious gossips. What other motive could there be? Could a child like Grace have enemies?

'I don't actually know but I do know that she deserves better than this. Grace has my full unreserved support.'

'And mine Jill, and I think that I have kept you long enough. Have a good weekend and thank you for your advice, it was most helpful.'

Jill glanced at the clock, she may well get to the hairdressers in time for her usual Friday appointment.

'And you Thomas. Don't go staying too late. All work and no play and all that.'

Meanwhile the longer May afternoons tended to linger into the evening and some at Wath Mill allotments took advantage.

Keith Shakespeare was umpiring a match at Newhill cricket club on Saturday, and he wanted to put in a little time on his plot. He had met Billy at the school gate, and they walked across the park towards the small bridge leading to the allotments. They walked easily, chatting about the school cricket team and Aston Villa and the subject of Rosangel came up.

'Do you think that I should ask her out Dad, what would you do in my place?'

'You have an old head on young shoulders but nevertheless you are still only eleven. Time is on your side Billy. Why not continue as you are, just be her friend. You may end up at different secondary schools and you may meet someone you like just as much. Don't rush these things, just enjoy your life now. You can always wait until you are twelve to get married. I was nearly fifty before I could pluck up courage to ask your mother to a local dance in Trinidad.'

Little Billy grinned, 'And you could be best man Dad. I think that Cressida, Miranda and Jessica will get married before me, all that wedding cake to get through. Mum will have you on a double diet.' he said patting his father's stomach. 'Anyway, you are only forty-seven now!'

Arriving at the gate leading to the allotments Keith scanned the site, as he usually did on entering. In the past he had looked to see who was working there, who to chat with, but lately he had looked round for intruders. The arson attack on his shed had cost him money. The site was not insured for such loss and his home insurance didn't cover it. A new shed was out of the question, but he was on the lookout for a decent second hand one, there was of course no guarantee that that also wouldn't be torched. He kept these thoughts to himself, no need to worry Billy.

Keith saw to his dismay that Kevin Bolton was already at Wath Mill but not on his own plot. He was on plot nine, talking with Charlie Poole, the twins Jamie and Annie were playing catch on the broad central path.

'Billy, do me a favour, take the twins up to our plot, keep them up there for a few minutes. I need to talk to Charlie.'

Billy was alerted by his father's quiet tone and looked around to see why his father needed to have the children, including himself, out of the way. He looked left to where Keith was looking. Kevin Bolton was talking in an animated fashion to Charlie Poole. This could be trouble. Billy knew that Kevin was notorious for stirring up distress and anxiety, not a nice man. Good job he was not at Newhill School.

'OK Dad but just shout if you need help.'

'That's good to know son', the large Trinidadian said, smiling to himself as he looked down at his diminutive son. 'I know that you have got my back, but we'll only be chatting, don't worry.' The boy did not want courage, just strength and height.

Billy ran to engage the boisterous twins by challenging them to a race up to the far end, plot seventeen, the Shakespeare's plot which was full of unusual Carribean and oriental vegetables.

Charlie Poole reflected that she would certainly not miss this unpleasant aspect of being chair of the committee, the confrontations with people such as Kevin Bolton who had sought her out with his complaints. It was eight years since old William Mullins had proposed her as chair to the shock of all concerned, she had been a shy and lonely girl working at the bakery, pleasant but quiet and unobtrusive, William had seen deeper qualities in her, an inner strength. Charlie missed William and once upon a time she would have wished for William to have been there to support her, But William was gone, and the girl was now a battle-hardened woman. Eight years in the role of chair had given her skills of diplomacy and determination, being the mother of five year old twins had given her strength and confidence in herself. Her new role at Newhill Primary, helping Sam Chlebek, gave her patience and her marriage to Chris Poole had given stability and a quiet enduring love. Charlie Poole was now a formidable woman yet even as she dealt efficiently with the unpopular Kevin Bolton's complaints, she was glad to see Keith Shakespeare approaching.

'Hello Keith, Kevin here was just asking about insurance at the allotments in view of the theft of tools and, of course the shed fires.'

'We should have proper insurance, isn't that why we pay an annual subscription. The last AGM said that our bank balance is healthy or are the committee enjoying perks at our expense?'

'The committee decided several years ago that the cost of comprehensive insurance was far too high to justify the expenditure. We have a public liability license in case one of us is injured or indeed a visitor or even an intruder is hurt. It would cover our legal costs. This is normal for allotments like ours,' Charlie calmly replied determined not to be cowed or forced into an angry exchange.

'Exactly, that's just my point. Keith here has lost a shed and contents and was badly burned with hot water from a Kelly kettle. If I hadn't acted quickly, he could have been scarred for life. What about compensation, he could have been off work for weeks, if not months.'

'I've told you millions of times not to exaggerate,' Keith grinned but his joke apparently went over the Snelston teacher's head. He decided to lose the levity and go on. Kevin had obviously had a sense of humour transplant which had failed.

'And for that intervention I am truly grateful but with all due respect I should remind you that you are right, it was my arm and my shed. More than anyone I should be the one clamouring for compensation, but accidents happen. I'm not going to seek financial gain from the allotments.'

Kevin Bolton had crossed swords before with the jovial but bulky Trinidadian so quickly changed tack. Intimidation was a well-worn tactic which would obviously not work here.

'And another thing, the regulations say quite clearly that dogs are not allowed on the site. You are chair it is your responsibility to enforce this rule. Two allotment holders bring their dogs up here regularly. It is for growing fruit and vegetables, it's not bloody Crufts. If children come into contact with dog muck it can cause blindness. We have three kids playing over there right now and my lad often comes up here to help. How many kids must be put at risk before you do your job properly?' Kevin almost spat the words out as he entered fully into his intimidating stride.

Keith replied quietly but with some firm gravitas, 'Now there's no need for unpleasantness is there? Charlie here has given more than her fair share as a volunteer on behalf of all of us. Eight years I believe. Yes, I've lost a shed and some burnt tools and gained a very sore arm, but this lass has my full support as she will at the next AGM. As for the two dogs in question, Billy and Meg are always perfectly behaved and under control. Tessa and Laura are very responsible about clearing up any mess.'

At that moment Tessa approached with her cocker spaniel, Billy, on a lead accompanied by Kyoko and Satoshi.

Kevin turned and said triumphantly, 'And that proves my point. Will you get rid of that dog or do I take this to the committee and force your resignation.'

Kyoko recoiled slightly at this show of anger. It would not have happened in her home of Japan. Public shows of anger were quite rightly frowned upon.

Tessa realised that she had inadvertently walked into a dispute and almost regretted bringing Kyoko and her son up to see her allotment plot.

'And what harm is my dog doing to you Kevin, tell me that.' Tessa challenged.

Charlie went for a compromise and said that she would indeed bring up the issue of insurance and dogs on the site on Kevin's behalf.

She went on, 'But I have to say that threats to me are a waste of time as I already intend to stand down at the next AGM. We need fresh leadership and ideas. Perhaps a chance for you to serve three years without pay, just lots of work and complaints.'

Meanwhile Billy and the twins had spotted the newcomers and ran to greet Satoshi and fuss the frantic tail wagging spaniel.

Kevin Bolton decided upon a tactical withdrawal, sensing that he was losing the argument even though he considered himself in the right as he usually did.

'I've got better things to do than stand here wasting my time, but you have not heard the last of this believe you me,' he snarled turning to walk angrily towards the gate.

Charlie felt some relief that this unpleasantness was over. 'Thanks Keith and you too Tessa although the appearance of your dog was somewhat inopportune.'

'Don't worry about it love, that man isn't worth worrying about,' Tessa answered trying to hold onto the lead.

Keith added, 'I did nothing I was just the eye candy as usual, but I was glad to have been here to offer moral support.'

This had lifted the gloomy atmosphere and Kyoko was introduced to Keith. Satoshi, he already knew from the school cricket team.

Satoshi turned to his mother, 'May I introduce Billy Shakespeare and Billy the cocker spaniel. One is obviously prettier and more intelligent than the other.'

Billy laughed and said, 'That hurt, I'm clearly the good looking one here but Billy is probably more intelligent at least at fetching sticks and swimming.' He had never quite mastered the skill of swimming despite lessons at school. Embarrassing really, he felt.

Kyoko was slightly confused she understood why the Shakespeare's would name their son after the famous English playwright but surely the dog was not named for the same reason. Tessa explained that the puppy had been named Billy in honour of a good friend, William Mullins. 'We'll have to take you to Stratford on Avon where the original William Shakespeare was born, it's a lovely town.'

Kyoko was thrilled, 'I would really love that, it would be a dream come true, and where were you born young Master Shakespeare, not Stratford I presume?'

Billy grinned, 'No, Birmingham so I could be near Villa Park.'

Sometimes English is so confusing she thought.

Keith offered to show the Japanese visitors round his plot, which stood next to Tessa's at the far end of the site. Charlie said that she would return to her hoeing of the unwelcome spring weeds, Jamie and Annie loyally stayed with her, although they would rather have played with the lively cocker spaniel.

As the group arrived at plots sixteen and seventeen near the native hedge Kyoko was amazed at the difference between the plots. Her mother-in-law's plot was tidy with robust spring cabbages, neat rows of emergent carrots, beetroot and a couple of rows of labelled potatoes, Jazzy, Tessa and Grahams favourite. It was the sort of plot which could be found on any allotment site in England. The comparison with Keith Shakespeare's plot was astounding. There was little sense of order, but it screamed of exotic productivity. Keith explained that he tried to grow the sort of crops he grew up with in his native Trinidad, but the climate of Derbyshire was not always suitable.

'I make up for it with other crops from cooler parts of the world, the Andes in South America for instance, I even have some Wasabi plants from Japan, I'm sure that you are familiar with wasabi paste, Kyoko. She nodded her head gracefully to show her agreement and Keith was entranced. Tessa smiled to herself noting the remarkable physical comparison between the two, the slim elegant Japanese girl she had grown to love and the large West Indian who was both her friend and neighbour at Wath Mill allotments.

Keith continued to point out his crops with some degree of pride. There were sweet potatoes, oca, yams, Pak choi and several varieties of sweet corn. The only downside was a large square of ash from the burnt shed, which cast a gloomy shadow which had little to do with the sunshine. The area still smelt of unpleasant burning, but Keith had utilised this ash to sprinkle on his onions. 'They do like a bit of ash. Every cloud has a silver lining.'

Kyoko was a city girl, brought up in the sprawling city of Tokyo in the Asakusa district and she loved the feeling of being in the country amidst so much growth and productivity.

'And what do you do with the oca Mr. Shakespeare?'

'Keith, please, no formality here. My wife Faith roasts them in a light oil, they have a nutty lemony flavour.' You will have to come round, and we'll prepare an authentic Caribbean meal for you and your family.'

Tessa felt delighted to be showing off her daughter-in-law and grandson, they were obviously making quite an impression in Newhill.

Kyoko was diplomatic, 'Both allotments are very different, one very English and the other almost tropical, and what do you do here, Billy?

He replied with a serious face, 'I'm the official food taster'

Chapter Eleven

Glass is Tougher Than it Looks

PC Eleanor Kent walked slowly around the back of Newhill Primary School, her radio crackling but not for her. She had been pleased to receive the call, it was always enjoyable to visit her old playground, scene of so many minor dramas. There had been new equipment added, it had after all been over twenty years since she had left. New equipment, new head and it was Thomas who had called her in, or at least not her personally. Nevertheless, it was another opportunity to meet him again. Perhaps she would offer him a security survey, preferably after school and before a coffee.

Outside Thomas's office she found shards of glass and looked at the broken window, well, that solves one mystery but adds another. She returned to his office, Jill Taylor had made Thomas and her a welcome cup of coffee. It was early June, but the air was still cool in the early morning.

'Thanks Jill,' Eleanor said smiling at her mum Eve's friend. It was odd being served coffee in the head's office by someone she had known since being a little girl. Surreal somehow.

Thomas looked with an appreciative eye at the young police officer. The last time she had been in his office she had been called away urgently by her radio and he had been on the verge of asking her out for a drink. The break-in had given him another opportunity. This time he would act, married or not.

'I've been round the school, as you asked and Jill and I could find no damage, no graffiti and the only thing obviously missing is a trophy, the Mullins Cricket cup. It has little monetary value so I'm mystified why an intruder would want just that,' Thomas reported.

'Well, I don't believe that you had an intruder, the broken glass is on the outside. The caretaker is sweeping it up now before the children arrive.'

Thomas frowned and looked bemused. 'I assumed a broken window would mean a break in. I should have worked that out for myself.'

'Don't worry, I'm trained for this sort of thing. I don't think there will be anything, but I'll dust for fingerprints anyway. Probably yours will be the only ones. I'll have to take your prints, I'm afraid, to eliminate you. People don't realise how difficult it is to break reinforced glass. This was given quite a strong, sharp blow from inside your office.'

Later Thomas quite enjoyed having his fingerprints taken, especially when done by such an attractive girl, He had been away from his wife for too long.

'I don't suppose that you wouldn't fancy a drink later, would you? We could discuss the break in when we've got more....'

He didn't finish before El, as she preferred to be called swiftly intervened, 'Yes, I would like that, coffee or a beer?'

And so, a meeting was arranged for the next evening to discuss this major crime. A meeting both welcomed but not with a crime solving agenda.

When Eleanor had gone Jill came into the office with the school diary. Thomas was usually organised with his own diary, but it was a morning ritual for them to correlate both to ensure no mistakes. It suited both their working practices.

'You have a meeting with Steve Shaw about installing new computers at ten thirty. Laura recommended him, she knows him from the allotments, but he is something of an ICT expert and better still has offered his advice for free.'

'That may be all we can afford unless we can attract more pupils or find a way to swell the coffers. Still its good of him to make the offer, he's not a computer salesman. They always say that everything is out of date and needs replacement.'

Jill went on,' You have the governors' meeting this evening at seven, in the staff room as usual I presume?'

'Yes, I'll get everything ready.'

'Don't worry I'll clear up a little after school. Nothing worse than dirty coffee cups to give a poor impression'

'Thanks Jill. Where would I be without you?'

The experienced and very astute secretary paused, wondering whether to speak her mind. 'Thomas,' she said quietly, it's not my business but be careful. I've known Eleanor Kent since she was a toddler and she's a grand girl but on the rebound, looking for solace in a new romance. She is divorced from her prat of a husband, but you are not divorced. A reconciliation with your wife is not out of the question and you don't need complications. I'm not trying to interfere, but I care about you and El and it could end in tears.'

Putting on her business face she went on, 'Well, I must get on, letters to type up and dinner money to count as well as registers to check. I promise not to say any more, the rest is up to you.'

As Jill returned to the school office Thomas sat contemplating the events of the morning. If there had been no intruder, it meant that someone he knew had stolen the cup. An embarrassment which he would have to reveal to the secretary of the cricket league. The issue of his date with El Kent was not a difficult one, they were both adults and it was only a drink not a lifelong commitment, but he noted well his secretary's kindly but firm warning.

That issue would resolve itself he thought, but it could cause a deep and inconsolable rift between himself and Beth. He looked at the photograph of them both on his desk and looked away.

Moving on, Thomas took the agenda for the governors' meeting out of his briefcase. There were the usual set items with a welcome to Chris Poole as a new parent governor, Thomas had met Chris as he was Charlie Poole's husband and a respected solicitor in Newhill. A good addition to the governing body. Andy Chlebek represented the county council as a governor and Thomas knew that he, like Chris, was committed to the school. Between them they had six children at Newhill, children the school needed in times of falling numbers.

It was a small governing body, but Thomas got on well with them all. The meetings followed a formal pattern, but they were held in an informal atmosphere. It suited everyone and the governors were very pleased with their appointment of the young and enthusiastic headteacher. Thomas wondered how this would change if his secrets came out. He would hate to let them down, this was his dream job

He went through his typed head's report. It had been checked for spelling and grammar errors by Jill and circulated beforehand.

His meeting with Steve Shaw went well, there was an immediate respect and liking between the two men. Thomas had noted the key pieces of advice and rough costings which Steve gave. This would be too late for the governors' meeting unless as an AOB at the end. It was unlikely that the school could afford large scale expenditure in times of economic tightening of belts. Nevertheless, he thanked Steve for his time.

Steve stood and paused, 'I'm getting married soon and my fiancé has a child from an earlier marriage, so I was wondering if there was space in year four for her. She's at Snelston at the moment and she's not particularly happy there but from what I can see Newhill is a much friendlier school. I also know Charlie Poole and Laura Watson from the allotments although I know that Laura is retiring at the end of the school year. They speak very well of you and the school.'

Thomas smiled, an added child would help, and it was good to know that the school had a good reputation. 'I don't have to look; I know we have a place and I'll keep it open for you until you've discussed it with your fiancé. Congratulations on your upcoming marriage by the way.'

The meeting concluded with happy outcomes for both men a pity about the high cost of computers though. Sponsorship and the Friends of School could not always be relied upon.

At the end of the day Thomas sat in the staffroom eating a sandwich and drinking a cup of tea. Jill had been as good as her word and delinquent cups had been washed and put away, the central coffee table cleared of papers and the notice board tidied. Old union notices removed and others re stapled neatly.

The meeting began after Thomas had offered coffee or tea to the governors, Jill had set out their best cups and a plate of biscuits was uncovered.

When it came to the Head's Report, Thomas did not read it out as it had been circulated already. He added the recent news of the loss of the Mullins cup and the broken window and a brief outcome of his meeting with Steve Shaw relating to new computers.

As he concluded the chair, Caroline Perryman, thanked him for his concise report.

'Does anyone have any questions for Thomas?'

Chris Poole looked round before speaking. 'I know that I am a new governor and I thank you for your warm welcome, but the report does seem full of worries about possible school closure. Falling numbers and an upcoming inspection seem to be real threats. How worried are you and what can we as governors do to help and support you?'

Thomas replied, 'I am seriously worried about the numbers at the school. Projections are reasonable about future intake, but parental perception is vital. It is easy for a school to lose its reputation and children move to what is seen as a better school. A good inspection would help enormously, and the inspectors will want to see you as governors with individual responsibilities for things like special needs and safeguarding as well as main subjects. They take results into account, but it is always based on the results from the previous Year Six.'

Caroline looked round and summed up the message clearly.

'We must all make sure that we know what is going on with our own particular areas of responsibility. Liaison with the staff is key, when we speak to inspectors we must speak with knowledge and authority. Make sure you all know the achievements and if there are problems is there a plan to overcome them, Thomas, you are obviously worried and as a new headteacher that is understandable, these are difficult times, but you are not alone we were unanimous in choosing you as head and nothing has changed. We stand four square alongside you, you have our full and positive support.'

There were nods and sounds of firm agreement round the table. Thomas felt a weight lifting from his shoulders but the governors were unaware of his dual secrets, and he would hate to disappoint them.

Andy Chlebek spoke quietly, and everyone listened, he was a man of few words, but they were always precise and to the point.

'You ask how we can help fight school closure and I would suggest that you come to the County Council meeting on Thursday, the agenda includes potential school closure. You may be able to speak and put forward the school's point of view. Solid well thought out arguments are better received than placard wavers and shouting of slogans. May I suggest that you arrange for a few children to speak to the council? That sort of thing goes down well.'

After the meeting concluded Thomas thanked everyone and he walked home in the warm evening air feeling as good as he could in the circumstances. The promise of a social meeting with El Kent on the following night held both promise and moral dilemma.

The following morning assembly finished, and Thomas asked Grace Bisby, Billy Shakespeare and Rosangel Chlebek to come to his office. They were puzzled and two out of three were intrigued but one felt a nervousness deep in the stomach.

With the added chair there was room for the three Year Six friends to sit. All looked concerned. What could this be about? All three noted the brand new sheet of glass in the office window. Of course, they had heard of the break in and theft of the precious Mullins cup.

'Thomas said, 'Don't worry you are not in any trouble, not that I know of anyway. As you may know there is talk of closing Newhill school due to lack of finances and falling pupil numbers. There is a council meeting tomorrow afternoon and decisions will be made there about our school.'

'Billy spoke first, 'Can they do that, is it legal?

Rosangel knew something more than the others as her father was on the council. 'How can we help? Thomas was touched by the simple statement which said so much about the girl. Grace thought it over, 'Where will we go if the school closes?'

'Well Grace a very practical thought but I can put your mind at rest on that score. Any closure would not happen before you three leave for secondary school. It won't concern you as such, but I do need your help.'

Billy felt relief and a rising anger. 'Tell us what we can do, this is our school we enjoy being here it should remain open, it's too good to be closed.'

Rosangel was shrewd, 'Is this about us going to the meeting tomorrow?'

Thomas was impressed, 'Spot on Rosie, I would like you three to speak to the council members to tell them why you think Newhill should remain open, if you agree, your parents have already given permission. If you would prepare a brief statement in your own words, I can look it over if you like and we can drive over to the council offices after lunch. What do you say?'

The three children looked at each other. Rosie spoke for them all, 'Just try and stop us. My father will be there and together we will all put a strong argument forward.'

Thomas felt a surge of pride in these, his children, his school. It was a school worth fighting for.

So it was that the next afternoon three children stood before the council members in the imposing wooden chamber. Thomas noted the plush carpets, solid carved furniture and plants, there was no shortage of money here, apparently. He stood and thanked the members for the opportunity to state the case for Newhill but went on to say that Grace, Rosangel and Billy would speak on his behalf.

All had short, prepared pieces which Mrs. Taylor had kindly typed for them.

Grace went first and she spoke of the support which she had always received and the commitment of teachers, especially their popular new head, The school stands for the best of primary education, and it would be a terrible thing for it to be closed. The members listened politely and carefully. Billy went next and explained that he had moved to Newhill from Birmingham, His school there was enormous and had all the facilities possible, Newhill was tiny by comparison and may not have nice new carpets and potted plants, but it made up for this with spirit and enthusiasm. 'Mr. Tiler has set up a cricket team and we were thrashed in our first game, but he encouraged and supported us. We still haven't won but we will, such is the fighting spirit and determination which he has given us,' A few members smiled at the improvised reference to the plush surroundings enjoyed by the council members.

Rosangel concluded their brief presentation. 'Thank you all for your time but we need more than time and good wishes. Schools like Newhill are the backbone of the English primary system. All three of us will be leaving for secondary school in September but we have been given a sound education and sense of what is right and wrong. Billy is of West Indian descent, and I am proud to come from a Polish family. At Newhill it doesn't matter where we are from, we are treated equally with love and respect, and we will shine next year because of what Mr. Tiler and his wonderful staff have given us. We are all part of the Newhill cricket team, but we are also part of a bigger team, the Newhill family. It should remain open for all time to serve the town as it has for generations before. Thank you'

Andy Chlebek was filled with a bursting pride, watching his beloved daughter giving such an impassioned speech. The tears in his eyes were luckily hidden by the warm applause of the members.

The chair of the council stood and thanked them for their time.

'Mr. Tiler, if these are an example of what you are achieving you should be a very proud man. Please pass on our congratulations to their staff and parents.' He glanced at Andy and smiled to himself to see such a father's pride.

'However, economics is a harsh mistress, and we are all affected by this reality. The council members here are responsible for all schools. Emotion cannot rule our heads. We have much to discuss but I would say that a good inspection will go a long way to ensuring survival for Newhill. Good luck with your inspection, we will watch with real interest, I cannot make promises, but my guess is that the equation is simple. A good inspection report will attract new parents, and consequently greater funding and in all probability keep the school open and, in my opinion, rightly so.'

The three children smiled and hugged each other.

Thomas knew that the challenge had been set, a good report would probably keep Newhill open, a bad one, well, that problem lay in the future. Today was a matter for pride in his three pupils.

Chapter Twelve

A Close Run Thing

It was a hot lunchtime on the school field yet that didn't stop games of football, skipping and catch games. The lunchtime supervisors did their best to calm the inevitable squabbles as heated arguments between equally heated boys boiled over.

Rosangel, Billy, Grace and Sam sat on the grass and discussed recent events. Mikolaj played football with energy and skill and not a little amount of sweat. Rosangel kept an eye on her younger brother, and it brought back one of her mother's sayings, 'Horses sweat, men perspire but ladies' glow.' She wondered if she had got that the right way round Mikolaj was no horse, but he was certainly sweating as he raced for the ball in the midday heat. Perhaps the saying should be horses and boys sweat.

Her thoughts were interrupted by Billy who was trying unsuccessfully to get Rosies attention.

'Are you listening Rosie.? We were trying to make sense of the recent news.'

'Sorry Billy, I was miles away.'

The three speakers at the council meeting had reported back and it was agreed that they had done well. The discussion about school closures and upcoming inspection meant that it was no surprise to them when Mr. Tiler announced the date of the inspection in assembly.

'It's only a few days away and on the same day as our first-round cricket match against Mapleton Road Juniors.' Billy said, picking at the grass. 'Do you think that it will be cancelled?'

'I don't think that they cancel Ofsted inspections because it clashes with our cricket match,' Grace reflected.

'Not the inspection, the match, silly.' Billy retorted.

'Anyway, we would be playing for a cup which has disappeared, the whole thing may have to be cancelled, that would be disappointing. I doubt if I will be good enough to get into a cricket team at secondary school, too many others to choose from, a pity I quite like playing.' Rosie said.

Billy's hopes rose as he had a thought, He was worried that he and Rosangel would be at different secondary schools. 'You could always join our cricket club, I play in a junior team and your bowling is getting better all the time, not quite Shane Warne but improving.'

'Thanks Billy, that's nice of you to say so.' Rosie said, shielding her eyes from the sun.

At that moment Satoshi came over and plonked himself down on the grass. 'Where have you been Satoshi, we looked for you, we thought that you would be playing football.' Grace said.

'I had second helpings of apple crumble, definitely the best thing about being at school here in England, and then I saw Mr. Tiler and asked about the cup match against Mapleton Road.'

This had the sudden interest of the friends and they looked to the Japanese boy with hopeful expectation. Billy spoke for them all. 'And...?'

'And he says that he has phoned your dad, Billy and asked him to umpire and take charge of the team. He thinks that he will be too busy with the inspectors after school.'

Billy smiled, 'The Shakespeare's save the day again. Why didn't we think of just asking Mr. Tiler.'

'Japanese ingenuity Billy with a touch of brilliance' Satoshi grinned. Like Rosangel he had been wondering about the possibility of playing cricket next year when he returned to Tokyo' It would be difficult but then he would be able to play baseball once more and go to see the Tokyo Swallows again, He loved being in England and his English grandparents and Billy the cocker spaniel and his new friends. but there were quiet moments when he missed Japan. He had realised that in September Rosangel, Billy and Grace would be going to a new school, but Mikolaj and Sam would still be here, and he could continue playing cricket next season, it wouldn't be the same though.

Mikolaj came over and threw himself down, shirt open, his blonde hair sweat plastered to his head. Rosangel disapproved and wished she had a towel and comb to make her younger brother more presentable for afternoon class.

Grace was thoughtful, 'Did Mr. Tiler say anything about the Mullins cup? Will it be replaced; it seems silly playing for a missing trophy.'

Satoshi replied, 'No he didn't mention anything about a replacement, but I don't think they have any idea who stole it.'

Billy sat up, 'Now that we are all here, we should put our minds together and do some real detective work. The bell won't go for another half hour.'

'Half an hour? If the police can't solve it in the time they have had, why would we be able to solve it before the bell?' Rosangel asked.

Satoshi said, 'You are right Rosie, but the police have much to do, a missing trophy is a small unimportant matter to them but to us it is very important.'

Mikolaj had cooled down somewhat, 'Who would want to steal the cup? he asked,' it's probably not worth much unless it's solid silver or an antique worth thousands,'

Billy said that this was so simple, a brilliant thought, what was the motive for stealing the cup?

Satoshi agreed. 'Anyone from outside would steal anything valuable, laptops or money or anything they could sell. What do you think Sam?'

Sam shrugged, looking at his sister for help. He felt uncomfortable with speaking out loud except to Rosangel. She in turn desperately wished that Sam could communicate with others. Even with friends he was not able to speak, she knew that he could if only in whispers to her. Next year this possibility would not be there. She could imagine the hell of being in a classroom in secondary school and worrying about her beloved younger brother.

As usual she tried to cover for Sam's silence. 'Sam and I agree with Satoshi, it is unlikely that the cup was stolen by anyone outside the school unless it was a mad collector of cups. Not really credible.'

Billy liked to be seen as agreeing with Rosangel but in this case he really did. 'That quickly narrows it down from billions on the planet to a couple of hundred.'

Grace was subdued but added, 'Then break the suspects down to possible groups.'

Satoshi warmed to the subject, he liked this sort of puzzle and English television was full of Agatha Christie mysteries 'That's good, Grace, we have teachers, other staff, visitors and Mr. Tiler himself.'

Rosangel added, 'Don't forget children.'

Billy asked, 'What time of day was the cup stolen?'

'Apparently it was after school,' Rosie said, 'so that would rule out the lunchtime supervisors and cooks, they would have gone home.'

Mikolaj spoke up. 'But they could have sneaked back in.'

Billy thought and said it was unlikely. 'Someone would have noticed them at that time of day. Mr. Tiler was away on a course all afternoon apparently so he could be ruled out.'

Satoshi agreed, 'He wants to win the cup and keep it for Newhill, not himself. I believe him to be innocent.'

'That leaves us with those with opportunity.' Rosangel added. 'Mrs. Taylor would easily be able to put the cup in a bag after school. She should be on our suspect list, what about cleaners?'

Grace said that they too had opportunity but what would be the motive, Same as Mrs. Taylor for that matter. 'The cup is clearly engraved, the Mullins cup, difficult to sell at a car boot sale.'

Satoshi sighed. 'That applies to all our suspects, what is the motive/'

'Were there any visitors from other schools that day?' Billy asked. 'We don't have enough information and I can't see anyone from Snelston creeping into school, their team will probably win the cup anyway.'

They decided that it was difficult to be detectives unless a motive was established. Agatha Christie usually had a small group of suspects to choose from. The bell rang for the afternoon session to begin, and they decided to give it further thought. They must find a motive.

The next evening saw the start of the Ofsted inspection process. The lead inspector, Mr. Henry Harlond, a retired headteacher, chaired a meeting for parents to gather their views about the school and its efficiency. Thomas Tiler sat in his office not allowed to attend as he might influence opinion and he found it difficult. He could hear the buzz of voices but could make nothing out. Charlie and Chris Pole were there as parents as were the Shakespeare's and Chlebek's. Non parents were not invited so Thomas spent the time trying to prepare for the actual inspection.

After several coffees, Henry Harlond came into his office to thank Thomas for setting up the meeting. 'I'm not really allowed to comment or feedback fully, but I will say that it looks good. Apart from the usual small number of off the wall minor complaints it was very supportive. My role was merely to note the parental feelings and as usual the few dissenters were quickly put down by counter arguments from the majority. You seem to have engaged the support of parents in a short time, well done. I will see you tomorrow.'

A bit like an executioner wishing the condemned man a good night. Still, it was good to know that he had the support of governors and parents, most staff were on board, but the issue of Mary Anderson remained.

The following morning was drizzly, and Thomas thought it appropriate as he arrived early at the school. Everything was as prepared as it could be. A timetable for the inspectors had been agreed and once lessons started there was nothing more that Thomas could do. He had his own meeting with inspectors about his management role, teaching and learning and health and safety.

He was deep in thought when the phone rang, and he jumped. More likely a reaction to the day rather than the phone call itself, he thought.

'Hello is that Thomas? I thought that you would be in early. Its Mary, Mary Anderson here'

Thomas felt his stomach give a sickening lurch, she should be at least on her way to school, if not here already. He drew a deep breath before answering.

'What is it, Mary? Not an accident, I hope.'

'I'm sorry to have to tell you that I won't be able to come in for a few days. I woke up this morning with conjunctivitis in both eyes. As you know it's highly contagious so coming in would not be advisable, I know that the inspection starts today but I've rung the doctor and he agrees. We wouldn't want it to spread, would we?

What could he say? He was gutted, his timetable and schedules in tatters. She certainly chose her moment to let the school down. Conjunctivitis...? Perhaps.

'Thanks for letting me know Mary. Get your eyes sorted out, your health comes first. More important than an Ofsted inspection.'

He felt something of a hypocrite not saying what he felt. She may well be afflicted but it seemed convenient. At that moment Henry Harlond knocked on his door and walked in.

'Good morning, Thomas, not a nice day and the rain might mean a wet playtime with children inside, not ideal.'

Thomas grimaced, 'It gets worse I'm afraid, one of my teachers is sick and won't be in. I'll take her class until we can get a supply teacher in. We have a couple of excellent ones, and I primed them to be ready in case of emergency. We'll just have to re jig the timetable.'

'Unlucky Thomas, today of all days. You get yourself sorted and I'll speak to the other inspectors before we begin observations. Don't forget that I've been in your shoes, it happens to the best of us, it's how we respond that matters.'

The next two hours were frantic, Jill phoned for teaching cover, lucky he had someone on standby. Hasty lessons were prepared, and everyone went to their classrooms in a nervous tense atmosphere. Somehow the news of Mary Anderson's absence brought indignation and anger amongst the staff, it was almost a unifying effect and all the staff pulled together, supporting each other, the Dunkirk spirit. Few believed in the very convenient conjunctivitis.

The day ended and the staff met up in the staffroom, almost too tired to go home.

'Well Laura I suppose that this will be your last inspection,' Charlie Poole observed. 'It is my first and it wasn't much fun, only tomorrow to go through. Thomas must be shredded.'

The teachers drank a welcome mug of tea, prepared by Jill, and a new tin of chocolates was opened, courtesy of the Friends of Newhill School, as a boost to morale and a sign of parental support.

Thomas didn't sleep well; the day had started badly but Henry Harlond had proved both efficient and understanding. That certainly helped but nevertheless Thomas felt at crisis point. Two cups of coffee replaced his normal breakfast, a sure sign that all was not well.

Later the warm summer sun broke through the thin cloud and the playground asphalt began to steam. Surely this was a sign that today would be a better day. A good supply teacher was there in place of Mary Anderson, and he could concentrate on his meetings at times throughout the day.

Everything seemed set fair, he was proud of the way his staff had responded to the pressure of being critically observed. He could not have asked for more.

There was just time to look quickly through the morning's post, most could wait but one caught his eye. He couldn't say why it looked different, but it did. Thomas quickly opened the white typed envelope and a small piece of paper fell out. It read. 'WE HAVEN'T FORGOTTEN ABOUT YOU. THE INSPECTORS NOW KNOW YOUR SECRET.'

Thomas Tiler slumped in his chair speechless and almost in tears. A second anonymous letter. The cruelty of life hit him hard. Resignation would be a luxury for him now, more likely an ignominious sacking. His humiliation would be complete and absolute.

He was too overcome to even stand when Henry Harlond, the lead inspector, knocked and entered his office.

'Good morning, Thomas, aah I see that you have had a letter as well. May I see it? 'He took the brief note from Thomas and read it carefully.

'Well, our letter was hand delivered, anonymous and somehow put in our room.'

'Our letter says that you have dyslexia and shouldn't be teaching let alone be a head teacher. What is your opinion?'

Thomas stared at the floor and felt the shame of hot tears filling his eyes. So many years of keeping this secret, at school and university and in his teaching career. He was lost for words, he had let so many people down, his wife, his parents, his staff and pupils. There was nothing he could offer as defence.

'Henry looked at the young head in a not unkind way. 'I take it that it is true then.?'

Thomas nodded slowly, 'I've hid it for so long I was desperate to teach and at university I struggled to keep up with the reading requirements. I barely scraped through my exams. When I applied for my first teaching post, I made it look as if I had a good degree, I lied and I am so sorry, but I really loved being with children and this was my dream job. I'll write my letter of resignation straight away '

'Thomas when I was a head, I felt the same excitement which you obviously feel. William Mullins was head here and I was head at Warneside, just down the road. That man taught me so much which has stood me in good stead over the years. We used to go on courses together and I was interested to see how his school was doing. His passing was a blow to education I can tell you. Yesterday I spoke to quite a few of the Newhill children and it was obvious that they are intensely proud of the school and defensive of you in particular. One young lad, claimed to be called Shakespeare, a West Indian probably, well he did all but threaten me if I wrote anything negative about you.'

'I'm sorry, I'll have a word with him.'

'You'll do no such thing, he showed me, as did many others, a fierce team spirit and determination, they are proud of you and their school. That doesn't happen by accident. Parents feel the same, A large chap, probably young Shakespeare's father was particularly vocal in your praise.'

'Aston Villa supporters, they are usually noisy,' Thomas smiled weakly without conviction.

Henry smiled. 'If William Mullins were here now and God knows I wish he was then he would tell me just what to do and I would agree with him.' Henry took the two letters and tore them up carefully before putting them in the bin.

'That's the place for any anonymous letters, not worth anything, a waste of paper. If you have managed your dyslexia for so long and so successfully you must have developed coping strategies of the highest order. The children in your care will benefit enormously from your understanding of dyslexia, its nothing to be ashamed of, just a condition to be managed with skill. As for exaggerating your degree pass, I think that you deserve every credit for overcoming your disadvantage. You have tackled something which would have defeated many of us, you have earned your place here.'

'I don't know what to say', Thomas muttered. His mind was a swirl of mixed emotions and he felt slightly queasy.

'Then say nothing lad. William Mullins would be proud to see you in his place. We have a day's inspection to get through, your school needs you, now get out there and lead, as far as I'm concerned, I've never seen any anonymous letters. This will go no further.'

A knock on the door was followed by the head of Billy Shakespeare looking round. 'I was just checking that you hadn't forgotten about our cricket match after school. I've a good feeling about this one, it could be a good day, it may even be our first win.'

Henry Harlond put on his sternest inspectorial face, 'Young man you are disturbing an important meeting and I was just telling your Mr. Tiler how well regarded he is by everyone including me. Schools need more of his kind, but I think that you know that already. I guess from our earlier talk that you were just checking that I wasn't being unkind to him. Us Birmingham City fans are never unkind, unlike the Villa ones' Billy was amazed, he opened his mouth to make an impassioned defence of his team but decided against it and just said, 'Yes Sir' as he closed the door behind him. He would never understand adults, especially Blues supporters.

And it did indeed turn out to be a very good day as Billy predicted. Thomas floated through on a cloud of relief and positive energy. The meeting with the inspectors was a good one, the outlined report made many good points with just a few items to improve on. Merely indicators for further progress. Thomas and his staff were elated. The tension of two intense, critical days was over and they could relax. There was a good feeling of togetherness, they were a team, his team.

Thomas shook hands warmly with Henry Harlond and thanked him for his compassion and understanding. He felt lighter than he had done for years. The question of who sent the anonymous letters could be put on the backburner, but it didn't seem to be important any more. He hadn't realised just how much his secrets had been affecting him and not in a positive way.

'Good luck Thomas, you are a remarkable man to have achieved what you have. I'm certain that you will go far. Good luck. Haven't you got a cricket match to go to?'

Thomas glanced at his watch;

He had almost forgotten in his euphoria.

'Thanks for the reminder, I can just get there unless we've lost quickly of course.'

Thomas drove in his blue Volkswagen Golf trying hard to concentrate on driving, but it was difficult. He realised that much of his rift with his wife Beth had come about because of his tensions. She deserved better. It was time to make amends. However, the thought suddenly struck him that his flirtation with PC Eleanor Kent might well make any reconciliation impossible. They had met off duty as it were and several drinks and an Italian meal, washed down with a shared bottle of house red had led to an evening at her house with almost inevitable consequences. Almost. Thomas could not in all honesty say that he had not enjoyed the thought of exploring El's body, it had been a long time and she was certainly enthusiastic. However, the warning words of his secretary Jill filled his head together with images of the photograph of his wife, Beth, on his desk. It had almost been a dreadful mistake albeit a very pleasant one. It could on the other hand have ruined his marriage. Thomas had mumbled his apologies and left. Eleanor sadly poured herself a glass of wine. She had been so close, so very close.

Arriving at Mapleton Road Juniors Thomas parked and walked over to the field, they were still playing. He greeted Andy Chlebek who asked about the inspection.

'It was fine, well more than fine really but more important how are the team doing?'

'We won the toss and decided to bat. 65 all out, our best score. Andy Mapplebeck, George's older brother top scored with 20, wild swings mainly, Satoshi got 14 before an unlucky

LBW, Billy got 10, Sam 7 and Mikolaj got 5. Rosangel and Grace got 3 each. Typical that they had the same score.'

'Crucial question, Andy how are Mapleton Road doing?'

'Rosie took four wickets with her spinners, the uneven pitch helped, Satoshi took a couple of good catches and Sam managed to engineer a run out. We need one more wicket in the last over, Mapleton need eight runs,'

Thomas looked over as Rosie prepared to bowl her slow balls. This was make or break. Two fours could lose the match. He could not resist shouting his encouragement and the Newhill players looked over and some waved. They were glad to see him there

Tessa Tinton had brought Billy the cocker spaniel as a mascot and to support Satoshi. The dog watched keen to join in the interesting looking ball game.

The first ball was hit for four with a particularly lusty blow. Thomas winced, he shouldn't have distracted them, the next three balls yielded just two runs as Newhill chased and fielded with determination to get their first win and a cup game at that. Two balls to go and just two runs needed. Rosangel took her time and adjusted her grip on the ball. No margin for error.

It was, however, a poor ball and the Mapleton batter saw glory and swung hard with a six or at least four in mind. However, he edged the ball, and it flew high into the sky. All eyes went up and then saw that Grace was directly underneath. It seemed a long time before the ball came down only to slip straight through Graces hands. There was a groan of disappointment.

Billy shouted from behind the wickets, 'Never mind Grace, we win as a team and lose as a team. Keep your head up. Only one ball to go and they still need two runs.' Rosangel felt really sorry for her friend Grace who was nearly in tears. She knew that the dropped catch could have lost the match for them.

Last ball and Rosangel watched the ball spin beautifully towards the wickets, but the batter stepped back and swung firmly and with authority. The ball smashed hard towards the boundary, but it never arrived there. Grace dived to her right and caught the ball cleanly low to the ground. Her hands stung but as she stood the whole team ran over and hugged, Billy shook hands with the opposing captain. He knew that good manners and the correct spirit of cricket were paramount.

Thomas led out a cheer and sought out the Mapleton head to shake hands and thank him for a fine game.

Thomas thought that this day had almost been a perfect one.

Later when they were alone Rosangel asked Grace what had happened with the dropped catch. 'You are usually a good fielder Grace, was the sun in your eyes?'

'No Rosie but I was distracted just before the ball went up. I saw someone at the far end of the field watching the match and I'm not certain, but I think that it may have been my Granny. I was scared, I still am, knowing that she is here in Newhill and watching us play.'

Chapter Thirteen

A Scary Meeting and a Confession

It was one of those glorious June late afternoons which promised to go on forever. Keith Shakespeare took a break from hoeing weeds where he could. His plot was certainly not regimented, there were no neat rows, but it was an abundant productive piece of ground, almost a little bit of his old garden in Trinidad.

He leaned on his hoe and breathed deep with satisfaction, all around was growth and summer crops ready for picking. His basket was filled with kohl rabi, lettuce, Pak choi some early broad beans and a handful of peppery rocket. Faith was always pleased to add his vegetables to her meals. She was a fine cook and a wonderful wife and mother. Keith thought that he had been so lucky to have met her.

Their marriage and later move to England had been full of risk, Birmingham had certainly been colder than Trinidad and the winters were something to be endured but they had worked hard and settled in well. Three fine daughters had been followed by a son and he felt his life complete, the move from the Second City to a small town in Derbyshire had not been without its problems and stress.

The Shakespeare girls had initially resisted the move from the urban sprawl of Birmingham with its concerts, cinemas, restaurants and markets. It was a lively ethnic mix, vibrant and full of opportunities, a green city with many parks and open spaces, belying its past dark industrial reputation. After many family meetings his three daughters had come round to the idea of a move, keeping the family together as they loyally supported their father as he had been successful in his job as a head gardener.

Billy Shakespeare had taken much more persuasion. He was moving away from his beloved Aston Villa and days at

Edgbaston watching England or Warwickshire. He was leaving his friends behind.

Keith had had to promise that they would still enjoy going to see the Villa and go to Edgbaston, he knew that Billy would always make friends easily, it was in his nature. The clincher came when Keith said that they would be closer to some away matches at Nottingham Forest or Derby County. 'Manchester is close, son, United and City. That would be great, wouldn't it?'

And so, they had moved, and Keith felt blessed with his home and family and an allotment which was coming to the peak of harvest time. It was a good to be alive feeling, he looked around and saw several others tending their plots, it was always easy on days like these.

Looking across the small river which formed the southern boundary of Wath Mill Allotments he could see the park where he knew Billy was with his friends. If Billy was there Rosangel would be close and if Rosangel was there inevitably Grace would be too, Sam and Mikolaj usually followed their big sister, Rosie and Satoshi would be there.

Keith chuckled to himself; they were a close-knit pack. 'Good kids,' he thought and was happy that Billy made such good friends since being in Newhill. Trinidad, Poland and Japan represented in one small group, and he had thought that Birmingham was multicultural.

Over in the park Keith saw that the boys had organised an impromptu game of football whilst Rosangel and Grace sat on a park bench enjoying the sunshine. There had been a sense of relief when the secondary places were announced. Rosie and Grace were to go to Moordale comprehensive and to Billy's delight he had a place at the same school. Satoshi would do his last year at Newhill Primary before returning to Tokyo. Sam and Nikolaj, being younger, would move up a year but still remain at Newhill. The Chlebek's had seriously considered a catholic girls school but Rosangel wished to stay with Grace, and it was felt that her point of view was important, Andy and Sherie gave their independent daughter the final say, so Moordale it was.

Whilst the boys kicked Billy's old football about Grace and Rosie were deep in conversation.

'We may not even be in the same class Rosie, but I believe that you are given some choice of friends to be in the same class with.'

'If we nominate each other, we will probably be allocated to the same class,' Rosie pondered.

Grace looked closely at her best friend and quietly asked, 'And what about Billy? He's going to Moordale too, would you choose him or me to be classmates?'

Rosie blushed but said firmly, 'You are my best friend and that will never change, I would always choose you. But what about Jason Bolton, he may be going to Moordale, might even be in the same class.'

It was Grace's turn to blush as she had once confided that she had a secret liking for the arrogant blond boy from Snelston. He was sometimes at his father's allotment and so their paths crossed occasionally but Grace had never actually dared to speak to him.

'He wouldn't notice me even if we were in the same class, anyway he's so full of boasting about how good he is at cricket.'

They were engrossed in their discussion and enjoyed the opportunity to talk without the presence of the boys. They often turned conversations round to cricket or football.

They did not notice a woman approach until a dark shadow blocked out the strong sun. They both looked up startled.

Grace felt herself go cold even in the warmth of the afternoon. Her stomach felt strangely empty, and her heart fluttered as her breath came in short bursts. Grace Bisby was afraid.

Rosangel quickly saw her friends' sudden fear and anxiety and spoke up bravely, 'A stranger approaching two girls in the park might be seen as suspicious, but I won't say any more about it or call over my two brothers and our friends if you move on. My dad is over there on the allotments, I can always call out for him.'

The stranger smiled, 'A brave speech Rosangel Chlebek but your dad Andy isn't actually over there, I know him well.'

Grace sighed deeply, 'It's OK Rosie I think I know who this is. I've seen photos of her, this is my Granny, Eileen Bisby.'

'Hello Grace, my darling girl you have grown since I used to hold you on my knee, you are a beautiful young lady now, I hardly knew you.'

Grace had thought long and hard how she would react after eight years. The hands that held her tenderly as a baby had been the same hands which had held a pillow over her husband's face. Her grandfather in fact. A grandad she would never know. Questions flooded her mind, and she was flustered, where could she begin with this stranger, she had no real memory of, just rumours and harsh facts.

Rosangel recognised the fragility of the meeting, obviously this was indeed the infamous Eileen Bisby, and her friend needed her. 'What do you actually want from Grace?'

Eileen felt her age and ignoring the spirited Polish girl asked if she could sit down and rest her legs. Sitting next to Grace she was almost overcome with the moment which had finally come, the moment she had dreamed of for the last few dreadful years.

'We have such a lot to catch up with Grace, I have missed you more than you could ever know.'

Grace found herself holding Rosangel's hand without fully realising that she had reached out for reassurance.

Questions held in for so long began to blurt out.

'Did you really do what everyone says? Why couldn't you have got doctors to help if things were that bad? Where have you been for the last eight years? You lost a husband; I lost two grandparents.'

Grace's pent up anxiety spilled out and gradually petered out, she looked closely at her Granny trying desperately to find anything she could recognise from their time when she had sat on this woman's knee, cuddling close.

'A lot of questions Grace but they are good sensible questions. May I begin to give you answers to help you understand. I have gone through this moment for so long and now it is finally here I feel somewhat tongue tied.'

Rosangel's organised mind wanted to list the questions and break them down, but instinct said that her role here was to support her friend if only by holding her hand. She glanced at her brothers and friends who continued to play football oblivious to the unfolding drama. There were several people on the allotments site, including Billy's dad. Help was at hand, but her fears were receding as she listened carefully.

Eileen Bisby desperately wanted to hold her precious granddaughter whilst giving the answers the girl obviously craved.

'Yes Grace,' she said quietly, 'I did help your grandfather to die, to stop his pain, each breath was an agony for him. The doctors tried everything, but the cancer was too far gone, and they tried to make his end comfortable with painkillers but even the strong ones were not enough. When I met your Grandad, he was a strong young man, he loved playing rugby in the winter and cricket in the summer. He would come off the rugby pitch battered and bruised but it didn't seem to matter to him. You seem to have inherited his love of cricket, I watched from a distance the other day. Your catch was magnificent, and I cried as I knew that John would have been bursting with pride to see that. I miss him so much. They say that time heals but they are wrong.'

Grace had no more questions but she whispered 'Tell me about him I need to know.'

I was young when I was lucky enough to meet him and I decided straight away that he was the one I was going to marry, it took me some time but finally he asked me to marry him, and I felt truly blessed. Your mother coming along was the icing on the cake, as they say. No one could have been happier.'

'And then...?

'We were happy for many years but then the cancer started, slowly at first but then began to spread. We had endless hospital appointments. The specialists tried everything, scans and radio therapy and chemotherapy and so many blood tests. Finally, we had a meeting with one of the consultants and he said that we should prepare for his ending. They suggested a hospice, but John wanted to stay with me at home. There were strong painkillers each day but his body or rather the cancer fought them off.'

Eileen paused, her mind now back in that sleepless bedroom. The nights were always the worse, she would lay awake trying not to move as each slight movement jolted his pain and he would cry out. He wasn't the man she had married, more a shell full of perpetual agony. In the end he didn't even know his beloved wife. It had broken her heart to see him like that.

Grace began to have a glimpse of understanding and began to share her pain. Rosangel wanted to ask how it had ended but wisely kept her silence, but Grace then asked the question which filled her mind. The two girls often thought the same thoughts.

'Grace hesitated, but finally asked, 'How did...?'

Eileen looked down at her hands which were clasped together as if to support her deep emotions. This was the question she had tried to answer so many times, not least to her daughter Amanda and now her granddaughter was asking the same. She had given this answer so many times to strangers, the police, and the courts, it had seemed a question which would haunt her days for ever.

'How did I put your grandad out of his agony,,,? It wasn't a quick decision, believe me. It went on for so long. I couldn't bear it, watching him slowly die in such pain. He was the man I loved and the only way I could help him was to end his life. One night it was particularly terrible and whilst he sort of slept in his agony filled mind, I gently put a pillow over his mouth and allowed him to pass peacefully away.'

All three sat on the bench and there were tears for all three. Eileen took out a handkerchief and dabbed at her eyes before going on. The girls were too young to have to endure the truth of the actual struggle to keep the cushion in place whilst her husband fought his last weak fight for survival.

'I was in prison for a short time but then had to spend time in hospitals and rehabilitation centres with people who didn't really understand. They had to ensure that I wasn't likely to do anything like that again. Finally, I was able to go free, but I felt that I couldn't go back to Newhill, the burden on your mother was too much and so I went to Sheffield to try to start a new life but each day I felt drawn back to you and your mother. They were unhappy lonely days, but I didn't have the courage to face my family. A fresh start wasn't what I needed. It was you and your mother, but I knew that I would be judged by some in Newhill.'

Eileen stood and put away her handkerchief. 'I know that I can never ask you to forgive me, but I hoped that you would understand a little of what we went through. If you wish, I will leave you in peace again.' Her voice trailed off as she hoped for an answer that would allow her to stay.

Grace stood and hugged her granny tight; no words were needed. Both were relieved having met and talked after all those years, the wasted years. Rosangel felt compelled by instinct to join in the hug, sharing the warmth of love.

Mikolaj came over and broke the moment.

'When are we going home Rosie? 'I'm hungry.'

Chapter Fourteen
This Stuff Makes Your Fingers Go Black

'I think that I passed an ice cream van at the entrance to the park, I think we could all do with something cold on this hot afternoon.' Eileen suggested, thinking how long it had been since she had had an ice cream or even desired one. A well filled cornet with a chocolate flake was a joyous thing, a celebration of summer and all its delights. Eileen felt lighter than she had for several years, she had a reconciliation with her precious girl, a girl who had grown and was sadly no longer the chubby cuddly gigging toddler she remembered. Instead, she had almost time jumped to a tall, good looking and perceptive girl. The in between years were gone and could not be retrieved.

The boys left their game of football and went over to see who the adult was, curious but not concerned. The game had taken precedence.

Introductions were made and Eileen was impressed with the good manners of Satoshi and the delightful way he bowed. Sam returned her greeting with a smile but of course no words. Billy began to ask questions but a slight frown and shake of the head from Rosangel silenced him. He felt like a sheepdog in the trials under the almost silent control of the shepherd. One girl and her dog, but he didn't complain.

Eileen took out her purse and chose three ten pound notes, 'Now who is the most sensible of you boys or at least the eldest.' Little Billy was certainly the eldest but not the tallest, Satoshi was probably the most sensible, but it was agreed that Sam should be the recipient of the money. Rosangel knew that Sam could be trusted to take care of it but could not bring himself to ask for ice cream. He would leave that to Billy, the spokesperson of the group.

Eileen smiled at the debate and handed the money to Sam, the quiet one, 'How many of us are there?'

Mikolaj began to count but Satoshi said simply, 'Seven'

'And how many can four boys carry if you have one in each hand?

This time Billy was quicker with the answer 'Three with two and one with one.'

A debate threatened to begin as to who should be the one carrying only one ice cream, but Rosangel intervened. 'Why don't you do the ordering Billy and Sam can be the treasurer, Mikolaj can carry one then he can concentrate on stopping it melting.'

Eileen thought that this girl would be a fine politician with her easy way of offering compromise. 'We will need seven ice-cream cornets then but make sure they are big ones with two flakes.' This good news ensured that the boys would scamper away looking forward to a cooling ice cream.

Eileen realised what she had been missing, seeing Grace with her friends and good friends too. She was happy to have a few moments extra with Grace and her special friend, Rosangel. She decided that Andy and Sherrie Chlebek must be so proud of their children and was even more pleased when Rosie informed her that she had another brother Jacob, but he was too young to be part of the gang. He was still under his mother's care, as the two boys were obviously under Rosangel's care.

Grace had been quiet for a few moments as Eileen sat in the sunshine with a girl on either side. She put an arm round both, and it felt right, almost as if she had gained another granddaughter.

'Granny,' Grace began, not sure how to put her feelings into words. 'Granny I'm really pleased to have met you again, it's something I have been dreading, I was confused and frightened, I wasn't sure how I would feel when I actually met you but now that you have been honest with me, I think I understand a tiny part of what you have gone through. 'I don't think that many people would have your bravery, I was scared that I was going to grow up like you,' she hesitated trying to find the right words, 'I thought that my DNA would lead me to a life of crime and even, prison but now I am really proud to be yours and part of you.'

Eileen was shocked at mention of Grace's deep fears, but Rosangel wasn't, they had discussed this previously. Grace's follow up words filled Eileen with more love than she ever thought she could have again.

'But now I can see that I was wrong, very wrong and I am extremely happy to be your granddaughter, we will have a good future together. Especially with ice cream,' she smiled. 'But I have a confession of my own to make and I'll do it quickly before the boys return.'

Eileen and Rosangel looked curiously at Grace who continued, 'I wasn't sure about whether I had bad blood in me, I don't know how to describe it, but it was a real fear, and I was confused. I see now that it was idiotic to think like that, but I did something really stupid. It wasn't planned or anything, it just happened.'

Rosangel glanced around to see if the boys were approaching with rapidly melting ice-creams. They were not, so she was able to concentrate whilst her mind rapidly tried to work out what Grace could possibly have done.

Grace shuffled her feet but continued in a strong voice. 'I was the one who stole the Mullins cricket cup,'

This bland statement was greeted with astonishment.'

Eileen broke the silence, 'Was that the William Mullins who had an allotment, the old headteacher?' As soon as she asked, she realised what an irrelevant question it was. Rosangel could only think of two questions, 'Why would you do that Grace, how did you do it?

'The how is easy, it was after school, I had gone back to pick up my lunch box and there was no one around. I saw the cup and quickly put it in my bag but then I panicked and went to see Mr. Tiler, but he wasn't there, and the secretary had gone home. I'm not sure why I did it, but I think that I wanted to see if I was really a bad person.'

'But what about the broken window, surely that wasn't you as wall?'

'My criminal mind said to cover my tracks, I tried to make it look like a break in so no one would suspect me, I really regret it now, but I didn't know what to do. The window was hard to break but there was a rounders bat in the office, and I hit the glass hard. It's tougher than it looks. I ran home and hid the cup in my room.' I'm not sure that I'm cut out to be a criminal.'

Eileen realised the gravity of her granddaughter's confusion and dilemma. Putting her arm around her shoulder she said, 'Well I know what to do, you have been most courageous to tell us about this, but you must return the cup and tell your headteacher what you have done and why, I'm sure that he will understand, the cup is safe and will be returned. There is only the matter of paying for the glass and I can help with that, you are not a thief or a criminal of any sort.'

'Thank you, I really do appreciate that but it's for me to make amends. Is glass expensive?'

Rosangel had just about recovered her astonishment. Grace liking Jason Bolton and now this. She began to wonder if she really did know Grace. What other shocks might there be? The sound of the boys returning made her think quickly. 'We'll tell the boys that you found the cup, you'll be a hero or is it heroine.?'

'No Rosie no more lies I'll tell them the truth and hope they forgive me. At least we have a cup to play for now.'

The next school morning Thomas went into school early as usual and was surprised to see two year six girls waiting for him, asking to see him.

Putting down his bag and ushering them into his office, he sat and listened to Grace's story which she told with clarity and considerable regret. The cup was produced from a bag which Grace had brought in. Rosangel and Grace sat and waited for Mr. Tiler to say something.

Thomas felt his heart go out to this confused girl. waiting anxiously for his verdict. He saw the agony of worry which she had carried and knew that meeting her granny had been a pivotal moment in her young life.

'What you did was very wrong Grace, but I think that you know that and have shown real remorse. I'm sure that having Rosangel as a supporting friend has helped.' At this the two girls smiled at each other. Thomas continued, 'However I cannot let this go unpunished. You should have come to me, or your mum and not taken such drastic action. The cup does seem unharmed, unlike my window,'

'I'll pay for that Mr. Tiler from my own money, not anyone else's,' Grace said.

'I did think that dropping you from the cricket team would be a suitable punishment but that would hurt the rest of the team and I don't think they deserve that, do you?'

The two girls were shocked at the idea of Grace not being allowed to play in the cup semi-final against Oak Tree Lane.

'Perhaps something even more appropriate would involve just you Grace and it would allow you to play in the match.'

'Thank you, Mr. Tiler,' Grace said with some relief.

'Don't thank me before you hear what I have to say. The cup seems to be unharmed but could do with some polishing.'

Grace could not resist asking if that was all.

'No Grace, I will arrange for you to polish all the Newhill Horticultural Society cups. They are probably very grubby, and Mr. Shaw would no doubt appreciate some help. I'll tell him you are a volunteer. He won't know that it is a punishment, that is between us, are we agreed?'

'Then I volunteer too,' Rosangel added, 'there must be over twenty cups for all the different categories.'

And so it was that the two girls plus Little Billy, Sam, Satoshi and Mikolaj sat in the village hall surrounded by cups and shields in varying degrees of dust and grime. Tins of silver polish had been given to them and after a while the cups began to shine like new. All agreed that Grace deserved help and what were friends for if not to support. Actions not words.

Mikolaj complained that the polish wadding made his fingers black.

'Well, mine are sort of black all the time so welcome to my world Mikolaj.' Billy said with a grin.

Satoshi was slightly confused by the words polish and Polish but decided not to ask and like the others he continued to rub hard at the trophies and cups.

That same morning Eileen Bisby walked slowly over the bridge by the ruins of the ancient mill and opened the familiar gate into Wath Mill allotments. It was a warm friendly sun which did away with the need for a coat. There was no one working at their plots yet and Eileen was glad, it gave her chance to reminisce and think about her future. She had had long deep conversations with her daughter Amanda. Years ago, she had moved in to live with her to support her after her errant husband had left leaving Amanda with debt and a three year old to care for. Back then Eileen had felt she was a useful support and a live in babysitter for the delightful toddler.

However, the shadows had followed her to darken her happiness as she feared police sirens which would shatter her life. Eileen's husband John's death had broken so much but today there were no shadows, no fear of police sirens and life felt good. Amanda had asked her to return to live with them but the wonderful recent reconciliation with Grace had also provided unexpected worrying twists. Eileen walked along the broad path towards her old plot by habit rather than design. She was deep in thought, The fact that Eileen's crime had had such an impact on Grace had never really occurred to her. Hopefully the return of the Mullins cup and a meeting with the headteacher would lay the ghosts of the past.

Along the path she remembered with clarity the finding of a dead swan and her meeting with Tessa Tinton, Terrible Tessa as they would call her, but not to her face. Eileen had been contriving a way to be elected chair of the committee and she remembered with a smile her pointless ambition. Her anxiety to be in charge, even if only at an allotment site, seemed pathetic looking back and she remembered the empty feeling when William Mullins had unexpectedly nominated Charlotte Poole as chair. William was gone with cups named after him and Eileen sighed missing the old man.

Arriving at plot seven, her old plot, she felt that she belonged there but strangely detached and it was obvious that someone had taken it over, it was eight years ago after all. Stupid to think that time had stood still and plot seven had waited loyally for her.

Eileen looked at the tidy plot with its lush summer vegetables and flowers. She felt glad that it had been taken over by someone who cared. To her left was the jungle of productivity that was Keith Shakespeare's. No two plots the same she had told newcomers and aspiring allotmenteers when she, as membership secretary, had shown them around.

The past, she increasingly felt, could be packed away. She had no regrets apart from being so long away from Amanda and Grace. The previous night she had gone over her meeting with her granddaughter and her friends. Every word, every tear and every smile were rerun in her mind, and it was a treasured time which she would never forget. It was the best ice cream she had ever tasted, and Grace's friends seemed to be real friends, especially Andy and Sherrie's girl Rosangel. Eileen had been truly happy for the first time in years. The forgiveness she felt from Grace was all she could have hoped for, the almost magical hug hopefully the first of many.

No, the past was just that, she decided and could not be changed any more than that dead swan could be resurrected all those years ago. Her future looked good, very good and today she had arranged to go to Newhill school to meet Grace after school ended to see how her meeting with the head had gone.

'Good morning, Eileen, it's been a long time. It's good to see you.'

Eileen jumped, startled, she had not heard or seen Tessa Tinton walking towards her. They had once been neighbours on the site and once before she had been startled by her sudden appearance. Then Tessa had been a bitter person driven by her son moving to Japan and marrying a Japanese girl to a life of online gambling and sharp-tongued confrontation.

Eileen was surprised when Tessa held out her arms and hugged her warmly. This was a new relaxed Tessa, and she returned the hug with equal warmth not having been sure how she would be received at Wath Mill allotments. The two women looked at each other smiling and Eileen asked if Tessa remembered the day, they had come across the dead stone cold swan. Tessa laughed.

'A lot of water has passed under the bridge since then, I was pleased to hear that you were back in Newhill. My grandson told me about you and your generosity with ice cream. The way to a boy's heart is through the stomach as they say.'

'I assume that Satoshi is your grandson then, a wonderful boy you must be so proud of him.'

Tessa beamed with pride as she always did when Satoshi was mentioned. 'You must come and meet his mother, Kyoko; I'm meeting her at the garden centre in an hour for coffee. I had come up to pick some lettuce for tea, but we can go over there together, and we can catch up, if you are not too busy that is.'

Eileen felt grateful to have been accepted so readily.

'No Tessa, I'm not busy at all and I would love to meet your daughter in law. We can catch up on all the changes there have been. I see that my old plot has been taken up,' she said almost wistfully.

'Yes, a nice couple from over in the estate, Jan and Don, but mainly Jan. He's a plumber I believe, and she works at the estate agents in the square. They've worked hard on the plot. By the way did you know that I'm the membership secretary now? I quite enjoy it, showing new people round.'

Eileen felt a slight twinge of jealousy, it had been her old role.

Tessa looked closely at Eileen, 'I don't suppose that you would be interested in having a plot again, would you? There are lots of new people, there always is a good turnover as you well know.'

Eileen had felt drawn back to Wath Mill and the friendly companionship but this time there would be no manipulating her way to be chair, no anxiety. Just a simple plot of her own.

'I would love that, 'she replied but I wasn't sure if people would want me back, after all that has happened.'

Tessa said firmly, 'No one, apart from possibly one will object, indeed you would be actively welcomed and if they don't, they will have me to deal with. The past is the past, just history.'

There was a hint of the old Tessa who could pick a fight alone in a lift with the mirror, but this was a more mellow warmer Tessa.

Tessa went on, 'Of course it wouldn't be your old plot, that would be unfair on Jan and Don to ask them to change plots. You could have plot four, Tolly Braithwaite's old plot. There have been several tenants there, but none have stayed the course. As you know Tolly kept his plot in an immaculate condition and the soil is beautiful. He put so much horse manure and compost on it it's like chocolate cake, speaking of which we should go to meet Kyoko, coffee cake and a good chat. Now how about taking on plot four, it would be lovely to have you back.'

'I would really like that Tessa and thank you.'

Tessa picked up her several Webbs Wonderful lettuces and put them in a bag.

'Oh, by the way I don't suppose you've seen a brown cocker spaniel on your travels have you. It's not like him to stray and I'm beginning to get a little worried. Billy is usually a home loving dog'

Eileen looked puzzled, 'Billy...?

Tessa laughed, I'll explain over coffee, and we can keep our eyes peeled for him on the way. He'll probably find his own way home. I'm not too worried.'

But she was and as it turned out with good reason.

Chapter Fifteen

I Do Like Your Apple Pie

Excitement was high at Newhill Primary School, the cricket team were preparing for the cup semi-final against Oak Tree Lane. The team had only won one game this season and that had been in the first round of the cup. As there were only eight local schools in the cup the first round had in effect been a quarter final. Having won the newly returned and indeed very well polished Mullins cup last year, expectations were high.

After practice Thomas Tiler sat in his office, as usual doodling on a pad of paper whilst he thought. Last year's cup win was before he had been appointed as headteacher at the school. The winning players had moved on to secondary school and this year's team were a mix of underage or inexperienced players, very small players i.e., Billy Shakespeare, a Japanese boy and two girls. To be fair Billy was a very good wicket keeper, the only one who had played before and both girls were capable, especially Rosangel who was becoming a good spinner of the ball, courtesy of google videos. Satoshi had great hand eye coordination and was a more than competent batter but little experience of cricket. His baseball skills were very useful, but enthusiasm could only take you so far.

Prospects were not good, and an unlikely win would only mean a very probable clash in the final against the mighty Snelston team, coached and driven on by Kevin Bolton and led by his son Jason, probably a serious prospect for county cricket in the future.

To make matters worse he would have to umpire as Keith Shakespeare was unable to take this on as he usually did. Thomas disliked the role of umpire/scorer/ coach. To say he was very mediocre at the task would be extremely kind to him, in fact he considered himself very poor and so was happy for Keith to be the umpire. As Keith regularly took charge of men's matches in the local league, he was able to fulfil the role very well. Thomas could score and coach his team from the side, a role he was much more comfortable with. But not today Thomas would have to take all three roles and, in a semi-final, to make it worse.

After practice, the gang of friends, cricketers and would be detectives agreed to meet at Rosangel's house the next day to discuss the mystery of the shed fires at the allotments and the theft of tools and watering cans. There was also the worrying issue of the apparent disappearance of Billy the cocker spaniel.

As Sherrie Chlebek was preparing the evening meal Rosangel came into the kitchen and asked if Billy, Grace and Satoshi could come round to discuss cricket. Although she had little understanding of cricket, Sherrie was always pleased to welcome her daughter's friends. Grace was a regular visitor, and they would sit in Rosangel's bedroom listening to music, at the same time shouting at Mikolaj to leave them in peace. Sherrie was aware of Billy's infatuation with Rosie and thought the bedroom may be slightly inappropriate. Satoshi, she adored with his impeccable manners and habit of bowing respectfully to her.

'Well, it's Friday tomorrow so there will be no homework so perhaps you could invite your friends to tea, your father and I will eat later, and you can have the dining room table to yourselves. I assume Sam and Mikolaj are counted as friends,' she asked with a smile.

Rosangel who had inherited her mother's beauty and sparkling eyes, grinned, 'Keep your friends close but your enemies closer.'

Sherrie was a little shocked at this quote. 'Are your brothers your enemies Rosie?'

The girl pinched a piece of carrot which her mum was chopping for a casserole and walked away turning with a grin to reply, 'Only when they are awake mum, the rest of the time they are my beloved brothers. But tomorrow we are team mates.'

Sherrie smiled and thought how lucky the boys were to have Rosangel as their protective older sister, particularly Sam who would worryingly be without Rosie next September.

Turning back to her preparation of beef and vegetables Sherrie wondered if Satoshi and Little Billy would need particular foods. No, she decided, beef burgers, chips and beans were international and didn't involve any raw fish or callaloo. An interesting mix. Feeding the friends early would also allow her and Andy to have a meal alone together later. Recently they had seen less and less of each other as Andy's work had taken up much of his time and her role as mother of four was time consuming.

Yes, baby Jacob could be fed and put down early and Andy would no doubt insist on driving the visitors home safely whilst she prepared a special meal, one of Andy's favourites.

Pierogi, cheese or blueberry filled dumplings and Golabki, boiled cabbage rolls wrapped around minced pork and rice and as a dessert szarlotke, apple pie and cream. Although Sherrie and Andy had been born and brought up in England, they had long enjoyed traditional Polish comfort food, simple and very tasty.

Sherrie began to plan their special meal, with a bottle of white wine to follow. Yes, she decided she and Andy deserved a little quality time together. They had become too remote from each other, and Sherrie realised that she was becoming distracted by the children's handsome young headteacher, Thomas Tiler. He was separated from his wife, and she had to firmly remind herself that she was a respectable mother of four. The meal was planned in her mind, and she decided upon her most enticing lingerie and a simple low cut black dress,

No doubt the perceptive Rosangel would question the dress as not practical and the special meal, but she was an intelligent understanding girl, a girl to treasure, a girl rapidly growing up.

Andy came into the kitchen and putting down his brief case kissed his wife's cheek.

'What's for tea?'

Sherrie smiled as much to herself as Andy, 'Tonight is beef stew but tomorrow night we will have visitors so we will have pierogi, golabki and szarlotke to follow.

'Visitors and my favourite Polish meal, it's not your family, is it? 'Andy asked suspiciously.

'No, it's just us and half a cricket team.'

'That sounds interesting, will I enjoy the company?'

'Don't worry, I'll make sure that you enjoy it especially the dessert.' she added mysteriously.

'I do like your apple pie; I'll look forward to that.'

Sherrie thought, Men! Perhaps I should get Rosie to explain matters of the heart to him. Andy was as honest as the day was long, kind, hardworking and a loving father but at times he could be so naïve and didn't at once pick up romantic messages,

So it was that on the following night when the burgers, chips and beans had been eaten and ice cream consumed, a meeting was convened of the would-be cricketing detectives. Satoshi and Billy gallantly offered to help Sherrie with the washing up, but she thanked them and told them it was fine, she could manage. With relief the two boys returned to the meeting. Grace had brought a pad to write down any ideas or suggestions.

'Well, let's get this meeting started, Mikolaj, go and wipe the ice cream from round your mouth,' Rosangel said, taking charge as usual. Billy and Satoshi discreetly wiped their own mouths hoping that no one noticed.

'First on our agenda are the shed fires at Wath Mill. Any ideas?'

'Well at least we solved the mystery of the missing Mullins cup and the broken window.' said Mikolaj returning noisily to his chair.

Rosangel sighed and Grace blushed, looking down at her pad.

'I don't think we can actually claim credit for solving that one, I think we can put that to one side,' Rosie said glaring at her younger brother. He knew from experience that a blank silence was probably the best defence.

Satoshi explained, 'We are on item one, shed fires.'

Billy gazed at Rosie and thought that the soft dining room lights showed Rosangel in her best light, she was certainly worthy of his blossoming first love apart from his parents and possibly his sisters.

'I thought that we had decided that we had no evidence to work on,' Grace said, glad to have moved on from stolen cups.

Satoshi thought that Hercule Poirot had made detective work look so easy on television with so many clues to work on. 'Grace, can you write down what evidence we have so far?'

'Good idea Satoshi,' Rosangel said with her usual smile.

Little Billy wished that he himself had made that suggestion. He decided to take charge and look impressive. 'There are definitely no finger prints but the police say it was probably paraffin and we know the two sheds were set alight on the same evening or night. We should look at the owners of the two sheds, there are several sheds untouched between the two set on fire. Why were those chosen? What have they got in common? I think we should rule out random teenage vandalism.'

Rosangel looked at Billy, knowing his emergent feelings for her, 'That's good, now we are getting somewhere.'

Grace wrote down notes but looked up and said, 'Both sheds are owned by people from abroad, Billy's dad is from Trinidad and Leona is from Portugal, Porto, I think.'

Mikolaj reflected, 'But Spiros the chef is from Greece, he has a shed and they must have passed that one to get to the other shed.'

Satoshi said, 'Well done Mikolaj, that's an excellent point.'

Billy tried hard to look good in Rosies eyes.' Ben and Jenny are from Cardiff, but I don't think that counts.' As he said it, he felt a little silly although he was technically right, Wales was another country.

'Good process of elimination Billy.' Rosangel added, 'you have quite a talent for detective work. You should join the police when you are old enough,' She avoided the dreaded adults' phrase, 'when you grow up.'

Billy was pleased with Rosies response but the felt deflated by reference to the police.

'At my height, I don't think so.'

Rosangel sympathised, 'You will grow Billy, we all have growth spurts.'

Billy basked in the warmth of Rosie's words and looked forward to being called Long Billy Shakespeare or Big Billy.

Mikolaj looked at his friend, his older friend and said, 'That's unlikely we are the same height now and you are older.' This was said without malice but nevertheless it caused the two boys to get out of their chairs and stand back-to-back, both on tiptoes.'

'We are getting off the point,' Satoshi said. 'Anyway, I'm taller than both of you.'

Rosangel felt the meeting slipping away from her. 'Grace what do we have so far.?'

Grace looked up from her notetaking, 'We know the fires were deliberate, some foreigners were the victims, Sorry Billy, but I was the one accused, falsely this time.'

Billy murmured, 'But I'm from Birmingham,' using his thickest Brummie accent.

The meeting grew silent, they had forgotten that the ones who had alerted the fire brigade, the Boltons, had been the ones who had suggested that Grace was guilty by association with her granny.

Satoshi spoke up, 'Grace can you put down the Boltons as our only suspects if it wasn't teenagers. But what about a motive?'

Sam leaned to his sister and whispered. Rosangel was aware of time moving on and that her mum seemed keen on an early night for everyone, 'Good point, Sam. Why don't you tell everyone?'

Everyone looked hopefully at the usually silent boy, but Sam looked down and didn't meet their eyes.

Rosie, as usual rescued him, 'Sam asked what about Billy the cocker spaniel, Billy has been missing for some days now.'

Satoshi looked at the clock on the wall, 'Let's all think of a motive for the Boltons to set fire to two sheds, it's our only lead at the moment. I think we can safely rule Grace out.'

'Good idea Satoshi let's all bring ideas to the next meeting; Billy should take priority he's our mascot and usually comes to our cricket matches. We can all keep a look out for him in the meantime, we need him for the semi-final.'

Three days later the big match was played during the afternoon and the lucky mascot was still missing. The match itself did not live up to the hype of high expectations. Oak Tree Lane batted first and batted poorly, aided by good fielding, three catches by Billy behind the stumps and some spin bowling by Rosie which baffled the opposition batters. A score of twenty-three seemed easy to pass but four Newhill wickets went down cheaply, including Grace and Billy. Hopes of a final faded but Satoshi took matters into his own hands and his well-timed drives towards the boundary swung the match and it was right that he and Sam were at the wicket when Satoshi hit a firm shot to mid-off for two to win the match.

Thomas Tiler had been flustered trying to umpire and score and look neutral as his team rose to the challenge, however towards the end of the game he was totally distracted when he saw one of the Oak Tree Lane teachers walking to the boundary's edge. It was Beth, his wife. Thomas felt a surge of emotion. The opposing coach and umpire was Declan, the same Declan who Beth was supposedly having an affair with. Thomas observed the traditions of the game and went to shake hands and offer condolences. Win with humility, lose with good grace.

Declan was outgoing and friendly and congratulated Thomas on his team.

'Almost an international team there, the little Japanese boy was the difference today and your wicket keeper, three good catches. The girl spinner is quite a find. Where does she get her coaching from?

'Google, actually.' Thomas smiled, finding himself liking Declan and could quite understand Beth's attraction to him. In other circumstances he could happily enjoy a pint with him. As they spoke Beth hovered, obviously waiting for one of them. Thomas organised the lifts for his jubilant team but could not share their joy.

Beth said, 'Well done Thomas you must be pleased with your team.' She turned and asked Declan if she was still alright for a lift home. He agreed casually and they turned to walk back to the school together.

Thomas felt bleak and empty. He had wondered how he would feel seeing Beth with another man. Now he knew and it didn't feel good at all. How would she have felt seeing him with Eleanor Kent? Guilt was suddenly added to his swirl of emotions.

Beth turned, 'Oh, by the way Thomas I came across a couple of your things at home, could you come round sometime to collect them, they are only gathering dust.'

Thomas found anger and self-pity and despair a strange mix which tangled his tongue. 'How about tonight around seven, if you are free that is?'

After a celebratory tea of cheese on toast with a marmite topping Thomas drank a mug of strong coffee. He tried to interpret everything that had been said after the cricket match, but the overriding image was of Beth climbing into a car, with Declan. He sighed and wondered if Declan would be there in his house sitting on his furniture. The turmoil in his mind worsened the more he feared the worst. He had foolishly lost his wife, the girl he truly loved. Eleanor had been a distraction, a willing and delightful distraction but it had been a one off although it was obvious that Eleanor wanted a more serious relationship.

Thomas showered and chose his clothes carefully without knowing why. A spray of deodorant and a touch of aftershave or rather before shave completed the picture. Cord jeans and a blue checked shirt with a light-yellow jumper was chosen. Was this the correct outfit to be humiliated by Declan's presence? The last rites of a dying marriage.

As he approached his old semi-detached house he wondered if he should ring the bell or just walk in. He decided the bell was more proper. It was answered almost at once.

'Hello Beth, it was nice to see you again today, how are you?

Beth Tiler stood to one side to allow Thomas to enter, he glanced round and could see no sign of Declan. Should he ask? Would that sound desperate?

'What is it you want me to collect?' he said noting a small box in the corner. The last vestiges of their once happy marriage. His heart sank but at least they were alone, he sat down as Beth left, returning with a light blue cardigan.

'It's a lovely evening Thomas and I've had a long day. I could do with a walk and a chat if you have the time.?'

Thomas agreed, a little surprised, and they headed towards the park and as they walked, they talked of the reasons for their separation. Thomas agreed that he had become immersed too much in his work and his school. He had almost forgotten the reason he had married Beth. He told her of his increasing fears about his secrets and the anonymous letters. His words flowed easily, again at ease with his beloved yet estranged wife. They walked slowly savouring their time together, enjoying the soft summer air.

'Would you tell me your secrets even though we are apart now?' Beth asked, somewhat shyly. It was like a first date. Perhaps in some ways it was.

Somehow it felt easy and he spoke of his dyslexia and his upgrading of his qualifications in order to get a teaching job. He hoped that she would not condemn him too much, but the level of his guilt had been lifted.

They had come to the old mill and bridge leading into the allotments.

'Would you like to see our school plot Beth?'

'Yes, Thomas I would like that but first I have to say that any falsification of your applications is now irrelevant. I could see from your manner with your cricket team that you have made a great career for yourself. As for the dyslexia, well don't forget that I am a special need teacher. I suspected that you had a problem and had developed ways to manage it.'

As they crossed the bridge Beth confessed that she had missed him terribly and felt very alone in their house without him.

'But what about Declan, I thought... well feared really when I saw him, I could see why you and he...,' his voice trailed miserably away not sure of his words.

Beth laughed,' Declan gives me a lift sometimes and he is a very attractive man and a good friend, but he lives with his boyfriend in a lovely house in Newhill. I have no interest in him and he certainly has no interest in me. You are the only one I ever wanted, and I asked to meet you, to see if we could try again.'

'I would like that very much, I promise that there will be no more dark secrets, no shadows no overwork loads. This time will be different, a fresh start.' They turned into the allotments and saw two youngsters walking towards them holding hands.

Rosangel and Billy at once let go of each other's hands and looked guilty.

'Hello Rosie, Billy....this is my wife Beth, and we were just going to have a look at the school allotment plot. She teaches at Oak Tree Lane and saw some of the game. You were pretty good today; we are in the final! A great day.'

Rosangel had turned pink, and Billy was lost for words, well almost.

'It was a great match Mr. Tiler, but we can't really stop to chat, we are looking for a missing dog, a cocker spaniel, same name as me as a matter of fact.'

Rosangel recovered her poise after being startled at being caught holding hands with Billy and by their headteacher at that. 'Come on Billy we must find that spaniel, he's our lucky mascot, we'll need him for the final if it's against Snelston. Nice to meet you, Mrs. Tiler.' The two youngsters crossed the bridge and walked away, holding hands again after a suitable and decent time.

Beth and Thomas watched them go smiling at the innocence of first love.

'Were we ever like that. Can we ever be again?' Beth asked, turning to face Thomas.

'No more secrets Beth I've had enough of them. I would love to try again with you, more than anything in the world but I have to confess to a slight, almost one night fling with a police officer, a woman I should add.' His bridges were burned, there was no going back, and he confessed all.

Beth gathered her thoughts, pleased that Thomas had not fulfilled his night of passion but saddened at the thought of him with another woman.

'Well, we were separated, and I shouldn't be surprised. You are pretty desirable after all. That's why I married you in the first place. It's beginning to feel a little chilly. Perhaps we could go home, we have so much to catch up on. There's a bottle of red wine at home with our name on it.'

They followed Rosie and Billy back across the bridge, allotments forgotten.

Thomas took Beth by the hand and thought that his life was suddenly good, very good.

Chapter Sixteen

The Cosiness of Tea and Toast

Steve Shaw, treasurer of Wath Mill Allotments, computer expert, twice failed husband and ex-alcoholic left his heavily pregnant third wife, Leona, asleep in their bed. Leona and her daughter from her first marriage, Belinha had moved into his house after their quiet register office wedding. The eight-year-old Belle was already up and preparing her packed lunch for school.

Steve dressed quietly, despite two marriages to startlingly beautiful wives he had no children of his own. The soon to be born baby would be his first but he regarded Belle as she liked to be called as his own. Formal adoption procedures were underway and couldn't come too soon for Steve. He had finally found love after many attempts, and he had been surprised to find that the instant addition of a daughter was a true pleasure and he doted upon her.

The pretty Portuguese girl looked up from making her cheese sandwiches with raw onion, her favourite with a smear of piccalilli. She had already dressed and prepared for school. A transfer to Newhill Primary from Snelston had been a risk but Steve had seen enough of Thomas Tiler, Charlie Poole and the soon to be retired Laura Watson to realise that the school was friendly. A good Ofsted inspection report had certainly helped their decision. Steve did not consider himself an expert in education, but he trusted his instincts in this case, Belle's education and happiness were important to him.

'Would you like me to make you a mug of tea Steve?' They had decided on her using his forename as Dad seemed inappropriate, at least for now.

Steve looked at his independent and capable daughter and as in so many instances his heart sang with a quiet joy. He had certainly missed her early years and he would have loved to have known her as a baby and toddler. That would however come with the new addition. A child of his own but Belle had already claimed a firm place in his heart. She would certainly not be replaced by the new baby.

'Thanks Belle but I'll make one for me and your mother in a few minutes. She is sleeping now but didn't have a good night, she reckons that he will be a footballer with his kicks.'

'Or maybe she will be a footballer, and play for Porto or Derby County, welcome to the 21st century Steve. Girls do play football you know,' Belle exclaimed raising her eyebrows.

'It's too early for arguments, Belle.'

'I'm not arguing I'm just explaining why I'm right'

Steve grinned, 'And I am wrong I suppose.'

'In this case yes but I will forgive you' Belle said putting her lunchbox into her school bag.

'Most generous of you, have you got everything ready for school?'

'Yes, I just need a piece of fruit and to get my bag ready.'

'Good, well done. How is school, are you still enjoying life at Newhill?'

'It's friendly and I am enjoying being there. We have a boy called Mikolaj in my class. He's Polish but has never been there. Satoshi is clever and a star cricketer, but he will be returning to Japan at the end of next year. I will miss him, but he has invited me to visit.'

Steve smiled, the transfer from Snelston school to Newhill had thankfully proved successful.

He popped two pieces of bread in the toaster and fetched the butter from the fridge. 'Have you had breakfast Belle, or should I get you something?'

'I've had bran flakes and orange juice, but I'll share some of your toast if you like.'

The two of them sat on the sofa and Steve's mind went back to the bad old days of drunkenness, fuelled by frustration and lazy unhappiness. All that was behind him now and he felt blessed to have met Leona on the allotment site. Her calm caring and very capable manner had won him over and brought him back from the dark side.

Leona's daughter was very much in her image and Steve enjoyed moments talking with her. In his earlier life children were not really considered. Seen but not heard was his opinion but the delightful Belle had changed his mind.

Steve buttered the two pieces of toast and enquired as to the topping.

'Marmite please,' Belle replied, smiling as Steve pulled an exaggerated face of disgust to show his dislike.

Steve spread the thick yeast extract and decided to have his toast with no spread rather than use the contaminated black knife. Belle grinned and thought how lucky she was to have Steve as an almost father. He was a good man, and she could train him to like marmite later.

They ate in companionable silence, apart from the crunching of their toast.

Steve asked the time-honoured question. 'Which would you prefer, a boy or girl?'

'Momma tells me that she thinks it's a boy but then she has had a scan. I asked but she said that she wanted it to be a surprise, so she doesn't know.'

'And your preference?'

Belle thought for a moment, 'Whichever it is the most important thing is its health...and Mommas of course. I'll be the older sister either way, but a little brother may be nice. What about you, or do you know already?'

'No, I promise you that I don't know, another girl as delightful as you would be ideal, but a boy would be acceptable. Have you thought of names?'

Belle answered quickly. 'Adele for a girl and Brendan for a boy.'

Steve laughed and wondered if she was serious. No wonder his mother adored her first granddaughter by marriage. Any doubts about his mother's reaction to a third marriage and a Portuguese care worker with a child at that were quickly dispelled. Steve knew that his mother had taken to Leona at once and was busy knitting ready for the arrival of her second grandchild. Neutral colours, grey, yellow or green.

Steve felt a sense of real well-being and began to prepare a cup of tea in bed for his wife. Life had improved dramatically for him, he had so much to look forward to. But today he was preparing all the arrangements for the Newhill Horticultural

Society summer show. Well organised schedules had been distributed and Steve had ensured that all those with a plot at the allotments had received a copy. Today was the day to confirm booking and details of the church hall which was the usual show venue. Table measurements were matched to entries in each category and hall costs paid for.

'Do you want a lift Belle, or will you be walking?'

'I'll just go up and say goodbye to Momma then I'll meet Mikolaj on the way. It's too nice a day to go by car.'

Steve decided to check the arrangements for the Britain in Bloom judges' inspection day which was due. His predecessor old Tolly Braithwaite had taken on the dual role as chair of the Britain in Bloom committee and being in charge of the Newhill Horticultural society almost single handed. Laura Watson and Keith Shakespeare had offered Steve practical help and it was gratefully received. Belle had delivered schedules with him, and Steve had enjoyed the time talking to his almost daughter. She worked cheap, a bar of chocolate and an ice cream at the garden centre.

Steve's normal efficient mind had been augmented by a sense of energy and purpose. His life, on reflection, had altered dramatically and all for the better.

The same feeling of contented well-being could not be said of Mary Anderson, Year Five teacher at Newhill Primary as she sat in her dressing gown in her small house, just off the High Street. It was a school day, but she would not be going in. Her conjunctivitis had flared up again, but she would have stayed away even without the eye problem. She had lost the heart for teaching and could not raise the energy necessary for a day with twenty-three lively ten-year-olds.

Mary went to the bathroom to bathe her eyes and apply the usual drops. The mirror image was not a pretty one. Her usual gaunt face with its thin mouth and wrinkled skin was not helped by puffy red eyes and a very sad demeanour. At fifty-six she had little if anything to look forward to.

Many years ago, she had worked as a personnel secretary to the education director at the county council offices. She had a husband and two fine sons in what she now saw as the good years. Life was full of potential, and she had decided to try her hand at teaching, it looked easy. However, as a wise man said anyone could be a teacher, well anyone with a reasonable level of intelligence. Anyone could spin one plate of a problem; the trick was spinning nine plates at the same time whilst responding to the stress of a mountain of bureaucratic unnecessary paperwork. The added pressure of Ofsted inspections drove many talented and dedicated teachers away from the profession.

Mary Anderson had regarded Newhill primary, her first and only school as her school and she had applied for deputy headships and even the recent headship, when Thomas Tiler had been appointed. Her two sons had left as sons often did, one to work in Beckenham on the fringe of Penge as a graphic artist whilst the other was in Perth, Western Australia working as something vague in an office. Neither were natural homing pigeons, but they always sent Christmas cards and sometimes a birthday card. Mary's husband saw only a bleak future with his increasingly bitter and frustrated wife. He had left in a spectacular blaze of shouted arguments which went down in legend in her row of Victorian terraced houses, Albert Terrace. Mary was alone with few prospects in teaching or indeed life. The mirror told her that a second marriage was highly unlikely even when her eyes settled back to normal.

Mary knew that she was isolated at Newhill, the friendly team spirit developed quickly by Thomas Tiler, the new head did not include her. She sat aside, taking her frustration out on her unlucky pupils. When she had phoned school to report her highly infectious conjunctivitis on the first day of the Ofsted inspection, she knew that few would believe her. It was so unfair. She could not share the warm feeling which the staff had after the inspection. She was an outsider. Alone and increasingly resentful of Thomas Tiler as head in what she unrealistically felt was her job. Parents respected her firm discipline, and her class were quiet and subdued but it was rule by fear, not respect. Learning was an input of facts and not learning to be a lifelong learner. Learning for short term achievement, for tests and not learning for the joy of curiosity.

She rang the school to report that she would not be in that day, and she felt the disbelief in the secretary Jill Taylor's voice, but she was past caring.

Mary Anderson was deeply depressed and needed help, but she decided to get dressed and write her letter of resignation, certain that it would be greeted with elation by Thomas and his staff. It was his school now, no longer hers and there was no longer any place for her brand of dull negative teaching and glass half empty attitudes.

After a cup of tea, which did little to improve her gloom she dressed and prepared her resignation letter. It would be properly signed unlike the two anonymous notes she had sent to Thomas Tiler in a fit of anger at being side lined by a much younger rival, if she could ever really call herself that.

She had hated it when the school sign outside the gate proclaimed the name of Mr. Thomas Tiler B, Ed. and to make it worse, the word Headteacher had been replaced by Head Learner. Thomas had wished children and parents to see that the ethos of the school was one of learning for life. Learning went on beyond formal education. It was thought provoking and most agreed with this break with tradition but not Mary Anderson and a small number of small minded souls for whom the past was paramount and unchangeable. The dinosaurs who could not adjust their rigid mindsets, but they were thankfully few.

Mary had sat months ago in the garden centre café brooding over a cup of expensive black coffee. A bright attractive young woman sat nearby, and she vaguely recognised her as the wife of the new popular headteacher. Beth Tiler was using her mobile phone, too loudly in Mary's opinion. However, Mary's interest gradually increased as she realised that Beth was talking about her husband. It became obvious that she was taking advice about her husband's dyslexia, asking how best she could help him as he was keen to hide his condition and wished to deal with it alone.

Mary had no idea who was on the other end of the phone conversation but was gleeful as she realised that she had accidently been given information which could drive Thomas away from his job and conversely offered her a chance to put herself in her rightful place as head of Newhill school. A plan was hatched, a dark plan to match her rapidly cooling black coffee. An anonymous note or two would send the young pretender back to where he belonged. Head Learner indeed! What would William Mullins, her old headteacher have thought?

In fact, had she but known it William would have been delighted with this innovative thinking and supported it wholeheartedly. He might even have been a little jealous that he had not thought of it himself but back in the day traditions not forward thinking prevailed. Certainly, signs outside the school did not proclaim so openly the values now embedded within. The dinosaurs still ruled. William would have chuckled and said. 'Well done boy, a correct and courageous move.'

Later that night Mary had delivered the first anonymous letter to Thomas to unsettle him and make him nervous and less sure of himself. The inspection had brought a golden opportunity and she had managed to deliver a second accusing note direct to the inspection team. She had been ultra-careful not to be seen and had ensured that her fingerprints were wiped clean. Mary had watched the detective series 'Vera 'often enough to know what to do. Lonely television watching had finally proved useful.

The letter of resignation was surprisingly easy to write and without the need to wipe away fingerprints. Her signature removed the need for a Geordie female sleuth to work out the perpetuator. It soon became a long rambling list of accusations and perceived injustices real or imaginary. It rambled far beyond the point. Her sad lonely life was embedded in every word. It reeked of bitterness and anger and self-pity. A letter to contemplate and then destroy. It should have been a wake up call to Mary's need for help but it wasn't heeded as that.

Mary addressed the letter to the chair of governors, Caroline Perryman, and briefly contemplated a second letter to the local newspaper but couldn't be bothered. Her mood was dark, and she could see little light at the end of the tunnel. No husband or likelihood of one, sons far away and seemingly uncaring, a job she was not given due credit for and the silent contempt of colleagues. The television was becoming her only refuge and that, she decided, was fast falling into a trough of mediocrity and banal shouting.

A short walk to the High Street post office would follow and there would be a delicious finality about dropping the weighty envelope into the post box. If anyone saw her and queried why she wasn't in school, well firstly her conjunctivitis was obvious and secondly, she couldn't care less. The words, 'with immediate effect' meant that she did not have to explain her absence to anyone, least of all Mr High and Mighty Tiler.

That night Mary knew that her resignation letter would not arrive until next day but strangely she felt little elation as she had expected. There was only emptiness, and a plan began to grow from the depths of despair, a seed of a plan which ate away at her, and her mind was reeling as she went into her bed.

Not everyone was in bed that night. The sun did not set early in the long summer evening, but a few souls were patient as they observed the last of the allotmenteers leaving Wath Mill Allotments. Spiros Papaioannou had finished his lunchtime shift at the restaurant in Matlock and decided to spend an hour on his plot before heading home. His working hours meant that he was not often seen by others and his name was synonymous with absence, but he didn't really mind. Hectic sessions in a noisy heat filled kitchen were soothed by an hour hoeing in peaceful tranquillity, full of fresh Derbyshire air.

Spiros was seen leaving and the small group entered the allotments site secure in the knowledge that they would not be seen. They headed straight to plot one, the Newhill school plot by the small river and communal area. The marrows were ready for picking and one was to have been chosen for its size and perfectly unblemished markings to be wrapped with love and care to be the school's entry in the specimen marrow class. For a few minutes the sound of knives chopping into the fleshy marrows seemed to fill the air. There was no need to completely destroy each marrow, that was surprisingly hard work. It was only necessary to score and slash each one to ensure that there would be no Newhill school entry in the Horticultural Show this year.

Chapter Seventeen

Water is good to look at

Thomas Tiler sighed. Caroline Perryman sat patiently in his office waiting for him to read again the rambling bitter resignation letter from the unpopular Mary Anderson. The sun shone through the window revealing slowly swirling particles of dust. The warm July morning was darkened by the letter.

As Thomas lay the letter down sadly on his lap his chair of governors put aside her cup of tea and asked what he made of the unexpected letter.

'Well, this has certainly come as a shock. I would have said that this was a good opportunity for the school.' His mind went to his SWOT chart where Mary Anderson was firmly in the threat quarter,

Caroline looked shrewdly at the young head. She saw her role as one of protector and adviser, guarding his back whilst he forged ahead with his progressive changes. She had been amused by the term Head Learner but on reflection she realised that this was exactly what Thomas was as a role model for children and staff. He had bravely nailed his colours to the mast. Caroline had quietly smoothed the small opposition amongst the traditionalists. This had been done gently and effectively without Thomas being fully aware of it.

'Why an opportunity Thomas?' Caroline asked knowing the expected answer.

Caroline didn't regard herself as an outstanding chair of governors and she was Thomas' only one so no one to compare with. Every Friday morning Caroline came into the office for her regular meeting with the Head Learner and they would go over events of the week and upcoming events. It was kept brief and business like, afterwards Thomas would go to take assembly and Caroline would stay to listen to children reading. As a good chair should, Caroline knew what was happening in the small school, she was a familiar figure in the staffroom and staff were on first name terms with her. She knew the names of most of the children and once a month sat with them for their hot lunch where she gauged the mood of the school by chatting with the children and assessing the school meals. She was indeed an outstanding chair although she would modestly deny this.

Thomas paused before answering. 'Any vacancy is a chance to appoint someone who will improve the teaching, whether experienced or newly qualified. I would always look to add someone who is a team player. Unfortunately, Mary is not, in my experience a team player. She is negative and rigid in outlook. Ordinarily I would say that it would be great to lose her and take on someone who fits the Newhill ethos of togetherness and flexibility, but....'

'But you are as concerned as I am with the tone of the resignation letter, that does you great credit Thomas. The accusations and bitterness mask a very unhappy lady who, I believe needs professional help.'

'Yes, I agree, I always thought that I would regard this letter as merely an opportunity to move the school forward, but we have a duty of care. Rather than quickly accepting Mary's resignation perhaps the two of us should seek advice from the education authority and explore avenues to help. The fact that she has resigned with immediate effect and not given a term's notice is irrelevant in this case.'

Caroline agreed and Thomas left to take an assembly with the theme of 'helping others' somewhat appropriate he thought.

The following day was Saturday and the sun rose early bathing Newhill in a glow of bright light and clear blue skies. It was a day of promise, a day to get up early to make the most of this glorious weekend. Plans were made, adventures were organised and the town basked in the glory of summer sunshine which energised most residents in a dazzling burst of optimism and happiness. But not for Mary Anderson. She had had a fitful night when sleep eluded her for any length of time. When sleep came there were darkly darting repetitive dreams and she was restless. Part of her regretted putting her resignation letter in the post box but another part of her was relieved and a heavy burden seemed to have been lifted.

Mary dressed almost automatically without caring about her outfit. It didn't seem to matter anymore. Breakfast was replaced by a few gulps of cranberry juice. It was sadly time to end the charade of her life. Sitting at the table with writing pad and pen she began to write a note for her two sons. It seemed only right and traditional to leave a suicide note but she wasn't sure if anyone would care. It turned out that suicide notes were surprisingly easy to write. She could then turn her troubled restless mind to practical matters of how to carry out the final task.

Dark thoughts were far from the minds of the Newhill children. It was that wonderful thing a Saturday full of sunshine and empty of school, a day for adventure and walks and picnics. In addition, the summer holidays loomed in the near future, and all was good with the world. The Newhill cricket team however had the shadow of an upcoming cup final against the dreaded unbeaten Snelston. They were told that, they could only do their best and to just go and enjoy the experience.

Rosangel Chlebek did not accept these platitudes, Snelston had humiliated the Newhill team in their first game of the season, a friendly if playing Snelston could ever be called friendly. Rosangel had been the bowler who was smashed to the boundary in the first over as Snelston easily passed Newhill's meagre score of just eight. She had refused to accept the hard luck sentiments and swore darkly that this would not happen again. The Newhill team had indeed slowly improved as the season went on and they had managed to sneak into the cup final.

On the other hand, the Snelston team, led by the swaggering Jason Bolton and coached by his unpleasant bullying father, were all conquering. In league and cup, they had easily overcome all other teams with power and arrogance. Only Newhill stood in the way of an unheard-of league and cup double and as everyone knew Newhill were full of girls and younger children. Jason boasted that an all-English team would always beat a team full of foreigners. His father's influence was ingrained and deeply sad. He conceded that some West Indian cricketers were quite good but Japanese? Surely not. This was cricket not bloody origami.

Rosangel had certainly not forgotten the humiliation of defeat and her swearing an unlikely revenge. She suggested a practice in the park. Her younger brother Mikolaj wanted a picnic. As usual Sam said nothing, but Rosie organised a compromise. Practice then a picnic by the river Warne,

In addition to Little Billy, Satoshi and Grace they could only muster two other members of the team, family outings and visits to relatives and shopping in Derby took out the rest. However, Andy Mapplebeck whose wild rustic swings at the ball were a result of generations of agricultural labourers scything corn and Brian Braithwaite, grandson of Tolly and medium fast bowler promised to be there.

A practice in the park and a picnic by the river to cool down was organised. Sandwiches were made ready, together with a cake produced by Eileen Bisby and fruit added by Sherrie Chlebek. Billy brought along two bats an old ball and a few stumps together with his precious wicket keeper gloves. Marmalade sandwiches were added as an afterthought. Mikolaj caried two large bottles of lemonade, Sam the plastic cups and a blunt knife for the cake and fruit. Andy promised a bag of mini pork pies and possibly his younger brother George, lured by the promise of food. At the last moment Brian Braithwaite phoned to say that his mother was taking him in shopping at the Derbion shopping centre in Derby for new school shoes and shirts.

The day was set fair, and a light breeze kept the temperature down to near perfection. They met in the park and set up camp in an area away from others park users. The accumulation of food was covered with jumpers and George Mapplebeck stationed to guard the food from dogs, magpies and pirates. The promise of food as a reward was his motivation, he had little interest in cricket but had several Marvel comics to occupy him pre picnic.

Without their Head Learner, as they were becoming used to calling Thomas Tiler or Keith Shakespeare to coach them Little Billy took charge. He was captain, despite his size and he was the only one with actual experience of playing in a team. However, it was Rosie Chlebek who was the driving force. She was ruthless in her determination to defeat Snelston and they were not allowed to waste time messing around.

After an hour of good hard practice, they felt themselves slightly stronger but certainly not Snelston strong, that was a truly awesome team to measure themselves against. Rosie, to everyone's relief, called time for lunch. Perhaps they would have time after lunch for further honing of ball throwing and catching skills.

The hot team decamped to the allotments site, and they crossed the bridge to find a good spot for a picnic. Several blankets were produced and spread. Time for a feast.

George Mapplebeck decided to wander off to see the school plot and avoid work for a couple of minutes. He was a member of the school gardening club and wanted to check on their potential prize-winning marrows.

George was shocked by what he found and ran back to the others where everything was laid out ready for lunch.

'I think you'd better come and see this; I think our marrows have been sabotaged' exclaimed an outraged George.

'This had better not be one of your tricks to get at the food,' his brother Andy warned menacingly.

They stood at the edge of plot one, their plot where they had planted the Tiger Cross marrows in the spring. They had been about ready to choose the best for entry into the Newhill show, but there was no best anymore. The players stood in stunned silence at the scene of devastation. Slices and chunks of marrow lay everywhere slashed and trampled.

'What will Mrs. Watson say, she'll be really upset,', Grace said breaking the silence. Her use of Laura's formal school use name rather than the more familiar Laura which they used at the allotments site seemed proper.

'We haven't got her number, so we'll have to inform her on Monday at school. This is a disaster, a deliberate disaster.' Billy said.

'I had been hoping that we could win the best marrow cup as a sort of leaving present for her, she deserves it, and it would have been appropriate,' Grace added.

'Are there any survivors?' Billy asked and this led to a search amongst the foliage. Marrows were notorious for fast summer growth hidden away under the foliage. It seemed hopeless and most dispiriting until Satoshi cried out, 'Here's one. It seems to be untouched. Whoever did this must have missed it.' They crowded round the smaller marrow and decided that it had a couple of weeks to grow so they brought water over to pour around the precious surviving plant.

'Can we eat now?' George declared and they turned to him surprised, food was far from their minds. Who would do such a destructive thing, a crime without any sense. But George was right and Mikolaj agreed wholeheartedly.

They all walked dejectedly back to their picnic base and for a few moments ate in some degree of silence. The river was a lovely backdrop to their meal. The Warne was not a wide river, but it was surprisingly strong, not in a wild dramatic way but quiet and relentless in its movement to meet the mighty River Trent. It had once driven the medieval water mill and produced power to turn the heavy wooden mill wheel and thus enable the grinding of corn. The wheel was long gone but the river rolled on as it had for many centuries, before the mill, before the coming of the Normans and certainly before the Wath Mill allotments.

The peace of this tranquil scene was disturbed by the sound of someone crossing the bridge into the allotments site. They groaned as they recognised Jason Bolton. Only Grace did not groan, she was the only one pleased to see the object of her secret affections arrive unexpectedly.

'Well, well, well this is cosy,' Jason said noting the assortment of cricket gear. 'Been practising, have we? You'll need it for the cup final believe me. If I were you, I'd stick to picnics, more your style.' He laughed as he walked away and Rosie glanced at her friend Grace, no longer surprised to see her looking down and blushing slightly.

Rosie spoke out for them all, 'Yes, we are good at picnics, and you may find out that we are also good at cricket. Would you care to join us or are you too good for that?'

Jason was actually tempted especially when he noticed the dark-haired girl sitting quietly amongst the group.

Afterwards Jason said that he didn't know why he had done something so stupid but stupid it was. Jason had grabbed two cricket balls amidst loud protests, and he began to juggle them as he walked carefully back along the parapet of the bridge. It was a low edge, only one side warranted a rail. Normally he could juggle with three balls but today he glanced at Grace to make sure she was watching and hopefully admiring his skill. As he looked back his left foot slipped, and he and the balls entered the river with a tremendous splash. Jason shouted but found that underwater this didn't work. He surfaced, disorientated and afraid, the current was sweeping him away with frightening speed.

Little Billy reacted first, and he jumped up and ran along the bank to stay level with the flailing arms and strangled cries for help. Jason's long blond hair was swept around, his vision was impaired. He was afraid as he spluttered and tried to spit out the water.

Billy ran ahead of the drowning boy and jumped in to where he judged Jason would be to meet his dive. Unfortunately, Little Billy Shakespeare had never learned to swim properly

Billy surfaced just as Jason collided with him. There was a tangle of arms and desperate clinging on cries of advice could be vaguely heard but neither boy was clear as to whether they came from the bankside or themselves. Billy tried the traditional doggy paddle but was not strong enough and encumbered with Jason he began to go under. In a somewhat surreal moment, he noticed one of the cricket balls bobbling by and he thought of trying to retrieve it but realised that his life, and Jasons was in real danger. There were no overhanging convenient branches to grab to slow them down as there would be in a film. This was no adventure film, and the boys were being swept apart. Billy's trainers were weighing him dangerously down.

Jason tried to pull himself towards the bank, but he was shocked and quickly weakening. He heard a huge splash followed by a smaller splash and he became aware of others in the water ahead of him. Miranda Shakespeare had been walking through the park to meet her boyfriend when she saw her brother Billy diving into the river. She screamed his name, but it was useless. He could not hear, and she was fully aware that he could not swim more than two metres even in a calm swimming pool and this river was no pool. Miranda saved her energy and sprinted to where she estimated Billy would be, allowing for the current. She quickly noticed to her surprise a second boy in the water, but it was not her brother. Miranda was a strong swimmer and she dived towards the second boy, as she dived expertly in, she saw Rosangel doing the same from the allotments side. Miranda surfaced and grabbed the unknown boy and turning onto her back began to swim with Jason held firmly in front of her.

'Be still, I've got you, don't struggle.' Miranda ordered firmly.

Jason felt safer than he had a few moments ago and he was dragged towards the bank where Andy Mapplebeck and Satoshi grabbed his arms and pulled him to the edge and safety. Miranda turned anxiously and scanned the surface of the water for her brother. Strangely all she could see were Rosangel's legs going below the river. Billy was nowhere in sight. Miranda calmed herself, this was no time to panic, she swam strongly with the current and saw Rosangel's head break the surface. The girls left hand pulled and Miranda realised that she held on to Billy's Aston Villa shirt. Rosangel was struggling and in danger, but her stubborn streak would not allow her to let go. Afterwards she joked that she needed Billy as wicket keeper in the cup final but at that moment there was desperate danger. Miranda grabbed at the unconscious small body and steered him to the edge. Without Billy's weight Rosangel was able to reach the bank gasping for air.

With a concerted team effort Billy and Jason were pulled from the water. Sam helped his beloved sister out whilst Miranda scrambled clear of the water anxious to attend to the lifeless body of her young brother. Jason lay on his side coughing and spluttering. Miranda realised that he was relatively safe and so was able to concentrate on her brother. Laying on his back she held his nose and began to breath into his mouth forcing precious air into his water filled lungs. In her mind she screamed. Breathe for God's sake breathe, please breathe.

Satoshi calmly phoned for an ambulance, but it would be too late for Billy. Sam and Grace tried to keep Rosangel warm, but she was shivering and anxious as she watched Miranda desperately trying to revive her brother. Jason sat crying his knees drawn up and head down. He kept repeating, 'It's all my fault' but no one was listening. Mikolaj and George looked round for something to wrap round the very wet quartet. Some old sacking and fleece were found, and they ran to the tragic scene. Sam ran back to the more useful picnic blankets.

Miranda couldn't say how long she had rhythmically blown air into the small lungs, and she began to despair. How would she tell her parents? Her actions and thoughts were broken when Billy suddenly coughed up water and tried to turn naturally to clear his lungs. He was placed in the recovery position and water trickled steadily from the corner of his mouth.

Miranda's anxiety turned swiftly to anger at her stupid brother, diving into a fast flowing reiver with very rudimentary swimming skills.

When Billy began to breathe more normally in between coughing, his life saving big sister almost shouted at him in her considerable relief.

'What the bloody hell were you thinking pulling a stupid trick like that? You almost died. If the two of us hadn't managed to get you out, you would now be floating face down on the way to the Trent.' Miranda burst into tears.

Billy smiled weakly, 'I was trying to rescue our cricket balls, did you manage to save them?'

There were smiles of relief as they realised that Billy was back. Almost unnoticed an ambulance had arrived, and Ben Ellis ran to the scene. He professionally assessed the situation and prioritising the needs, sent his partner back for more blankets to wrap up the shivering quartet. There would be time later for serious questions but for now Ben knew that no one was in immediate danger as long as they were all kept warm.

Later the back of the ambulance was crowded with the exhausted four. Jason held out his hand to Billy.

'Thank you, you saved my life, and it was all my fault.'

'I think Miranda actually saved you. I didn't do much saving.'

Billy looked at his sister, 'If you ever tell anyone that you kissed me then I will personally disown you.'

'I certainly didn't kiss you and anyway you didn't turn into a handsome prince, you are still an ugly frog. I've missed meeting my boyfriend for this, thanks a bundle.'

Billy grinned and looked directly at his sister, 'Thank you Miranda. Without you and Rosie I would be a goner.' He looked at the very wet Rosangel and mouthed the words 'Thank you.'

Rosie shivered and managed to reply.

'I can see that I will have to take you for swimming lessons Little Billy.'

Billy felt it was almost worth it and he would count it as an official date. 'I wonder what happened to the picnic food?'

'Think about it, George and Mikolaj were left unsupervised, I doubt that there's any left, probably only crumbs'

After being checked over at hospital the four swimmers were released to their respective parents. All were shocked and mightily relieved to have the children safe. Saturday had started with a day of sunny promise and ended with early nights for three of the younger swimmers. Miranda got changed, showered and went to meet her boyfriend but not before receiving a huge tear filled hug from her parents. She reckoned that this would be good for a few late nights on the back of their deep gratitude. Billy snuggled down in the duvet, glad to be dry warm and alive. As he fell to sleep, he regretted the loss of the two cricket balls, what a waste.

Rosangel was driven home by her father and consigned to bed, and she did not argue. Sherrie insisted that she first had hot chicken soup. Rosie's mother sat at the edge of the bed as her only daughter sipped slowly at the welcome soup. Both had been deeply scared by the afternoon's events. Tragedy had been averted but only just

'Mikolaj brought back your share of the picnic, do you want any sandwiches or pork pie?'

Rosie declined, she felt exhausted but asked to see her brothers to assure them and herself that all was well. The boys entered, Sam went to hug his sister, difficult to do with a tray on her lap. He whispered in her ear.

'You are a hero Rosie, my special hero.'

Mikolaj kindly offered to eat the pies or sandwiches if Rosie didn't want them. 'Anything to help' he declared. Baby Jacob was popped into the bed alongside Rosie, glad to be the apparent centre of attention. The last thing Rosie remembered was kissing Jacob's forehead and smelling his sweet talc fuelled body before exhaustion forced much needed sleep on her.

The following afternoon the Shakespeare's and Chlebek's met up at Keiths house to discuss the events of the previous afternoon. In the middle of the accounts the doorbell rang, and Ben Ellis was ushered in. He had dashed the four to hospital in double quick time, ignoring red traffic lights with flashing lights and sirens.

'I just popped in to see how you are after your ordeal. I'll organise a fence between the river and the allotments. After yesterday I think help for this project is guaranteed. Andy agreed and said that he would speak to the council to propose a fence on the park side of the river. A warning notice and lifebelt would also be needed.

Ben left the happy scene to go up to his allotment plot to pick some beans for lunch. He was glad to have a job where he felt needed and able to help. As he was shown out Kevin Bolton and son Jason were just about to ring the bell.

Faith thanked Ben for his prompt actions and welcomed the Boltons in with a real warmth They were doing what she herself would have done. Faith took them into the lounge and left to prepare cups of tea. Mikolaj gallantly offered to help just in case there was a chance of cake or at least biscuits.

Miranda stood to make room for the new visitors, declaring that she had a meeting with her boyfriend to go to. He had finally accepted her reason for missing their meeting yesterday, initially believing it to be an excuse.

Kevin Bolton felt awkward, he had never actually ever been in a West Indian home before.

Kevin declined a seat and coughed before speaking to Miranda.

'Could you please wait a moment young lady. I have something to say. Without your bravery and skill my son here would be dead, and I could not have borne that. He is all I really have, my greatest achievement. I owe you his life and words can never say how I feel right now. I have been wrong for so long on so many levels and I would like to make it up to you.'

Keith recognised the relief and gratitude of a fellow father and he stood to shake Kevin's hand. 'We don't want rewards, we are like you grateful for the lives of our children, your being here sharing this moment is enough for us.'

Miranda mumbled her thanks and was glad to leave and enjoy the warm afternoon with her boyfriend. She had decided that he would later ask her to marry him but at that moment he didn't know that. But she was working on it.

Kevin sat down with a cup of tea and said that his son had something to say. Looking very different from yesterday Jason stood in his dry trendy green hoody and designer jeans His expensive trainers were at home stuffed with newspaper and left in the sun to dry, but the smell was atrocious. His hair was combed neatly back. Jason had had a long talk with his father after his warming bath and a plan was prepared.

It felt like a formal speech, but Jason meant every word.

'I have to apologise to you all. Firstly, I was the one and the only one to set fire to the two sheds, I wrongly believed that Dad would approve, and he would thank me, but he certainly didn't. I will pay you and Leona back for new sheds.

Kevin solemnly interrupted, 'I will pay at once for my son's actions and he will repay me over the next thirty years. I am so grateful to have him with me, money means nothing.'

Jason sighed and went on, 'A few of my friends from Snelston thought it would be a good idea to sabotage the marrows on the Newhill school plot, so we went and destroyed them all so the school wouldn't win a trophy at the show. I didn't really want to do it as I know what it means to grow something from seed and look after it to go on and win prizes. But I felt that I had to go with my so-called friends, it was hard to be different. I'm sorry, I can't make it right.'

Mikolaj, mysteriously eating a custard cream when no one else ate, said, 'It's OK we found one you missed in the dark, we still have an entry. Its small but has time to grow, like Billy I suppose.'

Jason went on, 'The missing tools and watering cans were not me; I believe that casual thieves or vandals were responsible for those thefts but it was me who sent an anonymous letter to the police. I'm truly sorry.'

At that moment the doorbell rang, and Faith stood to see who it was. Grace Bisby had gone to find her friend Rosangel and was welcomed in just as Jason was confessing to yesterdays near tragedy being totally his fault. 'I was showing off balancing on the edge of the bridge whilst juggling cricket balls, but I was trying to impress Grace Bisby in particular. Grace heard this as she entered the room, she wished the ground would open up to swallow her embarrassment, as everyone turned to look at her, she blushed but felt her heart pump with the joy of first innocent love.

Chapter Eighteen

Holding Your Stomach Isn't Real Acting

Rosangel and Billy were offered an extra day off school to rest and fully recover from their near fatal ordeal. They declined and met as usual on the school field at lunchtime.

'Well, we weren't much good as detectives,' Rosangel' said, 'I don't think we actually solved any crimes.'

'But we have the cup final to look forward to on Friday night, it's been played at a proper sports ground with a real cricket pitch.' Billy enthused.

Grace said quietly as was her way, 'We almost lost you and Rosie on Saturday, cup finals aren't important. When I saw you struggling in the water, I felt paralysed with fear. I couldn't move. Seeing you both diving in to help Jason was the bravest thing I have ever seen in my life'

'Almost as brave as Jason confessing to being responsible for the shed fires and destruction of the marrows,' Mikolaj added, looking at Grace.

Satoshi had been quiet and apart from the others. 'Have you forgotten about our dog. Billy is our mascot and he's been missing for ages. My grandmother is very worried. That's a crime we haven't managed to solve but I think we need to.'

Mikolaj said quietly, 'It may not be an actual crime, he may just be lost or worse involved in a car accident. We have lost one Billy and gained another in a way.'

'Thats a terrible thought Mikolaj, not about our Little Billy of course but about the cocker spaniel,' Grace spoke aloud their thoughts. They all loved the dog which attended most of their matches and was a regular visitor at the allotments or waiting with Tessa outside school for Satoshi. His frantic tail wagging welcome was a delight to everyone he met.

Rosangel looked up, 'I think I may have an idea, where do lost dogs go?'

Grace at once picked up on her best friends train of thought, 'Probably a dog's home. There's one near the industrial estate, we could look for him there.'

Satoshi immediately poured cold water on the blossoming idea, 'Sorry guys my dad and Granny tried there already.'

There was a group deflation as this good idea was quickly squashed.

'But what if Billy had wandered further afield and was taken to a different dogs home?' Rosie added'

Satoshi wondered what the word afield meant but this was no time for such thoughts.

Billy said, 'We need a computer to look up all the dogs homes nearby, he can't have wandered that far, but we haven't got one or even a phone, we have to hand them in before school and I can't see Mr Tiler wanting us to use the school computer for our own use.'

Grace perked up, 'What about Steve Shaw he's quite the expert with computers we should ring him and ask him to find out the addresses of dogs homes.'

Mikolaj said, 'Yes, he owes us for cleaning all those bloomin' cups, my hands are still black from that cleaning stuff.'

'Have you tried washing them, Mikolaj?' Grace said, adding that it was her fault that she had had to clean the cups as a punishment and that they had volunteered.'

Satoshi summed matters up neatly, 'So we don't know Steves's number, and we don't have a phone but apart from that all we know is that Mikolaj is a stranger to the world of soap.'

Rosie laughed with the others but said, 'That's right we don't have Steve's number, but I think that I know someone who probably will.' She looked across at Belle playing with her new friends across the field. Leave this to me.'

Rosie returned a few minutes later with Steve's home number written on her hand. Belle was in awe of the older girl, the hero of the river rescue and almost asked for her autograph, she had been delighted to help.

'That's good Rosangel but we still don't have a phone, just a number,' Grace said.

'Billy come with me,' Rosie ordered, and Billy jumped up happy to follow. 'Where are we going?'

'In to see Mrs Taylor to get our phones back, just follow my lead.'

Jill Taylor handed over the phones to the two children who had come into the office to ask for their phones as they felt ill from their ordeal in the water.

'You can use the school phone if you like, it's possible that you are suffering the after effects of swallowing too much water. Heaven knows what is in that river.'

'Thank you, Mrs Taylor, but we think fresh air would help, but we thought it best to keep our parents informed, a monitoring sort of thing,' Rosie added as an impromptu embellishment.

Outside Billy stopped holding his stomach in what he considered an accomplished act of fine thespianism. It wasn't but it was enough to ensure that the school secretary erred on the side of caution.

'Rosie, you are a bloomin' genius' Billy declared in admiration.

Once together Rosie rang the number written in biro on her hand. To their relief Steve Shaw answered almost at once and Rosie succinctly explained their need to find the address of local dogs homes. Steve's analytical mind saw the issue and promised to do what he could. He would report back when he picked up Belle after school.

They cheered but did not notice Mr Tiler walking towards them.

'I see you both seem to have made good recoveries. I would have hated to have replaced you for the cup final on Friday. However, you should have come to see me if there was a real problem.'

The emphasis on the word real made Rosie and Billy look slightly shamefaced even though they knew their motives were good.

'I'll take those phones back to the office now. Whatever you are up to I'm really glad that your adventure on Saturday or rather misadventure turned out well. It's good to have a hero or two in school. By the way Billy holding your stomach may have seemed like good acting, but the dinner ladies tell me that you had two helpings of steak and kidney pie and chips with sponge pudding and custard to follow. Not the usual action of someone with the after effects of almost drowning. Good to see you practicing your cricket skills though, we'll need everything we've got on Friday.'

Thomas walked away with the phones smiling to himself at the children' ingenuity and courage. He loved his job and his team, his first cricket team as a head, they would always be special to him.

Mikolaj watched Mr. Tiler walking back to the school.

'Head Learners seem to know everything.'

'That's because Head Teachers talk but Head Learners listen. T and L, my Granny says that we were given two ears but only one mouth so we could listen and learn twice as much as we talk,' Grace added, much to Santoshi's confusion.

The bell rang to herald the start of the afternoon and the children trooped off the hot field into the cool of the classrooms.

Waiting for the end of the day to see if Steve Shaw had been good to his word was going to feel a long time. It was a long shot, but it would be worth it to get Billy their cocker spaniel mascot back. It may prove their last chance.

Chapter Nineteen

Japanese intuition and Polish determination

True to his word Steve Shaw stood at the school gate at the end of the day. Belle reached him first and hugged him as she handed him her school bag. Before he could ask how her day had been or had she eaten all her lunch they were joined by an anxious group of expectant children. Sherrie Chlebek came across, pushing Jacob in his pram. Faith Shakespeare, Tessa Tinton and Eileen Bisby joined curious as to why the impromptu meeting was centred on Steve.

Satoshi explained to the parents and grandparents, 'We have been trying to find Billy, our mascot and we realised that we had tried the Newhill dogs' home but not others in the area. Steve has, hopefully got some addresses of more dogs' homes where Billy may have been taken if he was lost.'

Steve said, 'I did a little better than that, I rang round the local dogs' homes and found two who had cocker spaniels, but both had collars with their names. Neither was called Billy.' This drew an outpouring of disappointment. Their hopes were dashed, finally and completely.

Tessa Tinton was crestfallen; her hopes had been raised and suddenly dashed, life could be harsh at times.

Satoshi asked if Billy had a collar with his address on. Tessa explained that he only had his name on a disc and a telephone number, but no one had rung to report the cocker spaniel as being found.

Steve could see the disappointment and then threw in his trump card.

'However, I did find another dogs home a little farther away and they said that they had indeed had a cocker spaniel in recently but without a collar.'

The group at once perked up at this glimpse of a chance, a slim chance but nevertheless a chance. Rosangel, ever practical said, 'We should go and collect him before it's too late.'

'I'm afraid that it may already be too late, this particular dog was adopted by a couple in Ashbourne. They collected him yesterday, but the dogs' home would not give me their address. At least not over the phone.'

Steve hated disappointing them all, but Rosangel was not one to be daunted by difficulty. She said, 'Then a few of us should go straight there and try to convince them to give us the address where Billy has been taken.' She looked round, 'Who should go?'

Tessa spoke up, 'Well Billy is my dog so I will drive, Satoshi can come with me, I'll ring your mother to explain that we will be late.' She looked round and said that she had room for one more in the car, especially if they were lucky enough to reclaim Billy, if indeed it was Billy. Cocker spaniel descriptions over the phone were not easy especially without a collar.

Satoshi with his usual methodical manner said, 'It should really be Rosangel, all this line of enquiry was her idea.' He was pleased with the phrase, 'line of enquiry,' watching detective programmes on television was proving good for his fast-developing English.

Rosangel looked across at her mother who nodded her agreement. Others were disappointed not to have been chosen but Mikolaj was secretly pleased. One less at tea meant potentially more for him

'We'll keep your tea in the oven to warm for when you come back Rosie.' Sherrie said looking directly at Mikolaj, he was easy to read. The boy was slightly deflated. Mums!

Steve gave Tessa the address of the dog's home in Ashbourne and the rescue party set off whilst the others dispersed to their respective homes. The general feeling was that it was probably too late, even if it proved to be their Billy.

Rosangel and Satoshi sat buckled up safely in the back seat, helping Tessa look out for the right road. The North Derbyshire Dogs Home was luckily well signposted at the end of a lane which they would almost certainly have missed.

A few minutes later they walked past rows of cages with a variety of dogs, mainly bull terriers, greyhounds and terriers. All were curious about the visitors, some barked their anxiety, others whined pitifully, others, the longer term residents just lay with heads on paws beyond hope that their owners would return.

Satoshi wrinkled his nose and commented on how much dogs smell when together in large groups. He had often helped bath Billy at his Granny's house and in Tokyo he had seen many small dogs being carried about by their devoted owners or even pushed in prams. Those dogs didn't seem to smell apart from maybe special dog shampoo. This was different.

At the office a young receptionist with a name tab clearly marked, Sarah, politely listened to their account.

'It wasn't actually me who took Mr. Shaw's phone call but Rae, the other assistant left a note before going off duty. She probably told him that we are not allowed to give clients details out without their permission.'

Rosangel and Satoshi groaned. It had been a waste of time, a wild cocker spaniel chase. Well perhaps not so wild in Billy's case.

Tessa tried another tack, 'Would a donation to the dogs home help?'

Sarah was sympathetic to their case and said that donations were always welcome, but rules were rules

Rosangel pleaded, 'Billy is our mascot, we are part of the Newhill school cricket team and the cup final is on Friday'

Sarah brightened at this information. 'I went to Newhill when Mr Mullins was head. I was never anywhere near good enough to be a cricket player, but Mr Mullins showed me how to score so I went to all the matches as official scorer. He always taught us so much in assemblies. I remember when he said that it is always right to do the right thing even when it is seen by others as being wrong.'

Tessa smiled; it was amazing how often she came across positive references to Willliam Mullins.

Sarah scribbled on a notepad. 'I shouldn't do this officially, but I feel that in this case it is exceptional, and rules are made to be followed not rigidly enforced.'

The precious address was handed over and Satoshi bowed offering solemn thanks. Sarah smiled as they left, enchanted by the polite manners of the little Japanese boy, for a moment she wished that she were back at Newhill school. She would still have been no good at cricket, but she had enjoyed been part of the team as scorer.

Back in the car Tessa was able to enter the post code into the sat. nav. Thankfully it showed a short journey.

Leaving the car in Orchard Close the three walked up the path to number 27 and knocked. A dog within barked, a familiar bark. Hope rose and they glanced at each other, not daring to speak aloud their hope.

The door opened and an older lady answered.

Tessa told her briefly why they were there.

Surprisingly they were not only invited in but felt very welcome. Linda Appleton had bought the cocker spaniel from the Ashbourne Dog's Home for her grandson but to her dismay found that he was frightened by the enthusiasm of the dog. They had named him Cocker as no one knew his name. Sitting in the lounge the three would be rescuers sat and could hear a familiar whining and scratching at the door to the kitchen.

'We realised that it was a mistake as soon as my grandson met the dog but felt too stupid to take him back'

Linda went to open the door and was almost bowled over as Billy ran with desperately wagging tail to Tessa and then the two children. All were overjoyed and Linda said, 'Well it's obvious that this is your lost dog. I'd be very happy to return him to you. There is the small question of his fee of course.'

Tessa happily paid a refund to Linda to compensate for her loss of fee to the dog's home.

As they went to get in the car, Billy with a piece of rope to tie him safely, Linda asked how they knew where to find the cocker spaniel.

Rosangel smiled, 'Just call it Japanese intuition and Polish determination.'

Linda was puzzled but happy that she had her money, and everyone would be happy with the arrangement, especially the spaniel and Linda's grandson.

News of Billy's return to the fold quickly spread and anticipation of the big cup final was heightened. It seemed a good omen. The weather was set fair, and all arrangements made.

All the Newhill team checked their equipment and shirts, and trousers were washed and ironed. The rest of the week dragged slowly, seemingly never ending. Would Friday never come?

For Mary Anderson however the week did go quickly, and she knew that she had to make a big decision. Going back to Newhill and trying to be part of the team there seemed too difficult to undertake. Her bridges were definitely burned. Her attempts to force the head, Thomas Tiler out of the school with anonymous notes had failed, as she too had failed. Her teaching career seemed sour and full of self-generated bitterness. Her resignation letter had gone in. That part of her life was ended and there seemed little, if anything to look forward to. The loneliness of her life seemed to creep into all her thoughts. The very walls seemed to whisper darkly the word failure at her. A short suicide note had been written but she didn't know what to do next.

She sat in her dressing gown; getting up and dressing seemed a waste of time, as was breakfast. Mary slowly contemplated possible ways to end her bleak life, the sunshine outside seemed to mock her thoughts and for Mary there were only four walls and shadows. Who would mourn her passing? Her sons? Once her pride and joy, they had grown apart from her and rarely communicated. Mary was sure that they would be sad for a moment before moving on with their lives as they always had. Her ex-husband? He had made it clear that he didn't care for her and had married again. The staff at Newhill? She had increasingly felt isolated and outside the team ethos. Possibly her fault. Maybe just a little.

Self-pity was overwhelming Mary Anderson, ex Year Five teacher at Newhill. The gloomy darkness of her very soul was closing in on her. It was time.

The sharp ringing of the doorbell made Mary jump and she felt a twinge of guilt as if her thoughts had been read. She could pretend not to be in but found herself trudging to the door ready to repulse whatever intruders on her space and time stood there.

As she opened the door the incoming shafts of sunlight forced Thomas Tiler and Laura Watson into an almost silhouette appearance.

Mary squinted and slightly recoiled.

'Hello Mary, we came to see how you were,' Thomas said gently.

Laura added, 'We are all concerned about you, can we come in for a moment?'

Mary silently stepped aside, not sure how to greet the couple. Their unexpected appearance had disturbed her deepening dark thoughts and it felt like an intrusion. Nevertheless, she led the pair into the lounge.

Thomas noted the sense of airless neglect and signs of squalor. Unwashed plates lay on table and floor. He wanted to open the windows and let in the air, let in the light, let in a sense of summer life.

Laura's practical mind took over. 'Let me make us all a nice cup of tea Mary, I'm sure it will do us all good. Nothing like tea to refresh us.' She walked into the kitchen and cringed at the state of it, dreading what she would find she opened the fridge. There was a small amount of milk in a jug, but Laura recoiled at the smell, a nice cup of tea was certainly off the agenda.

In the lounge Thomas sat looking at the woman who had tried to use his weaknesses against him and force him out of the job he loved. Mary sat dead eyed and dejected, looking down at her slippers.

Thomas felt only deep pity and hoped that Laura would return soon with the tea. He needed help to deal with this situation which was beyond his comprehension or experience.

Laura returned and glanced at Thomas, 'I think we need professional help here, this goes way beyond a nice cup of tea.'

Thomas picked up his mobile and requested an ambulance although he wasn't sure what to say. He summed up as much as possible and directions were given.

Laura looked round and found the shakily written suicide note, Mary sat staring at nothing. Thomas noticed Laura's silent call for help and leaving Mary he read the note with horror. How could things have got to this level?

After what seemed an eternity, an ambulance arrived, and Ben Ellis and his partner entered the house. They spoke calmy and gently to Mary as they assessed her mental and physical state. Wrapping a red blanket around her she was steadily persuaded to walk slowly to the ambulance. Help would be given but it would be a long journey back to recovery. Outside Thomas watched the ambulance go and he shivered in the warm sunshine.

'That puts everything into perspective Laura. What should we have done to give more support?'

'I don't think that anyone knew the full extent of her mental state, all we saw was the bitterness and anger.' Laura replied sadly. 'We'd better see about locking up and letting social services know. They will have to contact her relatives, not that they seem bothered from what I can make out.'

Reporting this matter to the chair of governors and staff would not be easy. But being in charge of a school was sometimes far from easy.

Back at school Thomas told his secretary, Jill, about what they had found.

Jill said, 'She'll get help now, good professional help. I don't think that you have anything to reproach yourself with in any way. Lots would not have gone to her house to check on her welfare especially after what she tried to do to you. You'll be ready for a cup of strong tea now.'

Jill's practical words helped but only a little.

A knock on the door heralded a visit from Rosangel and Grace.

'We just wanted to say that we managed to rescue our mascot Billy, you know, the cocker spaniel, not Little Billy Shakespeare.' They smiled at their joke and Thomas joined them rejoicing in their young lives, full of warmth and vitality. He really needed this visit from the two girls to remind himself that there were good things in the world.

'Thank you, girls, I'm really pleased. More than you will ever know. Perhaps we can get on with the cup final now.'

Closing the door behind them Grace turned to Rosangel. 'Well, I have to say Mr Tiler seemed more pleased than I expected with our news, must be a secret dog lover.'

Chapter Twenty

The Best Days of our Lives

The Fitzwilliam Hall cricket ground was idyllic with a backdrop of elegant trees and the old hall. It was to be the venue of the North Derbyshire Schools Cup Final, kindly offered as it was each year by the bank who owned the estate. The facilities and pitch were immaculate. Satoshi exclaimed that the pitch was actually level without any long grass.

'It's like a billiard table without the pockets,' Billy added

The Newhill team had arrived early as the ground was in Newhill itself. They changed in the dressing room and went to set up their camp at the side of the boundary rope.

Bats, gloves and bags were centred amidst a growing number of pop-up chairs set up by parents and supporters. Confidence was high and the newly returned mascot was fussed over by everyone, and the story of his rescue repeated many times.

Thomas went to greet the neutral umpires who had kindly agreed to officiate, Declan being one and Brian from Mapleton Road school being the other. The Newhill head felt more kindly disposed to Declan who he had once regarded as a rival for his wife, Beth's, affections since he had discovered him to be uninterested in females.

The Shakespeare's and Chlebek's were there in force and picnic blankets and chairs gave a festive air. Set further apart was a table for scorers, once again two neutrals were setting up their score books and sharpening pencils whilst chatting about past matches. Thomas handed his team sheet to the scorers and excitement began to build. The Newhill team practised at the side almost afraid to spoil the beautiful pitch.

Keith Shakespeare stood with Ben Ellis and said that the pitch was alright but not up to their school pitch. Ben agreed, 'They've managed to cut all the pitch and outfield to one level.

We had two levels, long grass and slightly shorter grass for the pitch itself.'

'Yes,' Keith agreed, 'and they don't have any bumps for the spinners to use.'

The two men grinned as they appreciated that their efforts to produce a good cricket pitch needed more time and money than they could offer. It was indeed a beautiful ground and an immaculate pitch worthy of a cup final.

Cars began to draw up in the adjacent car park and the Snelston team disembarked. They walked together, tall and arrogant. The undefeated were coming to collect their cup. The formality of beating Newhill who they had thrashed in a friendly and in the league was the only thing between them and the William Mullins Cup. If they won the toss and put Newhill in to bat it would be over quickly and the celebrations could begin.

Thomas Tiler and Keith Shakespeare exchanged glances. Snelston had won the early exchange as the Newhill team and supporters were silenced by the menace of the much older and larger team. Suddenly the earlier air of anticipation and optimism drained away.

Parents mentally began to rehearse their talks of condolences to their defeated and deflated offspring. Their hearts went out to the sacrificial lambs. If they lost the toss and had to bat first this final would only last under an hour as Snelston skittled Newhill out for less than ten and then would easily smash the winning runs.

Thomas gathered his team together for a final motivational chat. He briefly thought of using Henry the fifth's speech before Agincourt. He could build to a crescendo and end with the cry, 'For Newhill, St George and England!' But that would be ridiculous, Snelston could also lay claim to St George and England whilst having a Shakespeare in the team may infringe on some sort of copyright. The flashing idea was sensibly dispatched, and he told them how well they had done to reach the final and how proud he was of them, win, lose or draw. Finally, he reminded them of their first game of the season when Snelston had smashed them in a friendly. They had come a long way since then but probably not far enough he thought sadly.

Rosangel Chlebek did not need to be reminded about that defeat. Her face was set grim and turned towards the mighty opposition team. Her father, Andy, looked with considerable pride on his daughter. Generations of Poles had faced such great odds in their tumultuous history with the same resolve and determination. He looked across at Sam who mirrored his sister looking at the opposition with a burning desire not to be defeated. Mikolaj was busy finishing off a ginger biscuit or two to give him strength. Andy felt blessed and silently thanked his ancestors.

Billy, the captain's, speech was unprepared and short, 'We may lose today but if we do, we'll go down fighting. We'll make them fight all the way. They are a great team, but you've got Billy Shakespeare and Billy the cocker spaniel. What can go wrong? 'This lightened the mood and each one felt determined to do their best.

Jason Bolton, the Snelston captain and leading batter, came over to the Newhill team.

'All the best for today Newhill, without your help I would have been drowned and for that I will always be grateful. However, we'll be trying 100% to beat you today but it will be fought in the right spirit. The ones who cut up your marrows have dropped themselves from the team.'

Grace spoke for them all, 'We appreciate you saying that, but we too will be putting in every effort no matter who is playing against us.'

The umpires called over the two captains to toss the coin to decide who would bat first. Jason called 'Tails' and tails it was. Newhill were asked to bat. Snelston grew in confidence as they knew they could bowl the Newhill team out cheaply.

Satoshi's mother asked her husband Alex how many runs Newhill would have to get to win.

'Difficult to say, it's not a set number, just like baseball.' he called over to ask Keith his more expert opinion, but the Trinidadian was deep in conversation with Ben Ellis.

Ben had confided in his friend, 'Yes, we had a letter confirming it a few weeks ago, we've been accepted as suitable to adopt a child. It is unlikely to be a baby which would be ideal, but we don't mind, not really. Jen is desperate to be a mother and we've tried for so long, but nothing has happened. So far, we haven't dare tell anyone in case we are disappointed again.

Keith shook Ben's hand warmly, 'The two of you will be great parents. Any child would be fortunate to be able to call you Mum and Dad.'

'Thanks Keith, that means a lot'

'Boy or girl?

'Jen and I really don't mind, the adoption liaison lady said it could be either and maybe up to ten years old. We may have to have the child on a trial basis first to see if we are suited. It's important that its right for everyone. She did say that it would be unlikely to be a baby as they were the one's everyone asked for. It's not like picking out a puppy or anything.

The good news quickly spread and for a few moments cricket was forgotten as everyone congratulated Ben and asked him to pass on their congratulations to Jen.

Meanwhile the Snelston team carefully set their field placings and Andy Mapplebeck and Satoshi Tinton put on their pads and walked out to the middle of the wonderful pitch, their first real pitch.

Alex explained that it was a sixteen over game with four bowlers allowed four overs each. He then went on to explain the concept of an over.

Everyone settled down to watch what would hopefully be a good close game, but most felt that it would be far from that.

Kevin Bolton came over to the Newhill group of supporters. 'Good luck today and I mean it. He shook hands with Thomas as the opposition coach and with Keith Shakespeare.

''Whatever the result today I'd be honoured to buy you a pint and share a post-match chat.'

'No, you won't,' Keith said firmly, and Kevin was taken slightly aback. He hadn't expected this rebuff to his peace gesture.

Keith smiled, 'I will buy *you* a pint and if you are still willing you can buy the second, no matter who wins today.'

Both men had almost lost their only sons in the near tragedy in the river. Both realised that results of cricket matches were unimportant compared to the horror of what might have been.

'Is Miranda not here? I was hoping to thank her again for saving Jason, I thought a cheque to help with university or clothes or whatever, I am in her debt for ever. And another for young Billy over there, he was the one who dived in to help even though he could barely swim.'

'For God's sake don't tell Miranda that you'll never get rid of her but thank you that is a kind thought.' Keith said in his deep resonant voice. 'She's gone to the cinema with her boyfriend, a nice lad, we all like him except he's a Sheffield Wednesday supporter.'

'Ouch' replied Kevin, 'I feel your pain mate.'

Kevin looked across at Rosangel and caught her eye. He went across to where Rosangel and Grace sat, inevitably together. 'Good luck today, I hope that you do well.' He looked at Grace aware that his son had expressed his feelings for the Newhill girl.

'I hear that you are a fine fielder, we could do with more girls like you and Rosangel in cricket.' A breath of fresh air.' He moved on to speak to Andy Chlebek and passed on a cheque for Rosangel to be put in trust for her when she turned eighteen. Although initially rejected as there being no need, Kevin insisted, and it was eventually gratefully received. Four children were expensive, especially Mikolaj.

Kevin was happy with his peace-making and felt that he had drawn a line under his earlier life and certainly attitudes, he walked back round the boundary to the Snelston supporters. He breathed in deeply of the fine summer air and felt good about life.

Two precious overs had gone and only three scored when Andy Mapplebeck lost patience and tried to hit a six but only managed to snick it into the wicketkeepers gloves.

Things got worse as Satoshi tried to rescue the situation. He managed to score fourteen but by then Brian Braithwaite, Matt Down and Eddie Farquar had all been out without adding to the score. The Snelston bowlers were relentless and when Satoshi was caught in the slips things looked perilous. Twenty runs for five wickets,

Kyoko asked if that was a good score, 'Perhaps but probably not' Alex replied. Kyoko stood with an easy elegance which was the envy of most of the women there. She went to say well done to her son.

Little Billy Shakespeare saw the wickets tumble and feared the inevitable worst, but he felt that this was his moment, his chance to be a hero, to be a giant for once.

There was a group despondency amongst the Newhill supporters. The overs were going fast, and the score was not enough. All hopes rested on Billy Shakespeare.

Sherrie Chlebek cuddled her youngest, Jacob, on her knee when she glanced across at the car park where a distressed looking woman was coming over to them.

'Ben' Sherrie called out urgently, 'I think that's Jen and she looks troubled.'

Ben Ellis whose married life was blighted with troubles, looked up and began to stand, surely this couldn't be more disappointment. Had the adoption agency changed their mind. He noted with gathering concern the crumpled piece of paper in her hand. By the time Jen arrived she was breathless, and Tessa stood up to offer her a seat. Laura Watson poured her some tea from her flask. It was a few moments before she calmed down. Ben wanted to be alone with his beloved wife to share the usual bad news, but he could not wait.

'Has the adoption fallen through? If it has, we'll keep trying, rest assured we will keep trying. I will always be here for you.'

Jen was tearful and drew a careful breath. This was an important moment, one to remember. 'No, it hasn't fallen through, far from it. This letter came and we have been offered a chance to meet a two year old girl whose parents died in a car crash, there are no immediate relatives.' The adoption people seem to think that we would be ideal, and we can go to meet her next week if we wish,'

Ben thought that his heart would actually explode with happiness, but he was held back not daring to celebrate too soon. He was fully tuned in to Jen's moods and feelings as they had shared so many disappointments and he sensed that his wife was holding something back. He asked quietly, 'Are you happy with this, isn't it what we aways wanted?'

'Happy, of course I'm way beyond happy, if all goes well, we will officially have a daughter in a few months, perhaps in time for Christmas.'

The images of a family Christmas complete with a toddler to create memories was too much for Ben and he hugged his wife with joy. They savoured the moment. Congratulations poured in from all around them. Everyone knew how hard they had been trying for a baby and all were delighted for them.

Ben laughed and wiped away his tears. As usual he covered his feelings with humour, 'Well at least we'll have by passed most of the changing nappies bit and sleepless nights. A ready-made daughter for us and a ready-made family for her.' He relished the words, proud to say them out loud.

Jen calmed him down, 'I'm afraid not Ben. As you know I've been feeling under the weather recently and I went to see Doctor Fletcher. It seems that I have a condition.'

The blood drained quickly from Bens face,

'Oh God no, please tell me it isn't serious.' He had seen the attainment of his most precious desire, a child and now it seemed to be about to be dashed so cruelly away from them. The adoption agency would not accept Jen if she had a long term illness. Never mind that how would he cope without her?

'Yes, it is serious, and the doctor is certain,' Jen waited a moment before adding her second piece of news. 'I am pregnant, we are having a child of our own'

Ben was speechless and wanted to ask so many questions all at once his mouth opened and closed like a goldfish. Finally, he managed to ask how it was possible after so long trying.

'Doctor Fletcher reckoned that it was possibly due to being successful with our adoption. We were more relaxed. She said that this sometimes happened.'

Ben began to worry, 'But what about our little girl? It doesn't seem fair on her.'

'Her name is Lily, and the adoption people say it would be perfect for her to have herself and another baby growing up together. if we still want that of course,'

'Half an hour ago I had no children of my own, now it looks like I will have two, I am absolutely delighted, no man on this planet could be happier.' He gave out a great yell of primitive almost animal like exultation and the Newhill supporters clapped.

The umpires looked over with disapproval. This just wasn't cricket.

Billy assumed that the clapping and shouts were for him going out to bat.

Sam stood alone amongst the Snelston batters, having gone out to replace Matt Down. He was pleased to see Billy, his captain striding confidently towards him. Any company was good at that scary moment when nerves chased each other round his stomach.

Billy met Sam in the middle, and they touched gloves, neither of them knew why but they had seen the professionals do it.

'Just remember Sam, the first time we played them in our first match we only scored eleven. We have twenty already and we have five wickets left. Should make fifty at least.'

Tension was high, this was a key moment. Billy Shakespeare carefully and methodically took guard before looking round to see where all the fielders were. Picking his spot on the boundary careful not to look too closely in case the fielders noticed and covered that area.

The Snelston bowler ran in with considerable menace and the ball sizzled towards Billy's bat. But he missed and hit thin air. The ball however hit his pads and ran away quickly through the slips. The Snelston team shouted loud and long for LBW, but Declan said calmly, 'Not out. It was missing off stump'

Everyone stood almost paralysed by the action. But not Sam Chlebek. He shouted, 'Run Little Billy Run!' And Sam ran but Billy was so astounded to hear Sam call out loud that he did not move. There was a corresponding silence amongst the Newhill encampment.

Sherrie Chlebek could not believe what she had heard, her son had finally spoken out loud.

Billy woke up as if from a dream and his batting pads seemed suddenly heavy. The Snelston fielders realised that the batters were going to attempt a leg bye and the ball was sent quickly to the bowlers end where Billy was trying to get to.

The struggling batter both saw and heard the clatter of bails long before he reached the position of safety. Billy was out without hitting a ball.

Rosangel picked up her bat and joined her brother in the centre of the pitch.

'Well Sam, you've just run our best player out, so you'd better go on to make some runs now to make up for it, and I want to hear you shouting clear instructions as well.'

Sam grinned, 'I was ready, and I shouted for Billy to run but he didn't.'

Rosangel replied 'I've got a Polish flag in my pocket to give to Dad if we win, just make sure we do.'

For the next few overs, the Chlebek children proceeded to punch the ball all round the ground before Sam was caught out trying to hit a six.

Grace was sent in next for the last few balls, by Thomas Tiler.

'Just have a go and run for everything, no room for hesitation now.'

Grace joined Rosangel in the middle and Kevin Bolton thought how he would once have disagreed with girls playing cricket. Today was different and he found himself willing them on.

The two girls put on several runs before Grace hit one skywards only to see Jason Bolton safely underneath it. At the last moment he shielded his eyes and the ball dropped safely at his feet.

'Sorry, I was dazzled by the sun.' he explained to his team mates.

As he turned, he winked at Grace and she was flustered, so much so that the next ball exploded her stumps with a loud clatter.

The innings was over and Newhill had managed to scrape together fifty-four runs. Not a great total but respectable.

Time for a drink of orange and biscuits, or whatever was left by Mikolaj.

It was said later that in the Snelston innings Jason Bolton was like a wolf at bay surrounded by a pack of hungry dogs and the leader of the pack was Rosangel Chlebek.

When the Snelston innings began it did so with some considerable degree of confidence and rightly so. They were undefeated, did not know the meaning of defeat and their captain and opening batter was Jason Bolton who strode with real authority to the middle of the pitch.

Andy Mapplebeck took two wickets in the first over, one a catch behind to Billy. Jason could only watch from the other end powerless to intervene, but it was only two wickets and there were fifteen overs to go. But the slight element of doubt had entered the minds of some of the Snelston team.

Rosangel was handed the ball by captain Billy, and she measured up her run with quiet determination. The first ball was dispatched for one and Jason ran easily to the non-strikers end.

'Well bowled Rosie, I wasn't sure which way it would turn. You have got better.' Jason said as the girl prepared to bowl again.

'You've seen nothing yet Jason, I'm only just getting started, only warming up.'

True to her word the next ball clipped the top of the off stump, to the delight of the Newhill team and supporters. A perfect start. One run three wickets.

Wickets began to fall regularly, but not that of Jason Bolton. He was magnificent, at least Grace and half the watching crowd thought so. His long blond hair was tied back in a pony tail and he strode the pitch without fear, this was his domain, he would not taste defeat. He pushed the good balls away for two whilst the bad balls were dispatched without mercy to the boundary.

The score began to rise alarmingly, at least from a Newhill perspective. The great majority of the runs were scored by Jason but that didn't matter the total was rising like a flood tide, impossible to stem.

The overs were ticking by.

Satoshi, with a smart bit of fielding, had whipped the ball to Billy and the bails were removed well before the errant batter arrived. Sam took a good, low catch and shouted, 'Howzat.' to the umpire, quite unnecessary as he had caught the ball cleanly.

The Newhill team and contingent cheered as much for the appeal as for the catch. Charlie Poole went to quietly hug Sherrie Chlebek, no words were needed, all their work trying to get Sam to speak openly was beginning to bear fruit. There was light at the end of the long dark tunnel.

Rosangel rushed over to Sam and held him tight kissing him hard on the cheek.

'Good one Sam, and I don't mean the catch, that was easy.'

Sam blushed a deep pink at being kissed in the middle of a cup final. He decided that if this was what talking did, he would remain quiet but a part of him was thrilled to have spoken out loud, twice now. Only a few words but enough, for now.

Billy looked at the rudimentary scoreboard with a worried eye.

The score was desperately close. 52 runs for 9wickets and Jason was facing the bowler. Only three balls left in the match. Jason had been joined in the middle by a large boy called Stan who was the Snelston equivalent of Andy Mapplebeck. He was very capable of hitting the ball half way to Leek, if he caught it right with an agricultural scything shot.

Jason needed two runs to level the score and Stan was a dependable deputy.

Rosangel took her time, but the ball slipped badly from her tired damp fingers and the innocent looking ball was hit crisply by Jason. Satoshi and Mikolaj chased the ball with a frantic urgency. Mikolaj got there first and hurled the ball into Billy the wicket keeper's glove.

Two runs, the ties were level.

Kyoko looked curiously at the umpire whilst the Snelston supporters cheered what would now be a close but inevitable victory.

'Alex, what is the umpire doing, he has one hand touching his shoulder, Is he alright?'

Alex looked across and saw that she was right. At the same moment Keith Shakespeare shouted out the explanation. 'That's one run short. They only scored one not two. That signal is unusual, but it means that one of the batters didn't touch down behind the crease. Well spotted umpire.'

Declan felt quite pleased with this praise, it wasn't very often that umpires received any compliments, usually just a quick handshake at the end of the match.

But this wasn't the end of the match. Snelston still needed one to tie and two to win with two balls to go. It was probably the best cup final anyone could remember.

Rosangel wiped her fingers dry on a cloth produced mysteriously by Billy from the waistband of his trousers, behind him. He took the opportunity, as captain to talk quietly to his leading wicket taker. Rosie had already dispatched six Snelston wickets, one more would win the cup, but one mistake would lose it and Jason was confident.

Only Rosie heard Billy's words that late summer afternoon in the middle of the cricket match, in the crucial part of the cup final. She never repeated them to anyone, not even Grace. They were too precious to share.

'Whatever happens in the next two balls Rosie, win lose or draw you have been magnificent, and I will always love you, never more than at this moment. Whatever happens to us in our future lives I will continue to love you as you are now.'

He turned quickly leaving Rosie to continue the now unnecessary drying of the ball in some considerable astonishment.

Rosangel Chlebek took a deep breath and stared at her target. This would be her best ball and it was bowled with skill and intent, but Jason was better. He swung all his weight and power into the ball, and it flew straight towards Rosie's face.

The crowd gasped and Sherrie screamed. Billy was right behind the swift dangerous flight of the ball, unable to help. He cried out, 'Noooo' but to no avail.

Rosie saw the ball hurtling straight towards her and without thought instinctively put both hands in front of her face. Miraculously her hands grasped the ball firmly and she was knocked backwards still grasping the ball with red stinging hands. It hurt but for a moment there was a silence as everyone took in what had happened, what might have happened. This was followed by a guttural cry of joy.

Newhill had won the cup, the first team ever to keep the trophy.

Everyone rushed over to check that Rosie was not hurt. She was lifted and congratulated but she decided that that would be her last cricket match, she had made her point and dramatically so. Besides which her hands were still stinging and there was the matter of Little Billy Shakespeare to talk to.

Chapter Twenty One

Prize Vegetables and Autumn Days

The last day of primary school was always an exhilarating, frightening, exciting day for the Year Six children. It was full of heightened emotion, laughter and tears. It was the longest day and the shortest as they were hustled towards the long summer holidays and the looming dark unknown of secondary school. Instead of being the oldest with responsibilities and privileges they would be very small fish in a large pond. There would be many unknown teachers, strange and unfamiliar in their ways and new friends to make and break as the social structure settled down into lifelong friendships.

Little Billy Shakespeare lay on the grass at lunchtime with his hands behind his head. He looked up at the clear blue sky, 'It's not going to be the same is it, nothing's going to be the same.'

Grace and Rosangel sat alongside the West Indian boy and pondered on his profound words.

Rosangel finally said,' In a way everything changes and yet nothing changes. We'll all be together at Moordale next year as will Jason Bolton.' she said looking pointedly at her best friend. 'Sam or the chatterbox as we now call him, Satoshi and Mikolaj will still be at Newhill'

Grace smiled, 'I arranged it personally, he's not as bad as we first thought, and I believe that he deliberately dropped a catch in the cup final to help us.'

'Or maybe the sun did actually get in his eyes.' Billy said.

Rosie looked at him with narrow eyes, 'I don't think that there is a romantic bone in your body Billy Shakespeare.'

'Are you really sure about that Miss Chlebek?' Billy replied and she blushed remembering their first innocent clumsy yet somehow magical never to be forgotten kiss.

Satoshi and Sam joined them, to Rosie's relief.

Sam said, 'We have to go straight to the hall after lunch it's a presentation for Laura Watson for her retirement,' He sat, happy to have made a verbal contribution.

'Where's Mikolaj? Rosangel asked looking round.

Satoshi grinned, 'He's helping the dinner ladies clear up.'

Grace said, 'You mean he's helping finish off the last of the sponge puddings.'

Billy sat up, 'We ought to do something special after school to mark our leaving, but I think we should go to see Mr Tiler before the bell goes to sort of thank him. Without his help and encouragement, we would never have won the Mullins cup.'

'Thats a good idea Billy,' Rosie said. 'Let's go straight away before the bell goes.'

Thomas Tiler sat in his office getting his speech ready for Laura's retirement. On his desk were various bottles of wine, chocolates and unwrapped presents, gifts from leaving children and their parents. In the centre was a bottle of West Indian rum brought in by Billy.

A knock on the door was followed by the entry of an intrepid group.

As usual Rosangel spoke for them, 'We thought that you would be busy after school, so we popped in to say a big Thank You from all of us for all you have done for us.'

'No Rosie, it is I who must thank you all. You taught me so much about determination and courage. I will never forget you, my first team. You may wish to know that Mrs Watson and I had a little trip this morning. We took the Mullins Cup to the churchyard where William Mullins is buried. Mrs Watson knew him well and she told him about your win in the final. She said that he would have been delighted to see a team made up of boys and girls, different ages and representing several countries all coming together and working as one'

'The William Mullins Cup is back where it belongs in the hall cabinet, safe for another year. Perhaps those of you who will still be here would fancy another go at keeping it for a third year?' Grace cringed slightly at the mention of the cup being safe.

Satoshi declared that they would certainly try although it would be difficult without their star spinner, Rosangel.

Sam said, 'Can we keep her here for another year?'

Thomas looked straight at Sam, 'We both know that we would love that, but life moves on and we soon find that we don't need to cling to the past so much. We can both manage without your big sister, I'll try if you will Sam.'

Sam nodded his agreement.' We can both try our best.'

Rosie went over and hugged Thomas and he knew well why he had always wanted to be a teacher. His heart was full for these children, so ordinary and yet each so very special in their own way. 'Are you doing anything particular after school to celebrate your leaving?'

Grace decided for them on the spur of the moment. 'I think that we will go to check up on the school plot at Wath Mill Allotments. We have one marrow left which we've been specially looking after. We want Mrs Watson to win the trophy for best marrow as a sort of leaving present. The Newhill Show is in ten days. You should come.'

They all thought it a good idea, especially as it was off the cuff as it were.

As they left the office Thomas knew that he would seriously miss the leavers. He called after them, 'But definitely no swimming this time.'

The August Newhill Show, when it came, was a real success, the sun shone, and Steve had organised it to the point where everyone said it was the best ever. The people at Wath Mill had entered fully into the spirit and entries in the vegetable class were especially well represented. After the small church hall was cleared for judging, there was a good natured air of hope and anticipation.

At 2.00pm the doors were opened to the public and everyone went to check on their entries.

Charlotte Poole took the twins, Jamie and Annie and they were delighted to get second prize in the carrots section but best dessert for her rhubarb pie.

Eileen Bisby came up with Grace and her mother, Amanda. 'Well done Charlie that looks delicious a well-deserved win. Not bad with the carrots either.'

Charlie laughed, 'Just luck really.'

'And some considerable skill and knowledge I might add.' Eileen said..

Charlie took the opportunity to speak confidentially to the older woman.

'Eileen, I know that you have settled in brilliantly since you've been back at the allotments. As you know I am stepping down after too many years in the role and I was wondering if you would consider becoming chair. I have spoken to several people, and they agree that you would be perfect. At least give it some thought, the AGM isn't until October.'

Eileen smiled to herself. This was what she had once worked for and plotted for and aimed for. To be the one in charge for the first time in her life. Not to be second fiddle to anyone.

But things had changed in the intervening years, there were new perspectives. Eileen had changed and like Tessa Tinton had become more mellow, especially with her beloved Grace by her side. Raw ambition alone seemed empty, cold and meaningless.

'If no one else wants the job I'll be more than happy to serve as long as you are sure that I will be welcomed. I'll need a supportive committee to help me of course.'

'With your skills you will be welcomed with open arms.' Charlie smiled and gave Eileen a brief hug.

'Tessa will probably continue as membership secretary and we will be nominating Ben Ellis in a new role, that of site manager. He strims everything in sight as it is whether it's needed or not.'

'Now let's go and find the school entry.'

Grace said, 'Too late I've already been to look. Our marrow won first prize, there will be a trophy for Laura as our retirement gift to her.'

Andy Chlebek also won a trophy, a handsome cup for a small black tray with three different vegetables, two of each. They were carefully organised by Rosangel and Sam as their father was too busy with meetings and preparations for meetings. Two cucumbers, two tomatoes and two courgettes were chosen Andy officially won the trophy, and it would be engraved with his name, but his children did the display work and for this Andy was grateful. Rosie remembered that the handsome trophy was one of many which the friends had polished as part of Grace's punishment.

First, second and third prizes in the unclassified section were won by Keith Shakespeare and he was proud to spend time explaining to passers-by what the unusual West Indian vegetables were. Kevin Bolton asked for advice on growing the exotic looking items. A drink afterwards was arranged to exchange information and plant cuttings. Kevin had won the Tolly cup for the heaviest onion, a very heavy brass trophy on a wooden stand. It weighed more than the actual heaviest onion, one of the giant Kelsae variety

Tessa Tinton was pleased to get a second place with her chocolate cake. As expected, Nora Wilson from the bakery won first prize in this category. This was taken for granted each year. Second place to Nora was considered an honourable first.

Kyoko entered the handicraft section with an exquisite piece of Sashiko needlework. It was entered with some humility, but she was awarded a red ribbon for outstanding work in the whole handicrafts section. Her mother in law, Tessa, could not have been prouder at that moment not since Satoshi had done so much to win the cricket cup. Life for her was golden, a far cry from the dark days of despair and debt through online gambling when her son, Alex, had first gone to live in Japan.

Mikolaj looked at the blue Sashiko with tiny white stitching but told Satoshi that he actually preferred the look of Tessa's chocolate cake.

Ben Ellis had been too busy to consider entering anything in the annual show. It was hard work being a father he decided. Perhaps next year. Jen had stayed at home to rest, and she was certainly showing signs of her very welcome pregnancy. Ben led two year old Lily by the hand around the show, occasionally lifting her up to explain what things were.

Thomas Tiler watched Ben with his new daughter, both happy and laughing together. He turned to Beth and asked if they should try for a baby.

'Thomas Tiler, I thought that you would never ask. As long as it isn't just to boost numbers at Newhill school.'

Thomas smiled, 'That had never once occurred to me,' he lied, somewhat badly.

Postscript

Sixteen Years Later

Rosangel Chlebek sat at her father's desk and completed her annual self-allocated task, that of newsletter writer. The snow fell silently offering a good soft covering to the town of Newhill.

At twenty seven she was as stunning a beauty as her Polish mother. As she put the newsletter into the photocopier, she felt it a pity that her father had lost in his quest for a seat in Parliament at the General Election. It had taken a recount, and everyone said that he would achieve his goal next time.

It was early morning, but she heard the quick patter of small feet and her three year old son, William pushed open the door.

'I couldn't find you Momma, were you lost?' Billy said as he climbed up onto his mother's knee.

'No little Billy, I try not to get lost too often', she replied cuddling him close.

'What are you doing? Can I do it too?'

Rosangel continued to address the envelopes. Social media would have been much quicker, but she preferred the tradition of writing and each year used good quality stationery.

'Yes, you can help Billy perhaps I can teach you how to write first, this afternoon maybe after the Victorian Day in the square.'

Victorian Day on Christmas Eve in Newhill with snow. A good mix she decided.

And so, each newsletter was placed in the envelope each with a beautifully written personal message.

'Time for breakfast Billy, what would you like?'

'Turkey and hoops,' he declared firmly and very seriously.

'Perhaps we should leave the turkey till tomorrow, it is more traditional on Christmas Day. Go and get dressed but don't wake your father or sister up. I'll go and get your hoops.'

She smiled as the three-year-old trotted away with a parting shot.

'And some Christmas pudding on top,' he said hopefully.

Rosangel didn't always get to go home for Christmas, but she knew how much her mother, Sherrie, loved having her and the grandchildren there. It seemed unnatural somehow for Sherrie to have arms empty of a child or two. Billy and his younger sister, Eve, filled that space well and she was content.

Jacob was still at home and a keen cricketer. Sam would be joining them for their traditional Polish Christmas Eve meal later with his family. Rosangel thought it appropriate and wonderful that Sam was now a speech therapist in Derby. On occasion he gave motivational speeches at the university, offering real insight into his role. He had married Belle Shaw and said later that it was a perfect mix of Portuguese and Polish with a little English.

Mikolaj Chlebek had been best man at his brother's wedding and gave a sparkling witty speech. Moreover, he had supplied the very professional catering. He had opened a hugely successful restaurant in Croydon with a Polish food theme, his latest venture was a second restaurant based on Dickensian foods mentioned in the great writer's books. Tourists, especially Americans loved the menu.

Later that day the Chlebek's went on mass to Victorian Day and Rosangel posted her newsletters as she liked to do on Christmas Eve.

The letter to Satoshi would travel the furthest. Rosie had not seen him since he had returned for his granny, Tessa's funeral three years before but she kept him up to date with news. He worked at the University of Osaka and had a young daughter who he tried to teach both English and cricket to. One more successful than the other.

Ben Ellis had become site manager and later chair at Wath Mill Allotments where he was regularly helped by his son James, at sixteen the pride of his father as was the delightful Lily. Since Nora Wilson's retirement Lily worked at the bakery with the owner Faith Shakespeare. It had been something to occupy Faith's mind since her husband Keith had suffered the onset of senile dementia.

The newsletter to her best friend Grace was always special. Grace had married not the once hoped for Jason Bolton but a Canadian engineer, Jackson Leigh. They lived in a large lakeside house near Toronto and Rosangel had visited with her family. Grace had completed a series of detective mystery novels about a group of children solving complicated mysteries. The income from this writing was healthy and there was talk of a film or television series.

At secondary school there had been a brief and somewhat unhappy flirtation for Grace with Jason Bolton who suffered from a perpetual wandering eye. As expected, Jason now played county cricket for Nottinghamshire and his father, Kevin, went to every match. Jason had been batting and approaching his fifty playing away against Yorkshire when someone noticed Kevin slumped in his seat at Headingley. The assumption of sleep proved a dramatically wrong diagnosis.

The Victorian Day was a huge success mainly due to the atmospheric fall of snow. Rosangel chatted with Charlie Poole and husband, Chris, the twins were off exploring the fair with their partners.

Rosangel had mentioned their old headteacher, Thomas Tiler, although she had limited knowledge of him nowadays. Charlie confirmed that he was in charge of a large primary school in Suffolk and had three children. That information would have to keep until next year's newsletter. Charlie said that one of their old teachers, Mary Anderson, had gone to Australia to live with her son but little more was known of her. Of course, Charlie and Rosangel mentioned Laura Watson who had sadly collapsed and died putting on her coat ready to go on her annual trip to William Mullins graveside. To talk to the old headteacher, her deepest love.

Charlie said, 'She always said each year that that year would be her last, that it was too much for her failing body.' They both smiled as they remembered her retirement and her joy of having a trophy from the Newhill show for their solitary marrow.

Continuing around the fair Rosangel stopped to greet Eileen Bisby and her daughter Amanda. They hugged warmly.

'I was just posting my annual newsletter to Grace, I still miss her every day, she has never been replaced as my best friend, except perhaps by my husband.'

The two women understood, regarding Rosangel as one of their own.

They were proud of her achievements and been delighted when she had become a doctor in London at one of the major hospitals. Rosangel had married an Indian consultant, Sachin but never as she predicted, played cricket again.

There was no newsletter for Little Billy Shakespeare, wicket keeper detective that year or for the previous five years. A car crash had taken him and his wife instantly on a lonely Cornish road. Each year Doctor Rosangel Chlebek shed a tear on the anniversary of his death for the young Trinidadian with the thick Birmingham accent. She knew well how much he had loved her and treasured his quietly spoken message of love in the middle of the cup final all those years ago. She had never shared his expression of love that day with anyone, not even Grace. It was too precious and bitter sweet. Each anniversary brought memories of that wonderful day when she and her friends triumphed against the odds to win the William Mullins cup.

She sighed deeply then wrapped up her daughter Eve to keep her warm in her pram. Her own Little Billy slipped his hand into hers and he smiled up at her. Her future was secure and full of promise, yet her past was always with her. Memories of love and friendship sat alongside deep sadness and loss.

Perhaps on their next visit to Newhill she would take Billy and Eve to Wath Mill Allotments to tell them about her friends and those who had passed away, or perhaps not.

Rosie looked up as a solitary swan flew low overhead with strong rhythmic beats of his powerful wings. Rosangel had no idea where he was going but wherever it was it was his choice. He was wild and free.

Like her first love, the sadly missed Little Billy Shakespeare.

Acknowledgements

First and foremost, I owe a huge debt of gratitude to my long suffering wife of fifty years, Eve, who has given unstinting love and kindness together with determined support for my writing. Her advice and editing skills have proved invaluable.

Thanks to Willow Beeley Byrne who showed me what real writing is; to E.J. Murphy who showed me what determination and caring means and to my talented youngest granddaughter, Nora Murphy who taught me how to do jigsaws.

My brother Brian who was courageous enough to offer constructive criticism of my first book, 'Secrets Lies and Rhubarb Pies.'

For my daughters, Eleanor and Jessica who have been an inspiration with their bravery and brilliance. Their support and care have been a delight throughout their lives.

My gratitude must go to Lionel and Margaret Riches for their constant support, encouragement and friendship despite being Millwall supporters.

Thanks to all at Filnore allotments in Thornbury who were kind enough to take interest in my first book. Specific thanks must go to Chris who gave valuable advice on police procedures and my Polish friends, Aggi and Slawek who offered such patient advice with the Polish language and culture.

Finally, my thanks to all at PublishNation who helped turn my scribblings into published novels.

Printed in Great Britain
by Amazon